PRAISE FOR THE DCI RYAN MYSTERIES

What newspapers say

"She keeps company with the best mystery writers" – *The Times*

"LJ Ross is the queen of Kindle" – *Sunday Telegraph*

"Holy Island is a blockbuster" – *Daily Express*

"A literary phenomenon" – *Evening Chronicle*

"A pacey, enthralling read" – *Independent*

What readers say

"I couldn't put it down. I think the full series will cause a divorce, but it will be worth it."

"I gave this book 5 stars because there's no option for 100."

"Thank you, LJ Ross, for the best two hours of my life."

"This book has more twists than a demented corkscrew."

"Another masterpiece in the series. The DCI Ryan mysteries are superb, with very realistic characters and wonderful plots. They are a joy to read!"

OTHER BOOKS BY LJ ROSS

THE DCI RYAN MYSTERIES IN ORDER:

THE ALEXANDER GREGORY THRILLERS IN ORDER:

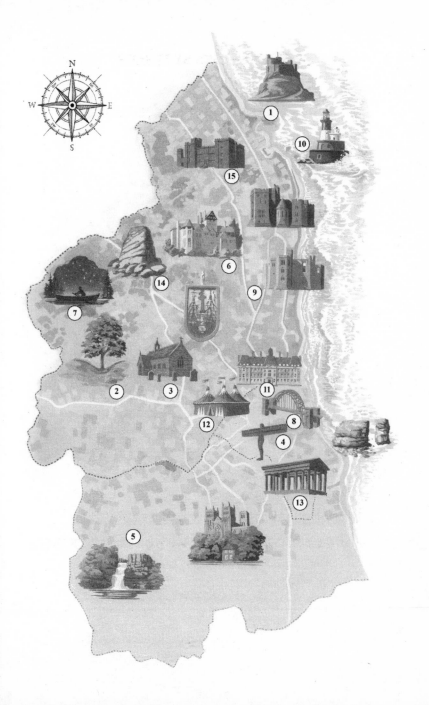

CUTHBERT'S WAY

A DCI RYAN MYSTERY

CUTHBERT'S WAY

A DCI RYAN MYSTERY

LJ ROSS

ISBN: 978-1-912310-17-3

First published in December 2020 by Dark Skies Publishing

Author photo by Gareth Iwan Jones

Cover layout by Stuart Bache

Cover artwork and map by Andrew Davidson

Typeset by Riverside Publishing Solutions Limited

Printed and bound by CPI Goup (UK) Limited

"Even if I could possibly hide myself in a tiny dwelling on a rock, where the waves of the swelling ocean surrounded me on all sides, and shut me in equally from the sight and knowledge of men, not even thus should I consider myself to be free from the snares of a deceptive world..."

—St. Cuthbert, from Bede's *Life of St. Cuthbert*

PROLOGUE

Priory of St Cuthbert, Durham Cathedral
December, 1537

"Fetch the chaplain—quickly, now!"

The novice bowed to the words of his elder and then, with a parting glance across the infirmary room to where Brother Edward lay pale and inert, left quickly to do his bidding.

As the young man's echoing footsteps receded along the flagstone cloisters, the two who remained spoke in hushed voices, their faces lit only by the dying embers of a meagre fire.

"The Commissioners left York last week," Brother William murmured. "It's said they spent a night and a day at Selby and will ride to Durham with all speed, if they're to return to London afore the New Year."

There was a small, crackling silence while they considered the threat that was, even now, thundering towards them from the south. By the King's order, Catholic monasteries throughout the land had been sacked; their authority dissolved, their riches and treasures confiscated or destroyed on behalf of the Crown, all in the name of a new, Protestant order. Thus far, the bishopric of Durham had escaped that fate which had befallen so many, but it seemed their period of grace was almost at an end.

Yet they feared the loss of something far more precious than gold or silver.

"They say the doctors amongst them are of lowly skill," Brother William continued, casting an anxious glance towards the doorway, lest anyone should overhear. "Given to destructive method—"

"Then we must act."

The Prior's voice was calm; its tone resigned. Hugh Whitehead was known as a fair and pious man, not prone to immorality of any sort; indeed, a model of monastic virtue. There had been temptations—siren maidservants to test his resolve and worldly accolades to test his vanity— all of which he had overcome. Yet only now, as an old and wizened man, had the Lord delivered his greatest test of all.

Prior Whitehead drew in a deep breath, his rough, weather-beaten hands forming a steeple as he sent up a silent prayer and sought forgiveness.

"Brother Edward must be afforded every rite," he said quietly. "As befits the passing of so devout a friend and son of God."

Brother William nodded, watching the laboured rise and fall of the man's chest as he fought the final stages of what would, one day, come to be known as pneumonia.

"'The chaplain has been sent for, and will stay with him until the end—'"

"He must die tonight, if aught is to be done."

William gave a strangled gasp. "Father—?"

"Think of the higher cause with which we are entrusted," the Prior said, as much for himself as for the other monk, whose hands had begun to shake beneath the cuffs of his habit. "Our brother would have borne this sacrifice proudly, had he the strength to choose."

Just then, they heard the sound of returning footsteps.

No further words were spoken. Brother William gathered himself and crossed the small infirmary room in three quick strides, pausing only to remove the thin pillow of duck feathers upon which Brother Edward's head rested. With a strength borne of righteousness, he held it over the man's face, shedding a single tear as the monk's body convulsed briefly before sagging back against the bed, barely offering a token resistance. He tucked the pillow beneath Edward's head again and closed his mouth, which gaped open in horrified accusation.

By the time the novice returned with the chaplain, the Prior and Brother William stood at the back of the infirmary, their heads bent in solemn prayer.

Brother Edward's body was dispatched to the Dead Man's Chamber, in the very bowels of the Cathedral, and thence to the Chapel, where it lay shrouded within the heavy folds of his habit. Two monks who had been closest to him in life now took it upon themselves to keep a silent vigil by his side in death, and knelt on the cold stone floor at his stiffening feet to pray for the departed's immortal soul.

Their prayers could not prevent the merciless advance of the Commissioners, who crossed the River Wear at sundown and entered the city of Durham bearing the King's banner. They made their way through its foul-smelling streets, past the miserable huts of townsfolk beaten down by pestilence and poverty, and wound their way upward to the summit of the hill upon which the cathedral had been built. Hundreds of years earlier, monks carrying the sacred body of Saint Cuthbert had built a modest 'white church' of wood, wherein they laid their charge to rest. Now, in its place there stood a towering edifice of carved stone, its Norman arches and columns a reminder to all who looked upon them of the wealth and power that lay within.

The men who entered its hallowed walls looked upon the architectural masterpiece with open stares, cataloguing and calculating its worth.

Doctor Ley was the first to speak, having drunk his fill from a cup of ale the Prior had, solicitously, delivered with his own hands.

"We will look to the book of accounts soon enough," he said. "But, first, by the King's order, we demand to see the body of Cuthbert."

The Prior affected an air of surprise.

"The body? 'Tis interred within the shrine," he said. "A place of holy rest, for that most holy of saints. Surely, sirs, you must have heard of Cuthbert's great healing power upon the afflicted—?"

"There's much that can be said, yet remains unproven," one of the other commissioners sneered. "It has been many years since any have looked upon Cuthbert's form. It may be a jumble of bones, not flesh and ligament, as many are wont to say."

There was a rustle of discontent amongst the small crowd of monks who had gathered in the nave, and the Prior held up an authoritative hand to silence them.

"You must excuse us," he said softly. "There are few in these parts who would question the power of our patron, whose deathly touch has healed the sick and the dying these many hundreds of years."

"Aye, and lined the Priory's coffers, no doubt, with lands and gold aplenty," the doctor replied. "So much the better, for now's the time of reckoning. Come! Lead us to where the man lies, and we'll have done with the matter."

The Prior inclined his head, and called to the Keeper-of-the-Shrine.

"Brother William? Lead these good sirs to Cuthbert's rest, and unlock the chains so they might look upon his form and behold it for themselves."

The body of Saint Cuthbert was kept in a raised iron casket in front of a magnificent shrine, as befitted the status of one of the world's most famous saints. In life, Cuthbert had been a Godly man; at times a hermit, a prior and a bishop, who lived a simple life in the Farne Islands during the seventh century. Years after his death, his coffin was reopened and his body found incorrupt, as though he were merely sleeping. As word spread of this phenomenon, talk of miraculous healing spread with it and people of all walks sought out the saint's divine power, bringing offerings in exchange for his favour. But when Viking marauders advanced across the North Sea, the monks were forced to flee the island of Lindisfarne with Cuthbert's body, travelling for seven years to protect him from those who sought to destroy all that he symbolised.

Five hundred years later, different marauders had come to pillage—and, this time, they brought with them a goldsmith by the name of Prycewinkle.

"You, there! Light up these candles and hold them aloft," Doctor Ley commanded of Brother William. "The light grows dim and we've a mind to see this bony-piece before nightfall."

William said nothing, capitulating to the demands of the King's men with all the humility he could muster.

"Prycewinkle! Bring up your hammer. The lock will not open."

"Sir, if I might help," William began, casting an anxious glance towards the hammer the goldsmith wielded. "What lies within the chest is of delicate condition—"

"Stand aside, man," the other doctor, Henley, said roughly. "Unless you wish to feel the King's displeasure."

William fell silent and watched the goldsmith heave himself up the wooden ladder to the top of Cuthbert's iron casket, where Ley waited impatiently.

"Strike!" he said. "I've a wish to find a warm bed and a warm woman, afore the day is out."

They shared a manly laugh and Brother William closed his eyes as Prycewinkle dealt the first blow, his iron hammer smashing through the casing and the inner coffin, connecting with the body within.

The goldsmith paused and let out another laugh.

"I fear I have broken the gentleman's leg," he called out. "Though I suspect he won't be needing it!"

"Aye," Henley laughed. "Mayhap he can heal it, himself!"

"Here, and I'll ask him," Ley boasted, clearing away the shards of wooden coffin to reveal the unfortunate recipient of their ministrations.

When he saw clearly what rested inside the folds of golden robes, now careworn with age and decay, the smile fell from his face and he let out a sharp cry.

"Good God!"

"What, man?" Henley called up, yawning widely. "I'm in no mood for japes."

"The body—I can hardly say, but it be whole!"

The goldsmith peered into the open coffin to see for himself, and then let out a similar exclamation.

"By me, but it's true!"

"It cannot be so!" Henley shouted.

"Come, and see with your own eyes!"

With much muttering and expletives, Doctor Henley joined his fellows on top of the casket and looked upon the pale, ghostly face of Cuthbert. His heart lurched against his chest when he saw, not a dusty skeleton but a body, wasted but whole, with a beard neatly kept, its fingers clasped around a magnificent pectoral cross of gold and garnet.

"What—what do we do?" the goldsmith whispered.

Henley recovered himself, eyeing the silver and gold trinkets tucked around the body.

"What, man? Have you forgotten your trade? Feast your eyes upon that cross of gold, then look to the rest. As for the corpse, we'll have it removed to the vestry while the King decides its fate."

"What of God's wrath?" Ley wondered. "There may be bad omens for those who move a saint."

He might not have believed such things, but finding a body instead of a skeleton after five hundred years could change a man's perspective.

"Then let us not be the ones to move him," Henley reasoned. "The monks can tend to the body, and we'll tend to the gold."

While the commissioners filled two horse-drawn carts with gold and silver, ivory and other valuable commodities to please the King, the monks filled another cart with a plain wooden coffin and covered it with caskets of ale and baskets of fish, intended for distribution to the poor. As night fell, the Prior came out to the courtyard to speak to the monks entrusted with its safe passage, knowing they should never meet again.

"Brothers," he said quietly, as each fell upon his hands to kiss the fingertips. "Kneel, and receive God's blessing."

He delivered a prayer, their bent heads illuminated by the pearly light of the moon, before a cloud passed over the sky and cast the landscape in shadow once more.

"William, George," he began. "May God grant you grace and fortitude, all your days. Only we three know of our saint's final journey, and so it must be until one of us dies. Only then can the knowledge be shared with another of our brothers, and they must be wise and true. Do not speak in haste, nor under any threat of worldly harm, for your Maker will decide your fate upon the Day of Judgment and will not look kindly upon cowardice."

The others nodded.

"Then, go, brothers. Seek out Elven Moor, for there are many there in need of hope."

"Hold!"

They turned, to find one of the commissioner's guards approaching.

"Who goes there?" he demanded.

"Alms for the poor, my son," the Prior told him. "Fish and a little ale, to ease their plight, for there are many running from the plague who are living wild on the moors, and many remaining to starve or else die a black death."

"Plague, you say?" The guard took an involuntary step back.

"Aye, they say it'll reach us, soon enough," the Prior continued, and it was no lie. The country was beset with a pandemic and many were already decamping the city, running for the sweet-smelling air of the hills.

"Soon? How soon?" the guard asked, all thoughts of checking the cart now forgotten.

"Any day now," Whitehead told him. "It would be as well for you to tell your masters to make haste, else none may live to return home."

The guard bade a hurried retreat, and the Prior turned back to his brothers.

"Godspeed," he said, and raised a hand in farewell.

He watched the cart rumble across the cobblestones, disappearing into the murky night until it was no more than an apparition, a memory of what once had been, and wondered if he had made the right decision.

Only time would tell.

CHAPTER 1

Crayke College, Yorkshire
Sunday 6th December 2020

All was blessedly quiet in St. Cuthbert's boarding house.

The boys had taken themselves off to attend 'Movie Night' in the main school hall, chattering and laughing as they crossed the grassy quadrangle and, as the hallways fell silent in the wake of their departure, Father Jacob could only thank God there was a double feature that evening, which meant he could look forward to at least four hours of restful, child-free contemplation.

Praise be.

Heaving a sigh of pure contentment, he followed the wood-panelled corridors towards his private rooms, where he took his time selecting a book from the overstuffed shelves in the small library he'd developed over the twenty years he'd been a monk and housemaster at Crayke. Given his vocation, it would, perhaps, have been more pious if he'd selected a religious text to while away his free time; however, when his hand strayed towards a volume of *The Adventures of Sherlock Holmes*, the matter was decided.

"To a great mind, nothing is little," he murmured, and settled himself down to read, cracking open the window to allow a steady gust of wintry night air to swirl around the room.

Father Jacob had barely finished the first page of *The Red-Headed League* before his solitude was interrupted by the sound of shattering glass somewhere on the floor below. He jolted in his chair, and half wondered whether it was God's way of telling him that he should have chosen different reading material, after all.

"Who is it this time?" he muttered, heaving himself up to go in search of the culprit.

Felix Haynes, no doubt. Perhaps Peter Alverton, if the others spurred him on...

It wouldn't be the first time either of them had been chastised for low-level property damage, but Jacob was disappointed to find that previous punishments hadn't been enough to deter them from acting up.

He'd have to call their parents—again.

Jacob lifted the sash window higher and stuck his head outside, where the bracing December wind rushed against his face, stinging his cheeks. The grounds were illuminated all the way to the trees lining either side of the manicured grounds, and motion-sensor security lights shone brightly upon the pathway skirting the perimeter of the boarding house.

They continued to shine, which told him that someone, or something, had activated the sensor very recently.

There was no sign of anyone there now and, when he opened the door to his study and stepped into the hallway beyond, there was not a soul to be seen nor a sound to be heard in any direction.

"Haynes? Alverton?"

He waited for the inevitable sound of scurrying footsteps and raucous laughter, but the air remained heavy and silent, as though the very walls were watching him.

Irritated by his own fanciful thoughts, Father Jacob trudged downstairs in the vague direction of where he'd heard the glass shatter.

"Who's there?" he called out, flicking on the lights as he went. "Honesty is the best policy, remember—"

A stream of cold air touched his face, and Jacob turned to find its source.

"You've been warned about this kind of thing before," he began again, for the benefit of any child who might be skulking in the shadows. "Come out now!"

Nothing moved except the rustle of Jacob's long, black habit as he wandered from room to room, following the stream of air which seemed to grow colder with every passing step. Eventually, he came to the laundry room, which carried the faint odour of adolescent sweat and dried mud. Rounding the corner, he was met with a strong gust of icy wind rushing through a gaping hole in the window, whistling past shards of jagged glass that clung to the pane while the rest lay scattered across the peeling linoleum floor. The window latch was open, leaving the frame to rattle on its hinges, swinging back and forth to clatter against the wall.

If he'd been a different kind of man, Father Jacob might have sworn.

As it was, he took several deep, nourishing breaths and picked his way carefully across the floor to shut the offending window. The air continued to flow through the break in the pane, and he cast around for a board of some description to prop against it until the janitor could be called. He thought of the notice board hanging in the common room and sidestepped the glass on the floor, thinking he would leave it there as the evidence of wrongdoing and ask the offender to clean it up themselves.

Preoccupied by thoughts of how best to uncover the guilty party, he did not see the figure at the end of the corridor until they were less than ten metres apart.

"Oh!"

Father Jacob came to an abrupt halt.

"I'm sorry, I didn't hear you—"

He peered along the corridor, struggling to make out the face of his brother. Their hood was drawn and the lights in the corridor had been extinguished, which he found strange.

"Brother John? Is that you?"

The figure said nothing, but began to walk towards him, very slowly.

"There's been another breakage, I'm afraid," Jacob said, gesturing to the room he'd recently left. "Sixth formers,

I suspect. They've been using the wood store on the other side of the rugby pitch to meet the girls and smoke. Some things never change…"

As the figure drew nearer, Jacob's unease grew stronger.

"Brother Simon? Are you feeling well—?"

But it was not John or Simon who came to stand in front of him.

Outside, the security lights flickered on again as one of the children ran beneath its sensor, not stopping to look inside the darkened windows of St. Cuthbert's House.

The light burst through a nearby window, casting a bright shaft of white light upon the floor between the two robed figures.

"Who—?"

Whatever Jacob had intended to say died on his tongue, the words turning to ash as the figure before him stepped forward into the light, illuminating a face that was not a face at all, but a grotesque mask, cut to resemble the image of a man who'd been dead for a thousand years.

But the eyes…

The eyes shone with madness.

"*Help! Help me, please!*" Jacob stumbled backwards, shouting and tripping over his own feet in his haste to get away.

Behind the mask, the figure smiled and said a single word.

"Run."

CHAPTER 2

Elsdon, Northumberland
Monday 7th December

Doctor Anna Taylor-Ryan awoke with a start.

The room was in darkness and she was disorientated for a moment, unsure of whether it was late evening or early morning. Automatically, she turned to her left, where a white-painted cot stood empty beside the bed.

Empty.

Rearing up, she let out a sharp cry as the action tugged at the scar across her abdomen, then struggled out of bed.

The baby was gone.

Oh, dear God…

"Emma," she whispered, gripping the edges of the empty cot.

Shaking hard now, Anna ran across the room, pulling open the bedroom door to search the other upstairs bedrooms, but found them empty, too.

Tears began to fall as she hurried downstairs and into the kitchen…

Where she nearly collided with her mother-in-law.

"Shh!" Eve warned her, pressing a finger to her lips. "There, now, everything's all right."

She took Anna's cold hand in her own warm fingers and led her through the kitchen to the conservatory area, which remained in darkness but for the gentle glow of the fairy lights hanging from the Christmas tree they'd put up the day before. There, Anna saw her husband sleeping in one of the easy chairs, his long legs crossed at the ankles while he snuggled their baby daughter warmly against his chest, his capable arms supporting her tiny body while they both slept.

Anna felt relief wash over her, followed closely by a fierce wave of love.

Emma Natalie Sara Ryan had been born on a sunny day in July, by Caesarean section. Whilst her mother was indisposed on the operating table, it had been her father who'd been the first to cradle her in his arms and whisper that he loved her, before holding her against Anna's chest so that she might hear her mother's familiar heartbeat. That first, special bond had only strengthened over the passing months and, more often than not, it was Ryan who volunteered to change nappies or do the late evening feed, so that he could sit quietly with his daughter and marvel at how he could possibly have been party to creating something so perfect. For these reasons, Anna should have known that no harm would have come to her little girl while she slept; not while Ryan had breath inside his body to prevent it.

The two women stood there for a moment watching the man and his child, both smiling at the sight of Ryan's blue-black hair sticking out at odd angles around his sleeping face. His daughter shared the same shade, but had inherited her mother's brown eyes, which would open soon enough for her morning feed, if Anna wasn't much mistaken.

"Ryan didn't want to wake you," Eve murmured. "Let's leave them to it for a bit longer, shall we?"

With a gentle hand, she steered Anna towards the kitchen, where they found Ryan's father, Charles, sipping a cup of coffee whilst thumbing through a copy of yesterday's newspaper.

"Good morning," he said cheerfully, while his sharp blue eyes made a quick assessment of Anna's face, alarmed to find it looking pale and drawn.

"Morning," Anna said, listlessly.

Exchanging a meaningful glance with his wife, Charles came to his feet.

"Well," he said, and made a show of checking his watch. "The corner shop will be opening in half an hour—I think I'll put my shoes on and take a wander down into the village to pick up some fresh milk. Need anything, while I'm down there?"

"No, I think we're all set," Eve said, and gave him a peck on the cheek.

Her husband was far from perfect, she thought, but, at moments like these, she was grateful he knew when to make himself scarce.

"Why don't we have a nice cuppa?" she suggested, casting a glance over her daughter-in-law, who remained standing inside the doorway, looking a bit lost. "Tea, or would you prefer coffee?"

Anna shook herself.

"Um, coffee, please. I can make it—"

"I don't mind," Eve said, tapping the edge of a chair to indicate the girl should sit down before she fell down. "Did you have a bad dream? You seemed upset, when you came downstairs."

"I—I'm not sure," Anna mumbled. "I woke up and—and when I looked across at the cot, Emma wasn't there. I just panicked. Sorry, I feel like such an idiot—"

Eve paused in the act of slipping a coffee pod into the machine and turned to look at her.

"Never apologise for experiencing a perfectly natural emotion," she said softly. "I can't tell you how often I worried about Ryan and—and Natalie—when they were young."

It hurt to say her late daughter's name, sometimes, but it was getting easier the more often she tried.

"Emma may only be five months old but, I'm sorry to say, you never stop worrying about your kids, no matter how old they get," she chuckled. "Especially the ones who decide to run off and become murder detectives."

That brought a smile to Anna's face. "Heaven forbid," she said. "I don't think my heart could cope with the stress of having two of them in the family."

"Try being the wife of a former diplomat," Eve said, not bothering to mention that Charles had been in military intelligence before that, when Ryan and Natalie were children.

Talk about sleepless nights.

She brought two steaming mugs over to the table, and decided the moment called for buttery croissants, too. Anna had always been a slim woman, but she was edging towards becoming *thin* and her skin was too pale, which spoke of anaemia.

Steak for dinner tonight, Eve thought, with a decisive nod.

"It's been a stressful time," she said, reaching across to give Anna's hand a quick squeeze. "Bringing a baby into the world is hardly a walk in the park, especially when that baby decides to come a couple of weeks early."

Anna took a swig of coffee.

"I'll never forget the look on Ryan's face," she said. "He's faced every kind of danger during his career but, I swear, I've never seen him look so terrified."

"That's all very well," Eve said, carefully. "But *you're* the one who's borne the physical strain. One day, that little girl will thank you, but, until then, it's a cycle of sleeping, feeding and changing...not to mention the constant worrying. Don't be too hard on yourself, Anna. You're doing a wonderful job, and you're a wonderful mother, already."

Anna's eyes glazed over and she set her cup down, battling sudden tears. At times like these, when she doubted herself, she missed her mother terribly; Sara Taylor had been taken years before her time, by the hand of a madman. Most days, she managed to forget that part and remember her mother's voice and sometimes her smell, if she closed her eyes and recalled old sensory memories that grew more distant by the day. When her own daughter had come into the world, she'd longed to share the occasion with Sara, to seek her advice and reassurance during those first few weeks, whilst they adjusted to the shock of becoming new parents.

But, of course, she couldn't.

It was thanks in no small part to Eve Ryan's unstinting warmth and kindness that she'd been able to overcome any sadness that threatened to spoil those precious first moments. Aside from loving Ryan, the two women shared a common bond, both having lost significant people in their lives: Eve, her daughter, and Anna, her entire family. There could never be any substitutions for those they had lost, but they had forged new bonds of deep and abiding friendship.

Not only did she *like* her mother-in-law, Anna thought.

She *loved* her.

How often could that be said, of modern families?

"Thank you," Anna replied, with feeling. "I don't know why I overreacted the way I did, just now. When I woke up, I just had this sudden, *awful* feeling that someone had taken the baby. It felt so real…I should have known it would have been her daddy, of course."

"We're programmed to know where our babies are at all times," Eve soothed. "You were acting on auto-pilot, and you were probably still half-asleep. Besides, after everything that's happened—"

She cut herself off, thinking it may be unwise to bring up a subject best avoided.

"You're thinking of what happened at the cathedral?"

Eve could have kicked herself. The previous March, Anna had been an unfortunate bystander during a large-scale heist on Durham Cathedral, during which a priceless artefact had been stolen. Much worse, Anna had suffered serious head trauma and extensive injuries in the process, which had threatened her life and that of her unborn child. She'd come through the worst, but her hair had only recently grown back to cover the scar on her head and, instead of her usual long style, Anna now wore a fashionable crop which happened to suit her very much. But then, when you had a face like hers, you could wear your hair however you liked, Eve thought tenderly.

"I shouldn't have mentioned it," she said, and moved off in search of sugar and pastry. "It does no good to relive it all."

"I don't often think of it," Anna admitted. "Or, at least, I don't think about the explosion. I think about the reasons why it happened."

Eve didn't pretend to misunderstand. "Even after all this time, Ryan still thinks there's a danger—?"

Anna nodded. "He doesn't talk about it too often because I think he's trying not to worry me, but by not talking about it…"

"He's worrying you?" Eve finished, with a crooked smile.

"Exactly," Anna murmured. "Ryan knows the cross they recovered was a fake, but he doesn't know why anybody would orchestrate such an elaborate, high profile theft, if it wasn't the real thing they planned to steal."

"It could be that the thieves didn't know it was a fake," Eve suggested, but Anna shook her head.

"Ryan's considered that, but he's fairly certain DCI Tebbutt was murdered and that forger—Faber, I think he was called— was tortured because they knew the cross was a replica…" Anna shivered. "Faber died before the heist, which means that whoever planned the robbery already knew they'd be stealing a forged copy. What we don't know is *why*. There's something much bigger happening, here, Eve—maybe a new organised crime group operating in the area, one that's well financed, with connections in high places."

Eve said nothing, thinking of the private conversation she'd had with Ryan months ago, while Anna was still recovering in the hospital. His message to his parents had been stark: if person, or *persons*, unknown had seen fit to commission the assassination of a prominent chief inspector for no reason other than the fact she'd found out about the cross being a fake, there was every reason to think they'd do the same again, if word should ever get out that Ryan was in possession of the same information.

That meant he was in serious danger, and so was his family.

Yet, what could he do?

If Ryan pressured Anna to leave with the baby and stay with his family at their home in Devon, the action would look suspicious to anybody watching their movements, placing them all in greater danger than before. Besides, if the person or group responsible for the Durham heist had money and connections, it made little difference whether the object of their wrath was in Northumberland or in Devon.

So long as the world believed Ryan was conducting a regular investigation into the death of his former colleague, they maintained a status quo. But it was not a long-term solution, and they could not live with the Sword of Damocles hanging above their heads, so he'd asked his parents to stay for as long as they could—to help with the new baby, and provide him with some reassurance that there would be people he trusted to watch over that which was most precious to him in the world, while he went about the business of quiet investigation to uncover the threat which now lay dormant but could erupt at any time.

Eve worried for her son, thinking of how much responsibility he bore in his private and professional life, but mustered a smile and set a warm croissant in front of her daughter-in-law.

"I'm sure Ryan will get to the bottom of it," she said, lightly. "In the meantime, you need to take care of yourself."

Anna raised the pastry half-heartedly to her lips, but her hand paused mid-air when there came the unmistakable sound of a baby's cry, followed by the much deeper rumble of Ryan's voice as he chattered to Emma on his way through to the kitchen.

"...and, Old Macdonald had a duck, ee-aye, ee-aye, oh..."

He appeared with the baby in one arm, his bright, silvery-blue eyes still misty with sleep as he gave a wide, jaw-cracking yawn. Spotting his wife, Ryan broke into a smile.

"Good morning," he said, and leaned down to brush his lips against hers. "I was hoping you might have managed another hour's sleep but, since you're awake, Madam here is ready for some milk...is everything all right?"

He noticed that Anna looked tearful all of a sudden and moved quickly, shifting the baby in his arms to sit on the chair beside her.

"What is it, darling? What's the matter?"

Anna merely shook her head and reached for Emma, who held out her chubby arms for her mother's embrace.

"Nothing's the matter now," Anna said, rubbing her cheek against the baby's soft, downy hair.

Ryan touched a gentle hand to his wife's face.

"I love you," he murmured, and smiled as the baby cast her deep brown eyes up at him, in accusation. "You, too, little one."

Across the kitchen, Eve turned away to mask the fear which must have shown clearly on her face. For, if Ryan was right, everything could be taken away from them in a single stroke, and she could hardly bring herself to imagine the devastation that would cause.

CHAPTER 3

While Detective Chief Inspector Ryan revived his sleep-deprived body beneath the spray of an ice-cold shower, the headmaster of Crayke College watched the sun rise from his office window. Long, hazy rays of pale amber light spread across the frosted lawns, while clouds of mist rolled over the moors and blanketed the valley in white, leaving Father Peter with the lingering impression of having been cut off from the rest of the world. Which was, he supposed, exactly why he'd chosen a life in service to God, and why he'd come to Crayke in the first place.

But, for all its safety and seclusion, their small community was not without its fair share of drama.

"You say there's been no sign of Father Jacob since last night?"

Peter turned away from the window to speak to Father Samuel, who was chaplain at the school and a key part of its monastic community. Crayke was a rare beast in the modern world, being both an elite, co-educational Catholic

26

boarding school set in acres of stunning landscape, as well as home to one of a dwindling number of active Benedictine monasteries, with the abbey providing a shared focal point for both sides of the community.

"No," Samuel said. "He hasn't been seen since around five o'clock, yesterday afternoon, which is when the boys went off for their movie night in the main hall. When they came back to the boarding house later on, they couldn't find Jacob anywhere, so they came to me, instead."

"I'm amazed they had the presence of mind," Peter was bound to say. "We must be doing something right, after all. What steps did you take?"

"I had a look around but, apart from finding the lights in his study blazing, there was nothing untoward…I assumed he'd been called away on some errand, so I told the boys to go to bed."

"There was still no sign of him after lights out?"

Samuel shook his head. "I stayed in Father Jacob's room, so that the children would be supervised throughout the night," he replied, with a hint of irritation. "I hope there's a reasonable explanation for his absence—"

"I'm sure there is," Father Peter said, forestalling any tongue-wagging. The chaplain was a good man but had a tendency to gossip. "I hope our brother hasn't come to any harm."

This last observation gave Samuel pause for thought, and unlocked another memory from the previous evening.

"There was one more thing," he said. "When I did my rounds, making sure all the doors and windows were locked,

I found a breakage in the laundry room. A windowpane was shattered and there was glass all over the floor."

Peter frowned at this.

"I thought it might have been one of the boys," Samuel said. "I know there've been one or two incidents with Haynes and Alverton, so I spoke with them first."

"And?"

"They strongly deny breaking the window," Samuel said. "And, I must say, they seemed genuine, this time."

"Perhaps," Father Peter murmured. "In which case, there might have been an intruder. Has anybody at the abbey seen Father Jacob?"

It was unusual for any member of staff to go AWOL, let alone an experienced monk and teacher of more than twenty years' standing, in possession of an impeccable track record.

A ripple of unease crept along the headmaster's spine; something Ryan would have recognised as a forewarning of bad things to come.

"I've spoken with all of our brothers," the chaplain told him. "Nobody has seen Jacob since yesterday."

Peter was silent for a long moment, then came to a decision.

"Assemble the staff for a search party," he said quietly. "Something isn't right."

When an initial search elicited no clue as to Father Jacob's whereabouts, it became necessary to call in reinforcements.

The 'Captain of Beagling' was a spotty-faced youth of seventeen, whose love of beagles was matched only by his love of fried food and the yearly subscription he had for *Horse and Hound*. Though hunting for sport had been criminalised in the United Kingdom, it was still possible to kill small, unsuspecting creatures in the name of 'wildlife management' or 'pest control' and, for that reason, Crayke College had taken it upon themselves to appoint a dedicated youngster to lead the pack of dogs they kept for this purpose.

Some might have said it was overkill; however, in the rare case of a missing monk, having one's own pack of sniffer dogs proved to be a very useful asset.

So it was that a crowd of teachers, monks and senior students gathered on the lawn in front of St. Cuthbert's House alongside one of their most celebrated hounds, who answered to the name of Toby. It was somewhat ironic that a dog who'd been named by Father Jacob in deference to his appreciation of the works of Conan Doyle was now called upon to help in the effort to find him. As the crowd watched, the captain held one of Father Jacob's unwashed vests in front of the dog's face and gave the signal to pick up the scent.

"I've been training Toby to track different scents," the boy said, proudly. "He's got the best nose around."

He slipped the vest back into a plastic bag and then gave the dog another signal, following which he began to sniff the ground beside the entrance to the boarding house, tail wagging as he turned this way and that, circling around and around until the onlookers began to give up hope.

Father Peter was on the brink of calling things off when the dog let out a bark and began trotting along the pathway leading to the back entrance of the boarding house, his nose stuck to the floor as his tail began to wag even more furiously.

The crowd hurried after him, older members of staff struggling to keep up with the dog's lolloping pace.

"Tell the others to stay back," the headmaster ordered one of the teachers, feeling a familiar tingle of apprehension snaking up his spine. "Father Samuel and I will accompany the search."

By the time they rounded the corner of the boarding house, the captain and his beagle were halfway to the sports hall, and showed no signs of stopping. Picking up the cumbersome skirts of their black habits, the two men ran in hot pursuit, their boots crunching against the frosted turf.

When they finally caught up with them on the pathway running beside the sports hall, they found Toby circling again, having stuck his nose back inside the plastic bag to remind himself of Father Jacob's unique scent.

They'd barely caught their breath before the dog let out another series of barks and took off again, even faster this time, chugging across the lawn towards the orchard on the far side.

"He's definitely got a scent!" the captain called out in a puffed voice, as he struggled to keep up with the dog's bounding strides.

Father Peter and Father Samuel followed at a more sedate pace, dragging in great gulps of cold air as they cleared the main grounds and entered the orchard, which was an area rarely used by staff or children at that time of year. In season, it was an impressive sight, with rows and rows of lustrous trees bearing juicy red and green apples ripe for the picking, but now the trees were bare, their branches long and spindly, like skeleton fingers, such that the orchard felt more akin to a cemetery.

"Over there," the captain called out, from somewhere within. "Toby's heading towards the cider mill!"

"Mallory!" the headmaster called out to the captain. "Wait, before you go inside! Call Toby back—"

Peter dissolved into a coughing fit, age and lack of exercise taking their toll.

"Mallory—" he tried again, but it was too late. The boy was too far away to hear him.

As they wound their way through the network of trees, they heard a loud cry, and exchanged a worried glance.

"Mallory!"

"Hugo!"

Both men called out for Hugo Mallory to hold back but, in his eagerness to display his dog's skill—as well as his own—the boy had failed to remember what it was that one usually found at the end of a hunt.

Something that was dead.

The cider mill was a romantic building that would not have been out of place on the pages of a George Eliot novel.

Built of crumbling sandstone and with ivy running up one wall, it was a regular meeting place for errant sixth formers seeking the perfect location for a tryst, or somewhere to smoke a joint without fear of being caught. The acreage at Crayke College might have looked impressive in the prospectus guide but, in practice, it made for a hard job policing the older teenagers, many of whom had the means and opportunity to push the strict boundaries set by the teaching staff.

At that moment, Father Peter wished wholeheartedly that they would find a couple of kids smoking their way through a pack of menthols, or even that they'd stumble upon a pair of hormone-addled sixth formers *in flagrante delicto.* Anything was preferable to the sight which awaited them as they followed Hugo Mallory into the cider mill.

They found the boy retching in the corner, his body doubled over as it violently expelled the horror of what lay sprawled in the centre of the room. As Father Samuel rushed across to help him, grasping Mallory's shoulders to drag him away and back out into the crisp morning air, Father Peter remained standing inside the doorway and forced himself to look upon the waste of what had once been a man.

Father Jacob's body lay face-down on the flagstone floor and had been stripped of its clothing. Had circumstances been different, Father Peter might have mourned such an ignoble end, but that was far from being the worst of it. Jacob's skin bore dozens of slashing cuts, particularly around the sensitive tendons at the back of his knees and, had he been able to think clearly, Peter might have recognised these as clear signs of systematic torture.

But it was not the cuts that would replay in his mind's eye for the rest of his days.

Oh, no.

It was the sight of Father Jacob's head, contorted and crushed inside the heavy wooden vice they used to grind apples. Blood and brain matter lay splattered around it, forming a perfect arc, while congealed blood dripped into a waiting barrel.

"Deus adiuva nos..." he whispered, and fell to his knees to pray, with the stench of rotting flesh permeating the air around his bent head.

CHAPTER 4

Eighty miles north of Crayke College, in a quiet residential cul-de-sac on the western outskirts of Newcastle upon Tyne, Detective Inspector Denise MacKenzie raised her mascara wand to apply the final touches to her daily war paint. She'd almost completed this delicate task when the unexpected sound of a bedroom door slamming caused her to jump and jab herself in the eye.

Swearing bitterly, MacKenzie blinked and held a tissue to her streaming eye while she stuck an angry head outside the bathroom door.

"*Hey*! What's all the racket about?" she demanded of her husband, who stood on the landing looking flustered.

Detective Sergeant Frank Phillips lifted his hands and let them fall again in a gesture of frustration.

"You might know, it's non-school-uniform day, today," he huffed. "Well, Samantha came downstairs dressed in a pair of bleedin' hot pants and a crop top and I *told* her, no daughter of mine is stepping foot outside that front door unless she's fully clothed!"

MacKenzie smiled privately at how easily he used the word 'daughter', especially now that they'd completed the formal process of adopting Samantha as their own.

"Are you talking about her little denim shorts?" she asked. "Usually, Sam wears them with a pair of tights underneath and those new trainers she likes so much, with the gold star on the side. It's all the rage at the moment, Frank."

"I don't care if Kate Moss and half the known world is wearing them!" he raged. "*She* won't be!"

He jabbed a finger towards Samantha's bedroom door, which opened on cue to reveal a skinny girl of ten, whose long red hair fell in crimped waves down her back.

"Who is Kate Moss?" she asked.

"A famous mo—never mind that!" Phillips blustered. "I thought I told you to go and find some proper clothes!"

"And *I* told *you*, I'm already wearing them! Tell him, mum," Samantha appealed.

MacKenzie felt her heart flip over at the girl's endearment, the novelty of being called 'mum' not having quite worn off, but she was determined not to find herself in the middle of their battle.

"Frank, all the girls wear the same kind of gear at school, so get with the programme," she said. "Sam? Don't start crowing too soon, because you know we made an agreement when I bought you that outfit. We agreed that you'd be wearing it with tights for the winter, and a proper jumper over that crop top, *especially* if you're planning to wear it to school. You're not heading out for a day on the beach, so don't push it, young lady."

Both of them stuck out mutinous chins and crossed their arms with the kind of synchronicity an Olympic swimming team might have been proud of.

"Don't bother giving me that look," she warned them. "We've got exactly—"

MacKenzie checked the time on her watch, and groaned.

"—*minus* five minutes to get out of the house, otherwise we'll be late!"

Galvanised, all three members of the MacKenzie-Phillips household hustled towards the front door, only for MacKenzie to catch sight of herself in the hallway mirror and let out a small cry of alarm.

"Why didn't anybody tell me I've got a black streak running down my face?" she wailed.

Phillips and Samantha exchanged a guilty look.

"You can hardly see it—"

"I didn't even notice—"

"Oh, get in the car!" MacKenzie cried, and slammed the door shut behind them.

On the other side of the River Tyne, in the small, pretty village of East Boldon, Detective Constable Jack Lowerson and Detective Constable Melanie Yates awoke to the sound of a heavy crash.

Reverting to training, both sprang out of bed and into action, Lowerson throwing out a protective arm, which Yates duly swatted away.

"I can handle myself," she reminded him.

"Sorry, it's force of habit," he said. "You can go first, if you like."

It was on the tip of her tongue to make some smart comment about him being a real gentleman, but, given her recent complaint, she feared it would sound hypocritical.

"Happy to," she declared, and began making her way down the corridor towards the living room of the lovely new house they'd recently bought together.

Trailing behind, Lowerson dragged his eyes away from the appealing sight of Melanie's long legs cased in novelty Christmas shorts, and told himself to stay focused. There could be a dangerous intruder on the loose, or many a thing.

But it was not a murderous criminal who had wrought carnage upon their new home—that might have been easier to handle, in the grand scheme of things. The culprit was rather a tabby kitten, with markings like a tiger and a temperament to match, whom they'd rescued and named, 'Sir Pawsalot' in a fit of temporary insanity.

"Paws! What have you *done*?" Jack cried, while Melanie looked upon the devastation and began to laugh, a little hysterically.

The kitten was entangled in a long strand of red tinsel in the centre of their living room, amidst the wreckage of a fallen Christmas tree whose ornaments lay smashed and scattered across the floor. To top it all off, the tree had connected with their new flat screen television as it fell.

Lowerson whimpered.

No television meant no Nintendo…

On that score alone, Yates was already thinking of where she might procure some cat treats to reward their furry friend for his public service.

As for the rest…

"The damage isn't too bad, really," she said, hauling the tree upright while Lowerson checked the cat's paws for any nicks or cuts. "I can't understand how he managed to get in here, though. We keep the door closed at night."

Lowerson spotted a small mound of carpet fluff beside the door, where Paws had obviously tried to burrow his way in from the direction of the kitchen.

Probably best not to mention it, now.

He set the cat down and smiled as it wandered straight back towards the tree, having apparently forgotten the recent calamity.

"I think we may be fighting a losing battle," he said. "Cats like to climb trees, and there's a tree right there, decorated with all kinds of shiny, interesting things."

Yates looked down at the cat, who belly-crawled its way towards a stray bauble before scuttling back again, in an attempt to appear nonchalant.

"After my sister died, my parents didn't really bother celebrating holidays," she said quietly, dropping down to ruffle the cat's ears. "There were no more Christmas trees, no more Easter egg hunts or anything like that because… well, there was very little joy left in the house. Since having my own place, I've enjoyed being able to rediscover some of the magic again, but, if it means having to wake up to this kind of mess, every day…"

She shook her head.

"A cat can't help being a cat; he doesn't know he's not supposed to climb a Christmas tree, but we can't afford to keep replacing our television sets."

Lowerson thought of Melanie as a younger woman, repressed within the confines of her parents' home, and would never have denied her the simple joy of decorating a tree.

"I'll be in charge of Cat Patrol," he decided. "We'll keep the door closed, for starters, and I'll get him another scratching post and decorate that to look more like a tree, since he's too young to go outside and play with the real things."

Melanie looked across at Jack and felt a surge of emotion. They'd come a long way, she thought, and the road hadn't always been smooth. But, standing there together, surrounded by gaudy Christmas tat, with a cat playing happily at their feet, she wouldn't have it any other way.

"Jack?"

"Mm hmm?" he said, while he lifted the broken television up into his arms.

"Thank you."

"It's no trouble," he said, tapping the edge of the box. "I'll put it in the garage, for now—"

"No, I didn't mean that," she smiled. "I meant…thanks for all this."

She spread her arms to indicate the room, their home—the life they now shared. It was more than anything she'd ever had before, and it would take some getting used to.

"I'm so glad we managed to work things out, so we could get to this point in our lives."

Jack set the television down again and stepped carefully over the cat's tail to link his arms around her waist.

"Mel, there'd be no home without you in it," he said softly. "I should be thanking you for being so patient and forgiving. I know it hasn't been easy, at times, and I'm sorry."

Rather than answering him directly, she reached for a sprig of fake mistletoe that had somehow lodged itself behind one of the sofa cushions and held it aloft.

"Christmas kiss?" she offered.

"Let's keep it hanging all year round," Jack replied, and gathered her into his arms.

CHAPTER 5

By the time Ryan arrived at the Northumbria Police Headquarters on the stroke of nine, he'd lost count of the number of strong coffees he'd already imbibed that morning, but could be certain of one thing: there was always room for more.

He made a beeline for a trendy-looking vehicle, affectionately known as the 'Pie Van'. It might have rebranded itself and polished up its rough edges, but 'Stevie's Coffee Shack' would forever be known to the men and women of the Northumbria Criminal Investigation Department as the place to go for caffeine, sugar, carbs and questionable meat sources—which was just the way they liked it.

"Five coffees, please," Ryan said, and yawned again. "Three with milk, two without, and throw a couple of sugar sachets on the side."

It was a point of principle that he would never step foot inside CID without bringing his staff their first 'proper' coffee of the day.

"Cow's milk, almond milk, soya milk or goat's milk?" Stevie asked.

Ryan blinked. "What?"

"Cow's mi—"

"No, I heard you the first time. I was just shocked you'd ask me, after all these years."

Stevie stroked the beard he thought made him look 'hipster'—but which, in reality, bore a strong resemblance to the one modelled by Captain Birdseye—and crossed his tattooed arms on the serving counter.

"Sorry, mate, it gets to be a habit," he said. "Everybody's changin' their lifestyle, these days, and nobody gives you any notice until you've already frothed the milk. Take Frank—for ten years or more, he's been asking me for coffee with full-fat milk and two sugars; three, if Denise isn't lookin'. Then, out of the blue, he starts asking for a peppermint tea."

Ryan frowned. "You're sure this was *Frank Phillips*?"

"One and the same," Stevie said, and crooked a finger to beckon Ryan closer. "There's somethin' else, n'all."

Ryan's interest was piqued, a matter he put down to the fact he'd been spending far too much time watching episodes of *Peppa Pig* with Emma.

"What?" he asked, in a stage whisper.

"He hasn't ordered a bacon stottie for two weeks, now," Stevie said, triumphantly. "I asked him if there'd been owt wrong with the bread...but he said he just didn't fancy one."

Ryan could hardly believe his ears. "You're having me on," he decided.

"God's my witness," Stevie said, crossing his chest. "I was so shocked you could've knocked me over with a feather."

Ryan felt much the same way, and he accepted a tray of hot drinks with the look of a man who had been told the Earth was not round, but flat, after all.

Frank Phillips not wanting a stottie cake?

Peppermint tea?

Had the world gone completely mad?

There was only one way to get to the bottom of it, and that was to go to the source.

When Ryan entered the large, open-plan office that was home to the Major Crimes Unit, he found several familiar faces but none belonging to his sergeant.

"Jack? Mel? Have either of you seen Frank?"

Lowerson spun around in his desk chair with a friendly smile.

"Morning, boss! No, I don't think he's in yet—"

"I saw MacKenzie's car parked outside," Yates interjected, and smiled her thanks when Ryan passed her a steaming cardboard cup from the tray he still held. "Frank and Denise usually travel in together after dropping Sam off at school, unless they need two cars for some reason."

At that moment, Frank's wife—and professional senior, in the workplace—wandered back into the office, having taken a few minutes in the ladies' room to remove the black mascara that had been smeared liberally across her face.

"Denise?"

"Morning!" she said, shrugging out of her woollen coat. "How's the new parent doing, today?"

Momentarily distracted by thoughts of Emma, Ryan's face softened into a loving smile.

"Tired, which is an ironic thing for a lifelong insomniac to feel," he joked. "Pity it's taken me this long to appreciate the value of sleep."

Denise grinned. "Too late now," she said. "Mind you, we have the opposite problem with Samantha. It's more of a problem trying to get her up in the mornings. I thought it was only teenagers who liked to lounge around in bed all day."

"Teenagers, and me—if I could," Lowerson put in, with a wink for Mel.

"Chance would be a fine thing, with that feral cat running about the place," she shot back, with good humour. "Ryan, if you ever want to do a swap, just let me know. I have a feeling Emma is much easier to handle than Sir Pawsalot."

Ryan's lips quirked. "I'll keep it in mind," he said, and turned back to Denise. "Actually, Mac, I was looking for Frank. Is he in the office, yet?"

MacKenzie dropped down into her chair and took a grateful swig of the coffee he'd brought her.

"Yep, he's gone down to the gym for a quick, twenty-minute run before the briefing starts."

Three faces turned to her in shock.

First the stotties, now this, Ryan thought. *Perhaps there was something seriously wrong.*

"Is Frank ill?" he asked bluntly.

MacKenzie shook her head in amusement.

"No, he's just decided to start looking after himself a bit more," she explained. "I've already told him that I love him just the same, but he thinks that, now we have Samantha, there's even more reason for him to stay healthy. He's still a strong man and a good boxer, so he's started heading back to Buddle's every once in a while to spar with some of the old crowd."

Buddle's Boxing Gym was a legendary establishment located in the historic west end of Newcastle, in an area that was now run-down following the closure of all the old factories that used to operate on the waterfront. Although the place had seen more nefarious criminals than world-class boxers, it was also true that it had been a community lifeline for decades of youths—including a young Frank Phillips, who'd learned to channel his energies rather than roam the streets without hope or aspiration. Buddle's had little in the way of kerb appeal, according to Ryan's own recollection—which was somewhat outdated, as it had been three years since he'd stepped inside the crumbling seventies prefab—but what it lacked in that department, it more than made up for in heart and soul.

"Frank always had a solid right hook," he mused, lifting a hand to rub a phantom ache in his jaw. "Anything I can do to support the Health Drive?"

MacKenzie's lips twitched. "Apart from keeping the biscuits under lock and key? Have you got any chickens he can chase around?"

Ryan flashed a smile, which transformed the hard lines of his handsome face into something extraordinary.

"We've got a cat he can chase," Yates threw back over her shoulder. "Although, I can't promise it won't chase him, instead."

Laughing at the image in his mind's eye, Ryan left them to go in search of his sergeant. As he made his way down the wide corridor towards the stairwell, he realised that, for a few precious minutes, he'd been able to laugh with his friends and colleagues as if life were back to normal.

He'd almost forgotten what that felt like.

Ryan jogged down to the basement, where he found Phillips pounding one of the treadmills while singing along to whichever seventies disco classic was playing through the ancient headphones adorning his shiny, balding head. Sensing his arrival, Frank waved a cheerful hand and jabbed a button to slow the machine to a walk, his rounded face red and dripping with hard-earned sweat. He wore a pair of running shorts that were, at a conservative estimate, over thirty years old and spread alarmingly tight across the man's buttocks, and his burly chest was encased in a t-shirt bearing a logo Ryan could no longer make out, given the number of washings it had evidently seen since it was made at the turn of the century.

Grinning openly, Ryan reached for the towel slung over a nearby rail and tossed it over to him.

"Need this?"

"Aye, thanks," Phillips said, and scrubbed it over his face and neck before checking the clock on the wall. "Shaved off a minute or two since the last run."

Ryan tried not to goggle at this gym-going stranger, presently masquerading as his friend and sergeant.

"You didn't tell me you were getting back on the health wagon," he remarked. "Are you feeling all right…in the head?"

"Har bloody har," Phillips replied. "For your information, I'm feelin' top o' the bill."

Ryan raised a single, dark eyebrow, both in surprise and delight.

"I like jogging myself," he said, quite genuinely. "We could head out for a quick run at lunchtimes, now and then, if you fancy it."

Phillips cast a beady eye over his friend's six feet two inches of solid athletic muscle, then considered his own somewhat…*cuddlier* frame, and sighed.

"Well, the thing is, lad, that's a nice thought but…well, look at me, and look at you."

Ryan gave him a blank stare, so he tried speaking plainly.

"I mean to say…*look*, there's no beatin' round the bush. I'm a fat bastard, and you're not. I'd only slow you down."

His friend blinked, then let out a rich peal of laughter.

"Frank, I'd hardly describe you in those terms," Ryan said, recovering himself. "Carrying a few extra pounds here and there isn't the end of the world. Besides, I thought you said a bit of extra padding keeps you warm in the winter, and 'gives the lasses something to hold on to'?"

That was true enough, Phillips thought.

"There's a world of difference between a bit of winter padding and walking around wearing a whole bloody duvet," he said, with brutal honesty. "Anyway, I thought it was about time I shifted some of the bulk, especially as…"

He stopped and took a sip of water.

"Especially as—what?" Ryan prodded.

Phillips sighed. "Y'know I'm older than Denise," he said, quietly. "She might not mind, and I don't mind it *so* much, any more…but now there's Samantha to think of. I want to be around as long as possible for both of them—that poor lass has seen too much heartache, already."

As ever, Ryan found himself humbled by his friend. Despite his gruff exterior, Phillips was all heart and fiercely loyal to those he loved—qualities you couldn't teach down at the training academy.

"They're lucky to have you," he said simply. "And, for the record, you'd never slow me down, Frank. For starters, you're as stubborn as an old mule. When have you ever let me get one over you?"

"True," Phillips mused, rubbing a thoughtful hand over his chin. "All true."

"So, what do you say?" Ryan prodded. "Fancy a run around the block, tomorrow?"

Phillips narrowed his button-brown eyes, then gave a reluctant smile.

"Aye, you're on. But don't think I'll go easy on you, just because you haven't slept in five months."

"Wouldn't dream of it," Ryan said. "And, don't think I'll go easy on *you*, just because you haven't had a bacon stottie in three weeks."

Phillips gave him a knowing look.

"Might've known Stevie couldn't keep that one under his hat," he said, with a rumbling laugh. "Bet he's been burstin' to tell you."

"In the man's defence, I think he was worried you'd suffered some sort of mental break," Ryan said.

"He might be right," Phillips muttered, and began limping towards the shower room, grumbling under his breath about the things he did for love.

"Briefing in ten!" Ryan called after him.

"Aye, if I make it that far!"

CHAPTER 6

Nine months had passed since the robbery at Durham Cathedral, which had enabled a small band of criminals to steal what many believed to be Saint Cuthbert's original golden pectoral cross. To create a diversion while the theft was underway, they'd staged an explosion that had caused minimal damage to the cathedral, but serious damage to Anna. Ryan would never forget the moment he'd learned the news that she'd been taken to hospital nor the long hours and days that followed, when he'd thought he might lose his wife, his soulmate, best friend, and their unborn child, as well as all the dreams they'd had of growing old together. Luckily, both Anna and Emma had survived, for which he was eternally grateful.

Others had not been so lucky.

Detective Chief Inspector Joan Tebbutt, a respected and longstanding colleague based from the Major Crimes Unit in Durham, had lost her life on the same day. Assassinated on the doorstep of her own home, Tebbutt hadn't seen it coming—

nobody could have—and the shock of her death had sent a rippling tidal wave of grief and anger across all the local area command divisions.

In the immediate aftermath of the heist, and once he'd been reassured of his wife's status, Ryan and his team had devoted their collective energies to investigating who had killed Tebbutt, and, more importantly, *why*. At the same time, they'd done everything in their power to track down a missing artefact that was irreplaceable in historic and cultural terms.

To their surprise, the two lines of enquiry had converged.

Tebbutt had been gunned down by one of her own team; a young woman by the name of Justine Winter, who'd chosen to take her own life rather than face the scales of justice. That same young woman had been a party to torturing a man by the name of Edward Faber, who'd spent many years operating in the criminal underworld as a high-class forger, before turning informant. When their investigations turned up the fact that Tebbutt had been Faber's contact during her time spent on the Fraud Team, things began to unravel. Through a stroke of technological genius, they were able to triangulate the location of the robbers using their phone signals and track down the missing cross in the process, leading many to believe the case was closed, and their troubles all over.

Except for one, niggling fact...

The cross they recovered was an excellent forgery; a fact Faber had discovered and reported to the late Joan Tebbutt.

Ryan believed—right down to his bones—that Faber had been tortured until he'd confessed to sharing his knowledge of the forgery with DCI Tebbutt, thereby signing her death warrant. But, the questions of why a young detective of good standing would involve herself in perpetrating such violent crimes, and of why a gang of criminals would go to such lengths to hide the fact that the cross they'd stolen—in spectacular style—was a fake, were unanswered. Until they were, there remained the possibility that Ryan and other members of his team were targets in the same way Tebbutt and Faber had been. To protect himself, his team and their loved ones, Ryan had taken the executive decision not to make public their knowledge of the forgery, which afforded them a short window of time to try to find out the answers they so desperately needed.

Ryan had his own theories but, unfortunately, no proof—despite having spent several months conducting a covert investigation in the hope of generating new leads. In the meantime, there had been no further robberies, no further assassinations or reports of torture killings aside from the usual gang-related assaults, and 'The Powers that Be' were growing impatient with his methods.

It could only be a matter of time before the order came to shut it down.

With such troubling thoughts circulating his mind, Ryan made his way to one of the smaller conference rooms and prepared to deliver what might be his last covert briefing on the matter of the missing cross.

A little after nine-thirty, Ryan's small team of trusted men and women assembled for their bi-weekly briefing on what had come to be known as 'Operation Bertie'. Their meetings were held at irregular times on irregular days, quite deliberately; the reason for their absence being listed in the departmental diary as something innocuous each time.

Ryan moved to the head of the oval table in the centre of the room, having shut the door firmly behind them.

"Anybody ask where you were going?"

There were negative responses all round.

"Good," he said. "It may have been a few months, but we can't afford to get complacent. Tebbutt was one of ours and, like it or not, so was Winter. Whoever managed to turn Justine Winter infiltrated our ranks, and it could happen again."

"That was over in Durham—" Lowerson started to say, but one look silenced him.

"Winter was one of ours," Ryan repeated. "The fact she was based in a different area command makes no difference. If we've learned anything over the years, it's that almost anybody can be susceptible to blackmail or coercion."

Lowerson pulled a face, not wishing to remember some of his own demons on that score.

"Okay, let's get down to it," Ryan said, and cast his eyes around the table, looking at each of their faces in turn.

Phillips, MacKenzie, Lowerson and Yates.

Each one a trusted friend.

"We all know why we're here," he said, leaning forward to rest his forearms on the table. "But let me spell it out, in case anybody's forgotten. We know that the artefact we recovered back in March was a fake; that's been confirmed by Dr Ahern at Durham University, who's an expert on Cuthbert and his relics."

For the same reasons they were now sitting in a room under the guise of completing 'Continuing Professional Development', Ahern had agreed to complete confidentiality in the matter of the pectoral cross—for her own protection, if nothing more. The same applied to their Senior Crime Scene Investigator, Tom Faulkner, who was the only other forensic professional to know the truth of the matter.

"Our working theory is that whoever killed Edward Faber and Joan Tebbutt did so because of what they knew about the cross," Ryan said. "Faber was killed before the heist, which means they knew the cross was a fake *before* they stole it—but *why* would anybody want to steal something they knew to be a fake? The obvious answer would be to conceal the fact from the police, before Tebbutt or Faber had a chance to tell anybody else. The best way to do that was to steal their own forgery."

"What I don't understand is why they'd be so bothered about it," MacKenzie remarked. "Why would anyone care? So what, if we discovered the cross was a forgery?"

"Prison is still a deterrent, to some people," Yates said.

"Not to a career criminal," Phillips disagreed, having known a few of them, himself. "They'd do their stretch and chalk it up as part of the game, knowing their families would be looked after on the outside."

"True, but we've already looked into known operators," Lowerson put in. "We checked out national and international watchlists, spoke to Europol and all sorts. The fact is, high level jewel thieves or gangs fulfilling black market orders wouldn't wait around to be caught, and they wouldn't return to the scene to try to cover it up long after the fact. They'd disappear off to Brazil or wherever and live it up on Ipanema Beach."

"Doesn't sound half bad, when you put it like that," Phillips joked. "But I take your point, son. Career thieves might get nasty if they're caught out, or disturbed in the heat of the moment, but they wouldn't go out of their way to murder a police officer, or go and torture some poor old git who might have spotted the switch. It draws too much attention."

Ryan nodded.

"Which brings us back around to our theory, which is that we're not dealing with a regular career criminal, or even a high-calibre gang of jewel thieves. We're looking for someone with a *very specific reason* to have taken the original cross in the first place. Your average criminal wouldn't go to all the trouble of having the artefact copied— and not just any copy, either, but one that was good enough to fool ninety-nine percent of people."

"Aye, it took another top-class forger to spot the difference," Phillips agreed. "Faber threw a real spanner in the works."

Ryan nodded.

"Whoever perpetrated this didn't want to be discovered, but not necessarily because they fear prison. I think it has to do with the cult of Saint Cuthbert."

The region's most famous saint had died a thousand years ago on the tiny island of Inner Farne, off the coast of Lindisfarne. It was an area they were all well acquainted with; not least his wife, who'd been born on the tiny, atmospheric tidal island an hour or so north of where they were seated. In the years following Cuthbert's death, his body had reportedly been found 'incorrupt' and it was hailed as a miracle. He was venerated as a saint and, thereafter, a cult developed around the dead man's remains, which were said to have had miraculous healing properties. In Medieval times, to be in possession of a miracle-maker was a very powerful thing, bringing enormous wealth and prestige, so the Benedictine monks had guarded their brother's body through the ages, to preserve what Ryan would have called an enduring fiction. Yet, there were many who had believed, and who may *still* believe, that Cuthbert's relics had the power to heal, and that could be the key to everything.

"We need to find more connections," Ryan said, battling his own frustration with the lack of progress. "If the original cross was stolen because of what it represents, we could be dealing with something similar to the Circle."

He referred to a cult that formerly operated around the North East, consisting of prominent, influential people including their very own former Detective Chief Superintendent Gregson, who now languished behind bars at Her Majesty's pleasure.

"There was one key difference there," MacKenzie said. "Before it was disbanded, the Circle used to cobble together old Satanic and Pagan rituals, bastardising both to give themselves a kind of veneer of respectability and perpetuate the idea of there being otherworldly forces at work. It never had any substance; it was all smoke and mirrors, phony rituals that its followers could use to tell themselves that their actions were all in a higher cause, rather than admitting the truth—that everything they did, they did for their own personal gain."

MacKenzie paused, thinking of that fraught time in their lives, before shoving the memories to the back of her mind.

"In this case, if you're right about the original theft having something to do with the cult surrounding Saint Cuthbert, we might be dealing with a genuine case of religious fanaticism. Not something whipped up or mashed together to suit the moment, but a longstanding, historic belief system that's endured for a thousand years."

"I don't see how it's so different," Yates said. "Surely, both cults are used as a means of control?"

"It's true that any cult can exercise control over its followers," Ryan said. "Groups forged together on the basis of a common belief system, no matter how ridiculous or untrue, allows its leaders to exert power over people using the same methods we see in other areas, like County Lines.

There, you have drug dealers targeting vulnerable people, usually kids, to do their dealing well outside city limits. They bring them on board with freebies and promises, then keep them with threats."

Ryan lifted a shoulder.

"Same applies to dirty coppers," he said. "Some of them don't flip because they want to, but because they've been caught out. Maybe they pilfer a bag of coke during a drugs bust because the other officers are all doing it, egging him on. Later, those same officers tell them they're one of the gang, now, and owe a few favours, or else they'll be reported and lose their job, the respect of their peers, their family... the lot. Of course, there are exceptions," Ryan added, with a knowing smile. "Some people have more backbone than others."

Beneath the table, Yates squeezed Lowerson's knee in solidarity. Not so long ago, he'd found himself in a compromising situation but, rather than bow to the pressure, he'd come through for his team and had been instrumental in toppling one of the most powerful organised crime gangs in the country.

"Anyway, their methods might be similar, but their approaches are different because one carries more authenticity than the other, and has history on its side," Ryan continued. "The Catholic Church is a powerful force and, although its following might be diminished on a world scale, it still carries plenty of weight, particularly at a local level. If you have a group of people who really believe in

God, miracles, afterlives, eternal damnation and the idea of utopia, the bonds that tie are infinitely stronger than a bunch of self-interested quacks."

As somebody who was of no faith, but was a great believer in individual liberty, Ryan respected the rights of others to have faith in whatever they chose, so long as they did no harm to others. As a logical man, it didn't mean that he understood the enduring quality of religious belief systems; merely, that he acknowledged the right of every individual to have one, if they chose to. He could readily admit that, at times like these, when religious dogma might prove to be the reason why people had been murdered and others injured, his level of tolerance fell, along with his patience.

But he knew that both Phillips and MacKenzie had been raised in the Catholic faith, and he was nonetheless a thoughtful man, so he spoke with care.

"Why would people believe that Saint Cuthbert's body was still whole?" he asked, of nobody in particular. "I know there were early reports that the body was intact, repeated over the years, but those could easily have been fabrication, given what the Church stood to gain. Life experience has taught us that not all 'Godly' men act in 'Godly' ways—surely, people must have had their suspicions. Why would anybody suspend disbelief?"

MacKenzie smiled. "Why believe anything?" she said. "For comfort, or to feel that there's meaning and order in the world; or, perhaps because it makes living that little bit easier—as well as dying. If you truly believe in an afterlife, in Heaven and Hell, then it makes dying a little less frightening, doesn't it?"

"Because then, it isn't the end?"

"Exactly," she murmured.

Ryan leaned back in his chair, thinking over what she had said. If MacKenzie was right and their theories were correct, the person or group they sought answered to a much higher master than one who dressed in fake animal pelts and danced beneath a full moon. They would be prepared to die for a cause and had no respect for secular justice.

They would never stop, for fear of eternal damnation.

A dull ache began to throb at his temples and Ryan ordered himself to remain focused. Fear of the unknown, of coming home to find his family dead before being shot on his own front doorstep, like Joan Tebbutt, could be overwhelming. It clutched at his heart like a vice, squeezing its icy fingers until he could hardly breathe…

He looked up to find his team watching him closely, and bore down against rising panic.

"I believe in *people*," he said, pushing back from his chair to pace about a bit, working off the cortisol running through his body. "*People* fed the cult back when Cuthbert died, and it's *people* who are murdering to acquire his relics, today."

Ryan spun around, eyes blazing.

"We're not hunting for some spectre from the past," he said. "Whoever is behind this is made of flesh and blood, just like us. No matter how hard this gets, we need to remember that."

He turned to Yates.

"Mel, you were right when you said that whoever stole the fake cross was worried about us finding it and using it to trace them," he said, decisively. "But I don't think they're worried we'll trace *them*, as much as we'd trace the weak link that separates us from them."

"What weak link?" she asked.

"Whoever made the forgery," Ryan explained. "Whoever did this must have known we'd use the forged cross to try to uncover its maker and, from there, find the person who'd commissioned it."

"We've already looked into the forgers with that level of skill," Lowerson put in. "It's been tough to keep the investigation quiet and ask questions without raising suspicions but, from what we can gather, it comes down to two names: Edward Faber, street name 'Fabergé'—"

"Who's dead as a dodo," Phillips pointed out, in his inimitable way.

"Exactly, and then there's Mathieu Lareuse, street name 'Rodin'. The two of them were old rivals, apparently."

"In that case, when Faber saw the cross on display at the Cathedral and noticed it was a forgery, perhaps he had a good idea of the person responsible for making it," Ryan said. "Do you have any further update on Rodin's whereabouts?"

When months had gone by without turning up any leads, they'd been forced to assume Mathieu Lareuse had gone the same way as Faber—or. indeed, the dodo.

"Actually, there's been some good news on that score," Lowerson was delighted to say. "Rodin was picked up and brought into custody last night, down in London. He's been charged with various dishonesty offences and is being held on remand until he goes in front of the magistrates later this afternoon."

Ryan's spirits lifted, along with the general mood in the room.

Hope renewed.

"This is just the breakthrough we needed," he said, and began making plans to contact one of his former colleagues at the Met to set up a private meeting with the elusive Mr Lareuse. "Phillips, cancel whatever you've got planned this afternoon—"

There came a peremptory knock on the door.

When it opened to admit Chief Constable Morrison, Ryan took one look at the resolute expression on her face and knew immediately that their time had run out.

She'd come to shut them down.

CHAPTER 7

"Ryan? A word, please."

She didn't wait for him, and merely nodded to the rest of the team before stepping back outside and walking directly to her office at the end of the corridor. There might have been words to say, but Sandra Morrison was no fool; she'd wait until they were safely ensconced behind another closed door before speaking freely.

Ryan followed at a distance, his footsteps a fraction slower than his usual pace while he thought of what he would say to try to persuade the Chief Constable to change her mind and give them just a little more time.

In the meantime, he kept his counsel, and shut the door behind him with a soft *click*.

"You wanted to speak to me, ma'am?"

Morrison gave him a long, level look that was entirely devoid of emotion. He knew that look, because he'd employed it numerous times himself when imparting bad news, especially to grieving families.

"Yes. Have a seat, Ryan."

"Thank you, but I'd rather stand."

Morrison gritted her teeth, and changed her mind about sitting down herself. Ryan was one of her best detectives and, despite all his foibles, she happened to like his style and his results were second to none. However, he was not built to be managed; he was built to lead. Usually, they rubbed along well, having developed an understanding over the years, which made moments like these all the harder. His focus was always on the victims of crime and their families, his energy always reserved to avenge the dead and seek justice, whatever that might be. Her focus was the same, or would have been, if she were not also responsible for managing the precarious balance between those who operated on the front line and those who sat behind desks, lunching with politicians. Appearances mattered as much as substance, which was something Ryan found abhorrent. Still, despite their differences, they shared something in common.

Ryan did not suffer fools gladly and, as it happened, neither did she.

"How long have you been working on Operation Bertie, Ryan?"

Morrison's approach threw him, momentarily, until he realised that she was doing exactly what he would have done, were the situation reversed: encouraging him to come to the same conclusion she had, despite his better judgment.

Clever.

"Around nine months," he supplied, without a flicker.

"And what progress has been made during that time?" she asked.

Rhetorical questioning, he noted.

"We've determined how the original pectoral cross was switched for the fake," he said, keeping his tone as professional as hers. "The only possible time it could have been achieved without drawing unwanted attention was three years ago, when the exhibition space at the cathedral was being completely remodelled. Large teams of builders, scaffolders, architects, cathedral staff, security staff and other specialists were on-site at one time or another, giving scope for any number of people to have been party to it."

"Mm," she said, and cocked her head to one side. "What proof do you have to support that theory?"

Ryan swallowed. "We've compiled a list of all known persons who had access to the renovation works during that time, and have been investigating each of them in turn—"

"What proof, Ryan?" she repeated.

He fell silent, for she was absolutely right. There was no hard evidence, no smoking gun, only deductive reasoning which didn't stand up in court. As for the list of possible suspects, it was as long as his arm and almost impossible to investigate with any kind of rigour without raising suspicions and alerting the perpetrator.

"The CCTV systems weren't as robust as they are now," he said. "Part of the renovation project involved replacing the old security system with a new one. In any event, footage from three years ago wouldn't have been kept, and it would raise suspicions if we were to go rooting around for it."

Being a fair-minded woman, Morrison gave him the benefit of the doubt.

"Even if you're right in your assumptions about when the cross was switched, you're still no closer to finding a definite lead, or even a suspect," she said. "What about DC Justine Winter? Have you found out why she was involved in Tebbutt's murder?"

A muscle ticked in Ryan's jaw, which was the only outward sign that he was irritated.

"As you know, ma'am, when Winter committed suicide, she left a note written in runes that was later translated to read, 'SACRIFICE'. The only other thing Winter left was a copy of the life insurance policy she'd taken out, which guaranteed cover even if she died by her own hand. The beneficiary of the policy is her brother, who suffers from a particularly degenerative form of motor neurone disease. We believe she highlighted this policy to be sure that he'd be taken care of, following her death."

He paused, gathering his thoughts.

"Our current thinking is that the genuine cross was taken not for its monetary value, but because of its religious and symbolic significance—specifically, the idea that it may be imbued with healing powers. If that's the case, we can hypothesise a link to the cult of Saint Cuthbert, and that Winter was involved in some way for the benefit of her brother, over whom she had sole guardianship following their parents' death."

Morrison ran a weary hand over the back of her neck.

"Again, I have to ask—what proof do you have that any of this is true? Aside from one of your famous 'gut feelings'?"

Ryan's eyes turned flat. It was true that, many times during the course of his career, his intuition had preceded the evidence, but he had always deferred to logic when it mattered and never taken important decisions based on intuition alone.

Perhaps Morrison read some of the outrage on his face, for she relented on that score, at least.

"All right," she said, and held up her hands. "I retract that last comment, but my question still stands. Are you any further forward in understanding why DC Justine Winter was involved in all this?"

"We know it wasn't for any monetary gain," Ryan replied, coolly. "We were able to check Winter's bank accounts and searches were made of her home as part of the regular investigation. The problem arises when we try to focus on her relationship with her brother."

"Oh?" Morrison found herself asking. "You think he's involved?"

"Not in the crimes she perpetrated, but perhaps as an indirect motivator," Ryan replied. "We suspect Justine bought into the so-called cult of Saint Cuthbert, perhaps because she wanted to procure a miracle on behalf of her ailing brother. He's in a private care facility now, but, when

Justine was alive, he lived with her and had a home-help who came in when Justine was at work. She worked part-time for Durham CID and, on the days when she was caring for him, she and her brother attended regular hospital appointments and carer meetings. Patient confidentiality is a major stumbling block to our being able to find out much in the way of the names of people Justine would have come into contact with."

Morrison gave up on the pretence and slumped gratefully into her desk chair.

"Let me see if I have this straight," she said. "Although you suspect Justine believed in the cult properties of Cuthbert's relics, perhaps because she wanted to procure a miracle, you have absolutely no evidence to support it?"

"Not yet—"

"And, that's the best theory you can come up with? That the theft, the explosion and Tebbutt's murder was all perpetrated by a group of religious fanatics?"

"Yes," he said simply. "It's the only logical connection, because we've exhausted everything else."

Morrison shook her head.

"Ryan, I can't allow this to go on," she said. "You've had months, now. If something was going to turn up or if anything else was going to happen, it would have done so, by now."

"Something has turned up," he said quickly. "Before you came into the conference room, Lowerson told me the forger most likely responsible for making the replica cross has turned up in London and is being held in police custody for other charges, as we speak."

Morrison remained unmoved.

"I take it you have some sort of proof to support your belief that this person made the replica cross?"

Ryan kept his frustration firmly in check.

"Not yet, but that's the point; Mathieu Lareuse has been off-grid. We assumed he'd skipped the country or that he was already dead somewhere. We've had no way of questioning him or conducting a search but, now he's been found, I could easily head down there this afternoon—"

Morrison was incredulous. "You have to be joking, Ryan. I'm not giving you carte blanche to scamper down to the other end of the country without good reason. You say this forger made the replica cross, but you haven't given me anything concrete to support it. We need a causal link, not baseless theories."

"When I question him, he might talk," Ryan tried again. "Now the Met have him in custody, they'll be going through his personal effects and, with any luck, will have already secured a search and seize warrant. They might find something that links back to this."

"And they might not," she snapped.

"If I could speak to him—"

Most of the time, it was true that Ryan could charm the birds from the trees or, in this case, a confession from a criminal. But, Morrison thought, everything had its limits.

"You *won't* be questioning him, Ryan, because he's been charged for an offence outside your jurisdiction," she said firmly. "Leave it to the Metropolitan Police. If they turn something up, they'll let us know."

"Ma'am—"

"That's final," she said, and her tone brooked no further debate. "I want Operation Bertie shut down, effective immediately. Finish up the public-facing investigation, for the benefit of the press and for the people of this region and, for God's sake, put this business to bed."

When Ryan said nothing, she added a final piece of maternal advice.

"On the subject of beds, you look as though you could use one," she said, more gently. "I know you had a rough time with Anna in the hospital and that you've got a baby at home now, Ryan. You should know how happy we all are for you, but make sure you get a proper night's sleep sometime soon because, frankly, you look as rough as a badger's arse."

"Thank you, ma'am," he muttered.

"Anytime."

CHAPTER 8

Ryan was a man of his word.

When he agreed to a course of action, or acquiesced to an order from a senior officer, it was only in rare circumstances that he deviated. As he made his way back to the conference room, Ryan comforted himself with the knowledge that he had not explicitly agreed that he would follow Morrison's order to shut down Operation Bertie. It might be a technicality, but desperate times called for desperate measures.

Slippery?

Most definitely.

Necessary?

"Abso-bloody-lutely," he muttered, and resolved to follow the Chief Constable's bidding just as soon as the day's briefing was over, and all present lines of enquiry were exhausted.

"What have I missed?" Ryan asked, once he was back in the room.

"Nowt much," Phillips said, eloquently. "But, never mind what we've been doing—what happened with Morrison?"

Ryan blew out a long breath and told the absolute truth.

"She told me to shut Operation Bertie down," he said, conversationally. "Not enough progress, no real evidence, et cetera."

There was a momentary silence while the others considered this, then Phillips pursed his lips.

"Well, now, usually, I'd have my lunch break around one o'clock," he said, baffling them all for a moment. "But, since I'm on a bit of a health kick, I'd only be eating a quinoa salad at my desk while I try to forget the taste of bacon. Seems to me, I could do that a bit earlier, today—say, around now, since we're just sittin' around."

MacKenzie gave her husband a knowing smile.

"Now you mention it, I didn't have time for breakfast this morning," she said. "I'd rather eat something a bit earlier today and now's as good a time, as any. We could have something here and, if we happen to talk over a few things, it'd just be work colleagues chewing the fat, now, wouldn't it?"

Ryan leaned back in his chair, a slow smile spreading across his face.

"It would," he agreed.

"I could take an early lunch," Lowerson said. "My caseload is manageable, and anything urgent I can get to in an hour, or so. How about you, Mel?"

"Funny enough, my stomach was rumbling, earlier," she said, with a wink.

Ryan looked amongst them and felt like the most fortunate of men.

Ten minutes later, it became clear that Phillips hadn't been joking about the quinoa, which he pushed around with a plastic fork while they continued their friendly 'discussion' about the cult of Saint Cuthbert.

"What about the other relics at Durham Cathedral?" Ryan asked. "Have we made any progress in finding out whether any more of them were switched?"

If they were right about the motivations behind the original theft during the renovation works three years prior, there was a strong possibility that other relics belonging to Cuthbert might have been taken at the same time.

Lowerson had been chiefly responsible for that element of their investigation, and was sorry to be the bearer of disappointing news.

"It would add a lot of weight to the investigation, if we could discover whether other relics had been taken," he said. "The problem is, it's difficult for us to investigate without alerting anybody at the Cathedral. We'd need to gain access to the relics, for one thing, and have their authenticity tested. But, as we've said before, there's huge potential for an individual or a crew of people to have made a switch—especially if we're dealing with a group that has cash to burn, and who could bribe somebody already working on the renovation works to swap the originals for forged replicas when the relics were being moved to their new display cases, for instance."

"All right," Ryan said, and ran a frustrated hand through his hair, which was long overdue for a trim. "Maybe we've been focusing too much on the relics in Durham. What about further afield? Over the centuries, Cuthbert's bits and bobs must have travelled to different parts of the country, maybe for safekeeping—and what about other museum exhibitions? They often loan out important pieces like that, don't they? Perhaps they've been targeted by the same perp."

"I did a bit of digging around that," Lowerson said, with more optimism. "And, actually, I think you may be on to something there, boss."

Jack paused to reach for a cardboard file, rifling through the papers until he found what he was looking for.

"This is a picture of Cuthbert's Gospel of Saint John," he said, setting a colour print on the table. "It's sometimes called the Stonyhurst Gospel, because it spent over two hundred years in the library at Stonyhurst College, a Jesuit school down in Lancashire."

Ryan leaned forward to study the image of a tiny gospel book, its front cover made of distinctive red goatskin and which was, he would later learn, the earliest surviving Western book binding in the world.

"This was Cuthbert's?" he asked.

Lowerson made a rocking motion with his hand.

"People used to think so, because it was made pretty close to the time Cuthbert was alive and it was stored inside Cuthbert's coffin with his body for centuries, until around the time of the dissolution of the monasteries in the sixteenth century," he said. "Nowadays, people think it was made by the monks at the monastery in Monkwearmouth—"

"Down in Jarrow?" Phillips piped up, glad to be learning something new about his local heritage. "They made that little book?"

"Yep, the current thinking is that they made the gospel book as an offering to Cuthbert, to be placed inside his coffin. That's why it's known as St. Cuthbert's Gospel, even though the text is from St. John."

"Anna would be impressed with all of this," Ryan said, thinking of his wife, who was a leading local historian and fountain of knowledge about all manner of things. "Where's the book now?"

"The British Library bought it from Stonyhurst for a cool twelve million back in 2012," Lowerson said, and couldn't help thinking it should have been donated to the library for free, as a public artefact of national importance. "Anyway, the book spends half of its time in Durham and half at the British Library in London, under lock and key."

Ryan perked up at that. "Where, in Durham? We could take a look—"

But Lowerson shook his head. "At the moment, it's in London."

"It doesn't matter either way, does it?" MacKenzie observed. "If we're dealing with people who aren't afraid of large-scale heists, it wouldn't matter to them whether the book was in Durham or London—if they wanted to steal it, they'd find a way."

Ryan agreed, and was about to say as much when they were interrupted by the sound of his mobile phone trilling out a rendition of *Eye of the Tiger*.

"Sorry," he muttered, and started slapping his pockets to find the offending block of plastic.

He caught it on the last ring.

"Ryan."

The others watched his face slowly alter, his eyes turning cool and detached as he listened to the caller at the other end.

"I'll be there as soon as I can," he said eventually, and ended the call looking thoughtful.

"Well?" Phillips asked the question on all their lips. "Howay then—who's died?"

"A monk," Ryan said, and the light of battle began to shine once more in his bold blue eyes. "He's been found dead—tortured, they think, in a similar way to Edward Faber. The SIO wants us to go down there and see if it's the same."

"A monk," MacKenzie murmured. "Seems an unusual choice of victim."

"One who happens to be a leading authority on Saint Cuthbert," Ryan added, after a quick online search. "Now, isn't that—"

"A coincidence?" Yates said, teasingly.

Ryan smiled, and they already knew what he would say.

"There's no such thing."

CHAPTER 9

Phillips popped a handful of mixed nuts into his mouth, telling himself they were better than beefy Hula-Hoops, in many ways.

Many, many ways.

He didn't know what those ways were, yet, but that was beside the point.

Stuffing the offending packet of bird food back in his pocket, he looked over at Ryan and thought he bore the look of a man who needed more than a packet of crisps to see him through the rest of the day.

"If you want a break, I can take over the driving?"

Ryan laughed shortly. "Frank, if we want to get down to Yorkshire and back before midnight, it's best if I handle the driving."

"Y' nah, between you and Denise, I get nowt but cheek over my driving skills," Phillips muttered, and crossed his arms over his paunch. "I always get us there safely, and in one piece."

"As do I," Ryan said. "The only difference is, I don't drive like I've got *Miss Daisy* in the back seat."

Phillips let out a rumbling chuckle. "Aye, you've got a littlun' now," he said. "How's she doing? Missin' her Uncle Frank, I s'pose."

He watched the Ryan's face soften, and was glad to see it. The man might have been his professional senior, but Ryan was a few years younger than himself in age and, from time to time, it showed. Phillips had never wished to step into any fatherly shoes, especially since Ryan had a perfectly decent father of his own; all the same, he felt something like a father's pride when he saw his friend smile, for there was a time when that was a rare thing indeed. Maxwell Finley-Ryan, who preferred 'Ryan' at all times, was a stoic man with broad shoulders, a compassionate leader in the office, a loyal friend, loving husband and, now, a doting father. It took energy and commitment to become all of those things, and even more to remain so. Over the years, life had thrown a few curve balls that might have derailed the happiness Ryan now enjoyed and, amid the grief following the death of his sister, Natalie, he might have become a bitter cynic, unable to love or be loved in return.

But he'd chosen a different path.

"Frank, I can honestly say, I never thought I could love another being in this world as much as I love Anna," Ryan said. "I didn't think I'd have the capacity...but I was wrong about that. It feels as though my heart's expanded for Emma, and I have the same amount of love to give her, all over again."

79

Phillips put a hand briefly on the other man's shoulder as they watched the road ahead.

"Aye, it takes you by surprise, doesn't it?" he said softly. "After my Laura passed, I never thought I could feel the same way again—then, along came Denise. *Then*, just as I'm getting used to a new life, trying my best to keep up with her, along comes Samantha to shake us both up again."

Ryan chose not to imagine what his sergeant meant by 'keeping up with' Denise and focused on the safer topic of the man's daughter instead.

"She's a good kid," he said. "Full of spirit, and sharp as a tack."

"She's an absolute belter," Phillips agreed. "Y'nah, we were only sayin' the other day, it's as though Sam was made for us—right the way down to her red hair and freckles. Who'd have thought a little girl would turn up lookin' the double of Denise?"

He sighed, happily.

"I thought we were too late," he continued. "Denise thought that n'all, but it's never too late to give a child a good home."

Ryan knew the adoption process had been lengthy, fraught with bureaucracy and emotional turmoil. He'd been called upon to provide references for his friends, and the only problem he'd found in doing so was a lack of room on the paperwork, so he could list all the many and varied reasons why any child would be bloody lucky to have Frank Phillips and Denise MacKenzie as its parents.

"That's not to say there haven't been teething problems," Phillips said. "The thing is, you and Anna have known Emma from the very beginning. You'll be there for her all the way through, and get to know what makes her tick. With Samantha, we missed out on the first eight years of her life, and those are some of the most important."

Phillips shifted in his seat, thinking of how best to express it.

"Fact is, we might know her parents' names, and what they did for a living, but we also know they left all kinds of trauma for Sam to deal with—"

"It's not every baby who remembers its mother being killed," Ryan agreed. "Or has to live with the knowledge that their father was no good. Bearing in mind all that, she's adjusted to her new life incredibly well."

"We've tried to do our best," Phillips said. "There's been a bit of counselling on the side and, to be perfectly honest, son, I'm relieved her birth parents aren't on the scene, anymore. There's no chance of either of them popping up, out of the blue, to claim her back and upset her all over again. God, I feel awful saying that."

"It's understandable," Ryan said, and indicated to take the slip road off the A1 as they neared the junction east towards the Howardian Hills, north of the ancient city of York. "Do you think Samantha's settled in, now?"

"Aye, she's got her feet under the table, all right," Phillips chuckled. "Has us both wrapped around her little finger, that's the truth of it."

Ryan flashed his sergeant a smile.

"You and me both," he said, and heaved a theatrical sigh. "I don't know how we manage to get ourselves into these scrapes, Frank. We could have been living it up, out on the tiles every night…a pair of good-lookin' stallions like us would have cleaned up at Bigg Market on a Friday night."

Phillips laughed, knowing fine well that Ryan had never been to the clubs in Newcastle's legendary Bigg Market on a Friday night, or any other night.

He'd never lived…

"Aye, all very well for you, maybe. You've got half the women in CID still carrying a torch, not to mention Samantha, who's still got that crush—"

Ryan was a bit embarrassed. "On me? I'm old enough to be her father."

"Yeah, but you look like a bleedin' superhero and she's been watching all those Marvel films, hasn't she? Every time your name comes up, it's all, 'Ryan's so handsome' and 'Ryan's so kind'…it's enough to put me off my quinoa. Mind you, with the way you're going, you'll be looking more like Superman's older, knackered brother, soon enough."

"Flatterer," Ryan said, deadpan.

Phillips laughed.

"Seriously, though, I can't help noticing you've been burning the candle at both ends, lately, son. I know you've got Emma but—"

"It isn't that," Ryan interrupted him. "She's five months old now and sleeps really well, except when she's teething. Besides, we've had plenty of help from my parents."

"What is it, then?" Phillips asked. "Operation Bertie?"

Ryan gave a brief nod.

"I know it's been months now, but I feel it, here," he said, rapping a knuckle against his chest. "This isn't over yet and, until it is, I won't rest."

His words hung on the air as the landscape changed, and the car began to wind its way through the rolling countryside of the Howardian Hills, which undulated on either side of the road and were flanked by rich woodland, all tinged with a sprinkling of winter frost.

It might have been something from a postcard.

"Whoever killed this monk had an eye for window dressing," Phillips murmured. "What was the name of the place, again?"

"Crayke College," Ryan said. "Next turning on the left."

Phillips spotted a collection of ancient stone buildings peeping through the trees and prepared to revert to 'work mode'.

Before then, he had one final thing to say.

"You're not imagining it," Phillips said quietly. "I know, in our game, we've usually got things wrapped up quickly, then we're on to the next adventure. This is harder, because we still don't know who we're dealing with, we only know they're out there."

"Morrison thinks I'm overreacting," Ryan said. "She thinks I'm in the throes of sleep deprivation, and that new fatherhood has addled my brain."

"Whereas, we both know, you've never been quite reet in the heed, as my old Da' would say."

Ryan laughed. "Probably true," he admitted, feeling a little better than before.

Phillips looked out across the misty, snow-flecked meadows and then back at his friend.

"Anyway, all I want to tell you is that you'll never be alone, lad. You've got all of us here, ready and willing to help."

"Thanks, Frank. I might hold you to that."

CHAPTER 10

It was a little after one-thirty when Ryan and Phillips drove through a set of impressive pillared stone gates, where they were met by a police constable from the North Yorkshire constabulary bearing a clipboard and the eager, stony-faced look of one who'd recently left the training academy.

"Sorry, there's no entry to the College, today, unless you're a parent—"

Ryan held out his warrant card for inspection. "DCI Ryan and DS Phillips, from Northumbria CID. Your SIO is expecting us."

He wasn't sure whether to feel gratified or concerned when the young man's eyebrows shot into his gelled hairline.

"Right—sorry, chief inspector, I didn't recognise you. Carry straight on, and I'll radio DCI Patel to let her know you're on your way."

"You're infamous," Phillips whispered, from the corner of his mouth. "Maybe he'll ask for your autograph."

"Shut your pie ho—damn it, I can't even insult you in the same way, since you're not eating pies anymore," Ryan grumbled.

"Salad hole doesn't have the same ring to it," Phillips agreed, smugly.

They followed a winding driveway towards the main entrance of Crayke College, which formed part of a much larger estate belonging to the adjoining monastery that extended to farms, orchards, playing fields and equestrian facilities, in addition to the main school buildings and boarding houses, which were large enough to resemble a small village. The school catered to children from the age of seven and, having attended a similar establishment from around that age, Ryan was struck forcibly by the strength of his own animosity—towards establishments of that kind, and, sadly, towards his own parents for having left him there.

"Bringing back a few memories?" Phillips asked, with his usual insight.

Ryan nodded, but said nothing more as they crawled along the driveway, his eyes scanning either side to gauge the terrain.

"Must be hundreds of acres, here," he said eventually. "Plenty of ways for somebody to gain access without anybody noticing."

Phillips made a rumbling sound of agreement.

"There's a security lodge, back there, but there's miles of perimeter wall with a place like this," he said. "Easy enough to hop over it, if you know how to avoid the cameras."

"Exactly. Not counting the river and any other gated entry points."

They rounded a bend in the driveway and had their first glimpse of Crayke College. It was a majestic sight, by any standards: the gilded edges of it its clocktower shimmered in the early afternoon sunlight, while its patrician architecture sprawled in symmetrical columns made of warm, finely-honed sandstone.

"What a dump!" Phillips joked. "Wonder what the upkeep is, on a place like this."

Ryan was lost for words. As it happened, he had a very good idea of what the running costs were for a stately home the size of Crayke College. Whilst he'd never made any secret of his upbringing, which had been very privileged, neither was he in the habit of broadcasting it. He'd always preferred to be judged on his own merits as a person rather than on the trappings of his family's wealth, but he was no hypocrite. Thanks to an accident of birth, he'd enjoyed advantages other children hadn't. Others might have mentioned that personal qualities of integrity and dedication might also have played their part, but Ryan knew there had been inequality of opportunity, even if he hadn't asked for it.

His decision to lead a different kind of life than the one his father had mapped out for him was one of many contentious issues that divided the two men, and it was only in recent times that they had begun to rebuild their fractured relationship. Charles Ryan could not understand why his son would wish to reject his birthright, while Ryan could not begin to imagine a life spent within the echoing walls of his childhood home, playing Lord of the Manor whilst others survived on the bare minimum. He'd used a generous inheritance from his grandmother to fund several charitable ventures, which were managed by others to redistribute money he plainly didn't need. Aside from Anna, Phillips was one of only a handful of people who'd ever visited Ryan's family home in Devon—even then, only to attend his sister's funeral at the chapel on the Finley-Ryan estate. However, Phillips knew nothing about Ryan's other philanthropic ventures, and he would have been embarrassed to speak of it.

"It takes hundreds of thousands a year," Ryan said simply, and left it at that.

Phillips gave a long whistle.

"Think I'll stick to my campervan," he said. "Low overheads, for one thing, and you can go wherever the wind takes you."

There was a second's pause, then Ryan began to laugh—not at Phillips, but at himself. There were all kinds of riches, he thought, but some things were priceless.

"Did I miss something?"

"You haven't missed a thing, Frank," he said, warmly. "Not a damn thing."

When they approached the front entrance, which consisted of a large, circular gravel driveway in front of a pillared portico, they spotted several police vehicles parked off to one side. Assuming correctly that the local police were keeping the gravelled area clear for forensic analysis, Ryan followed their example and pulled up alongside the others.

Spotting their arrival, a woman in a plain black trouser suit peeled away from a group of police and forensics staff and crunched across the gravel to meet them.

"DCI Ryan? I'm DCI Dina Patel," she said, after he'd unfolded himself from the car. "Glad you could make it down."

Patel couldn't have been more than five feet tall, and Ryan found himself stooping slightly so as not to loom over her diminutive height. She wore a thick winter coat over her suit and, as the air began to penetrate, he decided she definitely had the right idea.

"Thanks for reaching out to us," he replied, shaking her hand. "This is Detective Sergeant Frank Phillips."

Patel shook his hand, too, and then gestured to the building at her back.

"Impressive, isn't it?" she remarked.

"Not bad," Ryan agreed, opening the boot of the car to retrieve his ski jacket. "I hear they've had some trouble, here, lately."

"Bad business," she muttered, and looked out across the lawns to clear her head of the images she'd seen that day and would likely take home with her, later that night. "As I said on the phone, we got a call from the headmaster around nine o'clock this morning to report a murder. Control dispatched a couple of first responders to the scene, who were here by twenty-past, at the latest. They took one look at the scene and called in the cavalry."

Her throat worked, as if she was still fighting nausea.

"Gets to you sometimes, doesn't it?" Phillips sympathised. "Thirty years in the business and it still turns my stomach."

She gave a brief nod, then seemed to pull herself together.

"Worse I've seen in a long while, and I've got fifteen years under my belt," she told them. "The man was tortured, possibly for hours, and aside from the Faber case you had a few months ago, it's the only one of its kind we've seen in these parts for a good, long while. That's what prompted me to call you—I thought there might be a link."

"It's appreciated," Ryan said, and meant it. Not all Major Crimes Units were as cooperative, nor were Senior Investigating Officers always as communicative as Patel appeared to be.

She nodded, rubbing her hands together for warmth.

"It benefits both of us to know if there's any connection," she said. "It makes sense to share what information we have, and perhaps you can tell me if there are any facets of the killing that strike a chord with what you've seen before."

"We'll help however we can," Ryan said, carefully.

"All right, then. Let's walk and talk."

Patel led them towards a narrow pathway running behind the sports hall, which bore a pretty, hand-painted sign marked 'ORCHARD & CIDER MILL'.

"Vic's name was Jacob Jamieson—or Father Jacob, as he was known around these parts," she said. "Born in 1968, he'd been a monk for the past twenty years. Prior to that, he worked as a history teacher."

Patel raised a hand to one of her team, who passed them on the way.

"From what we can gather, Father Jacob was well respected in the community here, and well-liked by the staff and pupils. He was housemaster of one of the larger boarding houses, named after St. Cuthbert," she said, pausing to point towards a two-storey, stone-built edifice on the far side of the sports hall. "It's that one over there."

"St. Cuthbert?" Ryan asked.

"Yes, funny for that name to crop up, after what happened in Durham," she remarked. "Actually, before he became a monk, I'm told Father Jacob was an authority on the life and works of St. Cuthbert, and it seems that he was able to maintain his interest as part of his monastic occupation."

Ryan and Phillips exchanged a meaningful glance.

"Really? I suppose it's not uncommon in Benedictine circles," Ryan said. "Cuthbert is a major saint, particularly in this part of the world."

"I wouldn't know much about it—wrong religion," she said, with a smile. "But we'll do a full dive into his background when the preliminaries are underway."

Ryan nodded. "What are the circumstances?" he asked, bringing their discussion back around to brass tacks. "You didn't go into too much detail, over the phone."

Patel gave him a watery smile. "It was still pretty fresh, when I rang you," she explained. "As far as we can gather, Father Jacob went missing from St. Cuthbert's boarding house while the boys were enjoying their weekly Sunday Movie Night over in the main school hall."

"So, he was left alone in the boarding house?"

"As far as we know—yes. My sergeant's trying to get his hands on any available CCTV footage, so we can check that against the statements we've had from the other staff at the school, as well as the monks who reside in the abbey. The problem is, the list of potentials isn't limited to people on school grounds," she said. "They publish the school timetable online, including when there's a movie night, so anybody could feasibly have planned the right time to pay a visit."

"What about the kids?" Phillips asked.

Much as Patel hated to think any child could have perpetrated so heinous a crime, she had to consider the possibility.

"Them too," she said, bleakly. "We're coming to this with an open mind."

They reached the edge of the treeline, where a natural opening led through to a meadow, inside which an enormous apple orchard had been planted.

"This way," she said, taking care to use the plastic walkway that had been laid out by forensic staff, rather than stomping over the soft turf as they meandered through the bare trees. "The abbey owns the orchard, and the monks have a cottage industry making their own cider from the apples. In the season, it's full of people, including external visitors who can tour the orchards. At this time of year, it's deserted. Father Jacob was found in the cider mill at around half past eight this morning."

"He didn't die at the boarding house?" Ryan queried.

"Highly unlikely," she said. "You'll see what I mean, soon enough. How he came to be in the mill is anybody's business, but we've found tracks leading from the back of St. Cuthbert's House to the sports hall that suggest he might have been running towards the main building. We found drag marks and some evidence of minor blood loss, where the pathway forks."

"Where the perp caught him, before he could call out for help?" Ryan wondered.

"It would fit," she agreed. "The forensics team have a job on their hands to cover this kind of area—they'll be here for days. Then, there's the problem of the dog prints."

Both men frowned in confusion.

"There's a dog?"

"There's a pack of them," she said. "The college keeps its own hounds—for farming and grousing purposes, *naturally*."

Another bone of contention with his father, Ryan thought sadly. He, who had grown up on the land and was a qualified firearms specialist, didn't like to kill another living thing—whereas his father had been raised to manage the land and, having served in the military, took a different view of the matter.

They tended to avoid any discussion of politics, as a general rule.

"When they couldn't find Father Jacob, they brought in the Captain of Beagling and his best sniffer dog," Patel was saying.

Ryan frowned.

"Wait a minute. You're telling me that, when they thought Father Jacob was missing, rather than calling in the police they brought in one of their pack dogs?"

Patel wasn't overjoyed about it herself.

"Destroying trace evidence, in the process. The dog scrambled all over the route Father Jacob took last night, not to mention the footprints of everyone who trampled after him. If they'd told us sooner, we could have used our own trained dogs, if need be."

"It's a self-contained community here," Phillips pointed out. "Places like this tend to close ranks, and they like to run things their own way, without outside interference."

"You mean, the kind of people who believe they're answerable to a higher power, rather than to man-made justice?" Ryan wondered aloud.

"Maybe," Phillips nodded, thoughtfully. "Maybe that's exactly the kind of place this is."

CHAPTER 11

There should be a word for it, Ryan thought.

A word was needed to describe the unique emotion a murder detective experienced when they looked upon the decaying carcass of what had once been a living, breathing person. It was another kind of privilege, he thought, because only a handful of people would see the remains of Father Jacob Jamieson in such a compromised, vulnerable state; only they would know how to treat those remains with respect and care—which mattered, whether or not the person who'd once inhabited that body turned out to have been good or bad.

Sadness, disgust, nausea, impotence...

Ryan felt them all, yet none of those words was adequate to describe the whole, raw experience. He, and every other murder detective, forensics officer, mortician and pathologist were the ferrymen, who carried the dead to their place of final rest.

At times, the burden weighed heavily.

Ryan stood alongside Phillips and Patel inside the doorway of the cider mill, which was protected from the elements by a large forensics tent that billowed in the breeze. As the air whipped through the cracks in its material, they were afforded an occasional reprieve from the ripening aroma of decomposing flesh and dried blood, which mingled with the lingering scent of rotting apples that clung to the walls of the mill and inside their noses.

"Poor bastard," Phillips muttered, and was forced to look away, or else embarrass himself.

Father Jacob's body had not yet been moved, the forensics team having decided to leave it in situ to allow them to complete their work as fully as possible. Moving a body ahead of time could mean losing vital trace evidence, so this was done only with the approval of the Supervising CSI and the SIO managing the case. It made for difficult viewing, but it was better to see exactly how the man's killer had left him.

"Somebody went to town," Ryan said, after a moment's silence for the dead.

They were kitted out in protective suits and, with Patel's nod of approval, stepped further into the large, barn-like space to get a better view of what had been laid out for them to discover.

Ryan stood there for long minutes, a tall, raven-haired man with an unreadable expression on his face, until Patel cast a concerned glance towards Phillips.

"Is he okay?" she muttered, jerking her thumb at Ryan's back. "Does he always just...stand there, silently?"

"Oh, aye," Phillips said, with a breezy wave of his gloved hand. "Don't worry, he does it all the time."

Ryan didn't hear their by-play, his attention being otherwise occupied with tracing the details of the scene. There was a sense of drama here, he thought; as though everything had been arranged to the killer's satisfaction. If one discounted the shattered and defiled body of Father Jacob, which took centre stage, nothing was unusual—but there were elements that struck Ryan as being out of place. For one thing, there were four multi-coloured jars sitting on one of the window ledges, no larger than perfume bottles, which most certainly did not look as though they belonged in a dusty cider mill.

"Have you looked at those bottles?" he asked, pointing to the ledge on the other side of the room.

"I'm sure the CSIs will get around to it," Patel said, frowning in their direction. "I don't see the significance—"

"Discounting the blood and gore, the rest of this place is covered in dust," Ryan said, sweeping a hand around the airy space. "You said its rarely used out of season, right?"

Patel nodded.

"Then those bottles are significant, because they've been polished—very recently," he explained. "It might be nothing, but—"

"It could be something," Patel agreed, and made a mental note. "Thank you, I'll see to it."

When she moved off to speak to one of the CSIs, Ryan looked around him again, this time noting the placement of a heavy wooden worktable. It stood to the left of Father Jacob's body and, judging by the marks on the floor, had been shifted slightly towards him.

Why, he couldn't fathom.

No bloodstains marred its wooden surface, and it held nothing but a single white feather that hung precariously from the edge, as though it might fall to the floor.

A feather?

Ryan moved closer, walking with extreme care until he came to the edge of the worktable, where he could study the offending object.

"Patel?"

She looked up from her discussion with one of the CSIs and moved across to where he stood.

"Found something?"

"Ask them to look at this feather," he said, flummoxing her again. "It seems out of place."

Patel looked between him and the feather, wondering why Ryan wasn't talking about the body and was instead wasting his time thinking about stray feathers.

"I'd be interested to know which bird this feather comes from," Ryan continued, thinking that, as with soil samples, bird samples could prove to be a useful source of geographical information. "I wonder whether the killer brought it with him, because I don't see any other signs of bird activity in here, nor any broken windows to allow a bird to get inside. Therefore, how did it get in here?"

Now, he had her attention.

"Another thing," he said quietly. "There's a steady breeze in here, but the feather hasn't blown away…"

He trailed off and dropped down to his haunches, craning his neck to try to see if the underside of the feather was stuck on a splinter of the wooden countertop.

Then, he spotted it.

Blood.

"Look here," he said, and drew Patel down beside him so she could see what he had seen. "They've used blood to keep the feather in place."

He was right, she realised. Whoever placed the feather there had very carefully dipped the underside in some of Father Jacob's blood, ensuring it wouldn't blow away. They knew this, because there were no other bloodstains on or around the table, which made their discovery all the more significant.

She called across to one of the CSIs, who rustled forward to photograph it.

"Why would anybody do that?" she wondered. "The bottles, the feather…what does it mean?"

"I don't know," Ryan admitted.

"Aye, well, I do," Phillips said, matter-of-factly, from where he'd been making a thorough job of inspecting the doorway. "It means we've got a fully-fledged fruitcake on our hands, that's what it means."

Ryan allowed himself to look properly at Father Jacob's body, wincing at the multitude of cuts and gashes against the man's waxy grey skin, then allowing his eyes to travel upward to where his skull had been crushed like a pumpkin.

"You know what, Frank? I think you might be right."

An hour after they'd first entered the stifling interior of the cider mill, Ryan, Phillips and Patel stepped back out into the orchard to find that a light snow had begun to fall, coating the barren trees in a film of powdery white. They stood there for a moment breathing in the cold air, allowing it to cleanse their bodies and their minds.

"So, what do you think?" Patel asked. "Are there any similarities with Faber?"

They began retracing their steps along the plastic walkway.

"In the method of killing? Not really," Ryan said. "Edward Faber was tortured with a knife but, unlike here, his killer used water beforehand."

"Maybe they didn't have an apple press handy," Phillips said, and patted his belly as it gave a loud, ill-timed rumble. "Seems to me, whoever killed both men liked to travel light."

Ryan nodded, acknowledging the truth of that. In both cases, all the killer seemed to have used was a knife, which hadn't been recovered from either scene. The water and the apple press were opportunistic.

"You've got a point," he said, and turned back to Patel. "Have the CSIs found much in the way of trace evidence?"

"Not yet," she replied. "They were careful, by the looks of things."

Just like Faber, he thought.

Ryan happened to agree with the old adage that killers always left traces of themselves behind—if not DNA or fingerprints, then something more subtle—which was why he looked at their mess and destruction with a discerning eye. In this case, he found the use of the cider press interesting; not merely because it was macabre, but because it was unnecessarily dangerous.

"I wonder whether killing Father Jacob in the cider mill was a matter of accident, or design," he said. "After all, if somebody wanted to kill him quickly, they'd have been far safer finishing him in the boarding house."

"But if the object was to torture, not to kill quickly, perhaps they didn't know how long it would take for him to crack," Patel remarked. "The question is, why torture him in the first place?"

Phillips opened his mouth to venture a reason to do with a forged cross, St. Cuthbert's cult, but one look from Ryan reminded him that there were some things they could *not* share.

"Ah, do *you* have any ideas about why?" he prevaricated.

She looked up at the school, which rose above them from the summit of a gentle hill, and wondered.

"Generally speaking, ultra-violent torture of that kind is perpetrated for one of three reasons: retribution, as a warning to others—usually, in gang warfare—or in order to extract information," she said, logically. "What was the reason in your case with Faber?"

Ryan and Phillips immediately donned blank expressions.

"Unfortunately, we're still trying to get to the bottom of that," Ryan said, making a rare exception to his rule about always practising honesty. "Our best guess is that Faber's underworld past came back to haunt him, and it was a case of a good deal gone bad. The investigation is ongoing."

In truth, they had a very good idea of why Faber had been tortured, and of the information he'd revealed under sufferance. However, telling Patel would be tantamount to a confession that the recovered cross—now reinstalled in its glass cabinet in Durham Cathedral—was nothing but a fake, and would blow their whole cover and the covert investigation that had been underway for months.

If Patel thought they were evasive, she said nothing of it.

"With his connection to Cuthbert and that cross having been stolen so recently, plus the fact he was tortured, I thought perhaps there'd have been something to link the two cases. Have you looked into the possibility of Faber having been connected to the theft of that cross?" she wondered, innocently.

Ryan gave her a smile that didn't quite reach his eyes.

"We've considered most possibilities," he said, blandly. "Perhaps there's another reason for Father Jacob's death."

"At first glance, he seems to have been squeaky clean," Patel said. "On the other hand, there's a bit of a stereotype about Catholic priests, and—"

She paused, trying to find a polite way to put it.

"This is a school, the Catholic Church doesn't have an exemplary track record where safeguarding is concerned, and there's no smoke without fire," Ryan finished for her.

"Exactly. As I said, we're coming to this investigation with an open mind, and we've barely scratched the surface.

No truer word spoken, Ryan thought, and hoped she didn't scratch too deep—for her own sake.

CHAPTER 12

Before they left Patel and her team to continue their investigation, Ryan made two requests. The first was to see St. Cuthbert's boarding house, where the late Father Jacob had spent much of his time, which afforded a brief opportunity to search for any obvious clue about what the monk had known, or been in possession of, that was so important as to have cost him his life. The second was to meet the man who'd decided that one beagle's nose was more reliable than the full force of North Yorkshire CID.

After an unproductive search of the dead man's rooms, the three police officers made their way through a wide, marble foyer and along corridors that were noticeably quiet, passing gilt-edged paintings of dignitaries until Phillips was forced to ask an obvious question.

"Where are all the kids? And why isn't their artwork on the walls?"

He'd expected to see a bunch of smart-looking boys and girls in straw boaters wandering around, but instead the place resembled a tomb.

Patel checked her watch, which told her it was shortly after four o'clock.

"Maybe still in lessons," she guessed, half-heartedly. "And maybe they can't paint for shit."

Phillips let out a booming laugh, which echoed along the hallway in surround sound.

Ryan said nothing, remembering the rigid scheduling he'd learned to accept during his school days. As he thought of it, memories floated to the surface of his mind.

Finley-Ryan! Is that tie an appropriate length?

Smarten up!

No mail today, Finley-Ryan. Perhaps next week, eh?

Truant again, Ryan? What will your father say?

"Ryan?"

He snapped out of his reverie to find Phillips and Patel staring at him.

"Sorry, I was miles away."

"Anything important?" Phillips asked.

Ryan's lips twisted. "No," he said. "Just ghosts."

They found Father Peter Larverne in his private office, which commanded a triple-aspect view of the lawns from its position directly beneath the main clocktower. It was a room the headmasters of Crayke had occupied for generations and he was now the proud incumbent, with the added distinction of being the youngest ever to hold the position, at the relatively tender age of thirty-seven.

When they knocked politely at his door, they found he was not alone.

"DCI Patel? Please do come in," he said, gesturing them inside his domain. "I don't know if you've met Father Samuel, our chaplain, here at the school."

A middle-aged man with a mild, unremarkable face stood up from where he'd been sitting in one of the easy chairs and shuffled forward.

"No, I don't think we've met," Patel said.

"I spoke with your sergeant," Samuel said, a bit nervously, then turned to the headmaster. "I'll leave you to it—"

As he bade a hasty retreat, Patel's calm voice stopped him in his tracks.

"Actually, Father, perhaps you wouldn't mind staying for a moment or two," she said. "It would be useful to hear from both of you, to get a fuller picture of what happened last night and learn more about Father Jacob."

"Of course," Samuel said. "Our brother was a very worthy man. I'll do all I can to help your investigation."

"Quite right," the headmaster approved. "Please, everybody, make yourselves comfortable."

He cast an enquiring eye over the two strangers in the room, making a brief inventory of their looks and demeanour. The younger man was taller, and of a military bearing—straight-backed, as though he were quite used to being inspected—and more than capable of conducting an inspection of his own, judging by the uncompromising expression marring his otherwise flawless face. He was arresting, if not a little unnerving.

Father Peter smiled at himself, thinking that he'd never quite shaken the artist's habit of studying line and form.

Old habits die hard, so the saying went—an unfortunate turn of phrase given recent events.

The elder man was equally compelling, for different reasons. His face was what he would have called 'characterful'; rounded, but not soft, he bore the look of a fighting man from another era, one who might have used his bare fists, if the need arose. And yet, the toughness of his stance was belied by the warmth of his eyes, which invited company and conversation.

Of the two, Father Peter didn't know which he'd rather sketch first.

"This is DCI Ryan and DS Phillips," Patel said.

She omitted to mention that they were visiting from another command area, because to do so would invite entirely too many questions, and time was running short. However, she needn't have bothered. For all that Father Peter was a monk first and a headmaster second, his title demanded that he keep in touch with the secular world outside the walls of Crayke College, and he recognised Ryan's name immediately.

For reasons best known to himself, he chose not to mention it nor to ask why a celebrated detective from

Northumberland had travelled all the way down to York.

"Welcome," was all he said. "Please, be seated."

Phillips and Patel took up the offer, while Ryan positioned himself beside the window, which had the deliberate effect of casting his face in shadow so that his expression could not be so easily read. Father Peter was an observer of people, it seemed, but, on this occasion, it was he who was the subject.

"First, I'd like to thank you both for your cooperation in this matter," Patel began, in crisp, professional tones. "We understand this must be a difficult ordeal."

Father Peter raised the tips of his fingers to his lips and expelled a heartfelt sigh.

"Thank you for your empathy, chief inspector. It is, indeed, a very difficult moment for all of us here in the Crayke community."

Patel paused for a respectful couple of seconds, before launching into her line of questioning.

"I understand you've both given statements to my colleagues, but I wonder if you'd be good enough to go over some of it again, for us? It's quite normal, during the course of a murder investigation," she added.

"Of course," Father Peter said. "I echo Father Samuel's words; we are all here to serve, however we may."

"Thank you. In that case, would you both kindly tell us when you last saw Father Jacob alive?"

It was the headmaster who answered first.

"I believe I last saw Jacob at early evening prayers, which began at four o'clock, in the abbey," he said. "I enquired after his day, we exchanged a word or two about some of the children in St. Cuthbert's, then he made his way back to the boarding house to oversee the boys' dinner, at around five o'clock."

"How did he seem?" Patel asked.

It was a question Ryan would have asked himself, but he was conscious that this was her show; they were merely invited guests.

"Perfectly normal," Father Peter replied. "There was nothing untoward, if that's what you mean."

"He didn't seem upset, or nervous, in any way?"

"Not at all."

"What about communications—to your knowledge, had he received anything that might have upset him?"

The headmaster smiled, with the kind of subtle condescension that set Ryan's teeth on edge.

"DCI Patel, our brother lived a quiet life, here at Crayke. He had very little contact with the outside world, and, therefore, scarcely had the opportunity to receive any communications that might have caused upset. He was a quiet, spiritual man, who enjoyed reading—"

"Mainly Sherlock Holmes," Father Samuel put in. "Our brother loved to read Conan Doyle."

"A man of good taste," Ryan said, from the edge of the room.

The Chaplain looked across at him, then nodded sadly.

"What about you, Father Samuel? Can you tell us when you last saw Father Jacob?" Patel asked.

"It was probably around the same time," he said, and pushed his glasses a little higher on the bridge of his nose. "I led the prayers at four o'clock and could see our brother sitting with the children from St. Cuthbert's House on the pews towards the back. We didn't have an opportunity to speak before he left, which I will lament for all my days."

"I'm sorry to hear that," Patel said, with apparent sincerity. "When did either of you first become aware that something was wrong?"

"Not until later," Samuel said. "A couple of the boys came to find me at around nine o'clock. They'd returned from their Movie Night half an hour before, to find Jacob missing. There had also been an accident in the laundry room, or a break-in, as we now fear, and they thought it best to report it."

"Why to you?"

"S—sorry?"

"Why report it to you, specifically?" Ryan asked. "Do you live near to the boarding house?"

"I—no, my cell is in the Abbey. The children came to find me in the Abbey Church, where I was spending some time in quiet contemplation."

"Part of the Chaplain's role is to provide ongoing pastoral support," the headmaster explained. "Father Samuel has been a source of guidance and advice to many of our children, over the years, and they find him very easy to talk to."

"Around what time did the children come to find you?" Patel queried.

"I'd say around nine o'clock, or shortly thereafter. I went with them to the boarding house and, when I couldn't find Jacob, I oversaw Lights Out and supervised them for the remainder of the evening. I communicated this to Father Peter at around nine-forty-five."

"Was anybody with you in the abbey?" Patel asked.

A slow flush crept up Father Samuel's neck.

"Not—not at the exact moment the children found me, no. But—"

"I, myself, was with Father Samuel in the abbey, directly prior to the children's arrival," Father Peter interjected. "I can vouch for the timing."

There was an infinitesimal pause.

"Yes, sorry, I'd forgotten," Father Samuel mumbled.

"Thank you," Patel said, with another of her unthreatening smiles that Ryan was growing to admire. "Father Peter, weren't you worried when you heard Father Jacob couldn't be found?"

It was remarkable, Ryan thought, but the man's face barely moved. It had remained fixed in more or less the same genial expression throughout, and didn't alter at the implied suggestion that there might have been grounds for action long before he'd taken it.

"Of course, I was surprised," he said. "However, I naturally assumed Father Jacob had been detained with some urgent matter, perhaps in helping another child or one of our brothers. As you can see, the campus here at Crayke is large, and it's not always possible to keep tabs on all people at all times."

"How about the children?" Ryan asked, ever so smoothly.

For the first time, a flicker of irritation passed over the headmaster's face.

"You may rest assured, the children at Crayke are always well supervised, chief inspector, and follow a regular routine."

"We're sure that's the case, Father Peter," Patel said, and her eyes flashed a warning for Ryan. *Don't push too far.*

He nodded.

"We understand a search was made for Father Jacob early this morning," Patel said. "Then a report was made to the police control room at…nine-oh-four."

She looked up from her notebook and fixed the headmaster with a stare.

"Can I ask why the decision was taken not to telephone the police straight away?"

Father Peter leaned back in his chair and linked his fingers over the front of his habit, favouring her with another of his mildly condescending smiles.

"As you may be aware, the grounds here at Crayke are extensive. They include various types of terrain, as well as a number of different buildings on the complex, discounting the abbey and monastery. It remained perfectly possible that Father Jacob had taken the opportunity, whilst off-duty, to go for a walk or something of that kind—only to find himself hurt or stranded somewhere, without the means to raise an alarm."

It all sounded so reasonable, Ryan thought.

"We were concerned not to waste police time," the headmaster tagged on. "The nearest police station is miles away and, besides, we had Toby to help us."

"Toby is…the dog?"

"Not just any dog," Samuel cut in, with a genuine show of enthusiasm. "He's the best hound we've had in the pack for years."

"Yes, our Captain of Beagling was able to guide Toby along the way until eventually…well, you know what we found," the headmaster said, and whispered a prayer under his breath before kissing the cross that hung on a long chain around his neck.

"How's he doing?" Ryan asked. "It must have been quite upsetting."

"Yes, Toby was quite upset at having to be dragged away from his find—"

"No," Ryan said. "Not the beagle. *The boy.*"

The headmaster turned a slow shade of red, giving Ryan all the answer he needed.

The boy was long forgotten.

CHAPTER 13

"Did I ever tell you about Hot Pants Harry?"

Ryan added a few kisses to a text he'd been composing to Anna, clicked 'send', then turned to look at Phillips, who'd insisted upon driving the return journey—much to their mutual relief. Whilst he could function admirably on chronic sleep-deprivation for long stretches of time, he was as human as the next and wasn't too proud to admit when it was time for a break.

"Who's that?" he asked. "Some collar from the olden days?"

Phillips smiled into the passing darkness. Despite it being only a little after six, the sun had already set, and the road stretched before them like an endless tunnel of blurred lines and flashing headlights against an ink-blue sky.

"Nah, Harry was a lad who lived on my street, growin' up," he said, casting his mind back. "Bearin' in mind I'm talkin' about the seventies, I s'pose you could say it was the olden days."

He reached across to turn up the temperature in the car, so that the warm air would thaw them both out.

"I'm surprised you can remember that far back," Ryan joked. "Why did they call him 'Hot Pants Harry'—or is that a stupid question?"

"Well, he never actually wore any hot pants, that I know of," Phillips said. "But he did occasionally like to wear his mam's dresses. Somebody caught him, one day, and word got about…not long after, somebody thought up a name and it stuck."

Phillips kept his eyes straight ahead, as they pootled along behind a lorry.

"I probably don't need to tell you, lad, but, where I grew up, people lived hard lives. They lived hand-to-mouth, most of the time, and only just scraped by—it was the same with us. Thatcher came along, the recession…there was a lot of anger amongst working folk, all round the country."

Ryan nodded.

"We saw the remnants of it, after that case in Penshaw," he murmured. "People have long memories."

"Aye, they do," Phillips agreed. "Fact is, most people back then were spoiling for a fight. We all knew Gladys down the road was gettin' beat up by her husband, probably plenty more, as well, who were too ashamed to mention it. There was a lot of people turnin' to drink, especially, which made things worse…"

Phillips thought of his own father, then shoved the memory away.

Nobody was perfect, after all.

"Growin' up around that, feelin' like you've got no way out…it was hard," he admitted.

There was nothing Ryan could say that wouldn't sound trite, so he simply listened. It wasn't often that Phillips spoke of his early life, so he knew the reason for doing so now must be an important one.

"Well, you can imagine, Harry got it in the neck more often than not," Phillips said, his voice full of regret. "Me? I went to Buddle's and made myself tough, so I could use my fists to fight off anyone and anything that came at me— but Harry?" Phillips shook his head. "He wasn't made for fightin'," he said. "God knows, he tried."

There was a long silence in the car, until he spoke again.

"One night, Harry's Da' came home early and found him playin' with his mam's clothes again. Ol' Terry, he'd had a skin-full and went straight for him. I know, because I heard Harry's screams from three doors down the street."

Ryan's stomach turned, as he thought of it. "What happened?"

"I ran downstairs to tell my Da' and ask him to help make it stop," Phillips said. "He told me to go back to my room and mind my own bloody business."

He let out a mirthless laugh.

"I was only young, and I did what I was told. I went back upstairs, put a pillow over my ears and my parents turned the telly up loud. Y' know what happened? The screams stopped, just like that," he said, and clicked his fingers.

Ryan felt his heart stutter, already knowing what his friend would say.

"Aye," Phillips said, turning briefly to look at him. "Turns out, Harry fell down the back stairs. Funny, as he'd never had trouble going down those stairs before. Police came, they heard Terry's version, and we watched them come and take Harry's broken body away in the dead of the night. Like he'd been nothing, and nobody."

He swallowed, hard.

"I've never felt more of a coward than the day I went back up those stairs to my room," Phillips said. "I've never felt more trapped or confined in a community that believed family problems should stay in the family. Harry's the reason I wanted to get out, the reason I joined the Force. The first day I walked into CID, I asked my DCS to re-open the case, and I kept asking, until Terry Fletcher was charged with manslaughter, back in '98."

"You never told me that," Ryan said softly.

"Aye, and you know why?" Phillips said, rhetorically. "I was doin' the same thing as my Da'. Thinkin' it was just my problem, thinkin' it was all about where I came from or the fact that we didn't have a pot to piss in…and that it was somethin' you wouldn't understand. But, over the years, I've realised that's only half the story. It doesn't matter if you come from a two-up, two-down miner's cottage in Elswick, or a rambling stately home that looks like Crayke bleedin' College. You can still feel trapped, and you can still be surrounded by folk who think there are some things best left unsaid."

Ryan spoke, when he could be sure he could trust his own voice.

"You're right, you know," he said, eventually. "About lots of things, it pains me to admit, but one thing, in particular—I grew up in a place like Crayke, away from my family and my home. I lived by rules, schedules, expectations…and craved love like an addict, whenever any was thrown my way. You talk about feeling trapped? I know that feeling, Frank, and what it takes to break free from the chains that bind you to it. You can't change the past, but you can live in the here and now."

Phillips nodded, and thought of one more thing he wanted to share, in the quiet space of the car.

"Before he died, my Da' talked about what happened that day," he said. "He told me he'd lived with the guilt and shame of having turned the other cheek, and was proud that I'd done the right thing by re-opening the case. I know he got a lot of stick for it from some of the neighbours, but he was instrumental in gettin' others to come forward and give statements. It made all the difference."

Ryan smiled into the darkness.

"I s'pose, now I'm a father, I wonder about how good of a job I'll make of it," Phillips continued. "I think about all the mistakes I'm makin' and ones I might make in the future. Then, I remember my old Da', and how, when he died, he was a better man than the one he'd been in the years before. It gives me hope."

"You don't need to worry—"

"I'm no saint," Phillips said, before Ryan could go on. "Another reason I never told you about Harry is because... well, it was me who thought up that awful nickname. It was me who labelled that poor kid, to get a few laughs from the other kids on the street. Little Frankie Phillips, with his big gob and his spotty chin, who wanted to be tough like all the rest—"

"Frank—"

"No, listen to me, lad, because this bit's important," Phillips said, more quietly now. "I've made my mistakes, God knows, but I've tried my best to correct them. I worry about Samantha, about Emma, about all the young ones because, in the world we live in, it seems like nobody's allowed to make a mistake and feel sorry about it. But how else do you get to be a better person? It's never too late to change...I'm livin' proof of that."

Ryan inhaled a long breath and let it out slowly, unaccountably thinking of his own father, and of whether he'd judged him too harshly over the years.

Food for thought.

And, speaking of food...

"Well, I never thought I'd see the day you chose quinoa over a bacon butty, so I'd have to agree," he said.

Phillips grinned. "See? It was *fear* of the quinoa that kept me from tryin' it, more than the taste itself."

Ryan gave him the side-eye. "And the taste?"

"Okay, bad example," Phillips admitted. "It still tastes like death, warmed up. But you know what I'm tryin' to say."

"I do," Ryan said, and yawned. "Doesn't all this warm air make you feel sleepy?"

"Nope," Phillips said. "You should rest your eyes for a few minutes. I'll wake you up when we're nearly there."

"Well, maybe…just for a minute."

Seconds after his eyelids closed, Ryan fell into a deep, dreamless sleep, safe in the knowledge that his friend watched over him.

Phillips drove on through the night thinking of all the lessons he'd learned during his lifetime, and of how much he owed to Harry Fletcher. Through the windshield, he looked up to see a blanket of stars overhead, glittering like diamonds.

"Rest easy, Harry," he said softly. "Things are gettin' better by the day."

CHAPTER 14

"Splish, splash, splosh!"

Anna stood in the doorway of the bathroom with the baby's towel tucked beneath her arm and a bottle of milk in the other, smiling.

"Well now, let's get that tummy all washed..."

She watched incredulously as Charles Ryan, a distinguished former diplomat and member of the minor aristocracy, bathed his granddaughter gently, making *quacky-quack* noises as he went.

"I think you're all done, baby girl...ah! Here's your mummy..."

Anna stepped forward to lay out the towel and swaddle Emma, whose indignant cries at being snatched up from her warm bath could probably be heard all the way from Land's End to John O' Groats.

"I just heard that Ry—ah, Maxwell's on his way home now," she said, awkwardly. It was a sticking point for Charles that his only son chose not to answer to his given name and had, instead, appropriated his surname for regular use, and she had no wish to stoke the fire.

Charles heaved himself to his feet with a slight click of the knees, which wasn't bad for a man over seventy.

"That's good to hear," he said, and began tidying the bathroom while Anna dried and dressed the baby.

He was about to head back downstairs, when his daughter-in-law called for him.

"Charles?"

He stuck his head around the door and in the dimly-lit nursery, just for a fraction of a moment, she caught a glimpse of how Ryan might look in a few years' time.

The idea of her husband as an older man brought no sense of sadness or remorse for the passage of time—in fact, if he was planning to stay as fit and healthy as his father, she'd be a very happy woman indeed.

"Yes, dear?"

"I was wondering if you'd like to give the baby her bottle? Eve happened to mention that you didn't have the chance to do it when Natalie and Max were babies and I thought—well, you haven't had much of an opportunity here, either, since one or the other of us is always fighting over the privilege. Would you like to try?"

Charles felt as nervous as a new driver. "Ah—well, yes. Yes, if you really don't mind—"

"Of course not!" Anna smiled. "Why don't you come and sit over here?"

She settled Emma's grandfather in the comfy nursing chair and turned the lights down low, before reminding him of the best position to hold the baby while she fed.

"I'm all fingers and thumbs," he muttered, while his hands shook slightly at unexpected responsibility.

"There you go," Anna whispered, stroking her daughter's head as she began to suck noisily at the bottle. "You're a natural, grandad."

Charles smiled, and might have been fifteen years younger.

"She's all right like this?"

"I'd say so, wouldn't you?"

He looked down into his granddaughter's beautiful brown eyes, and found himself smiling.

"She's a corker," he murmured. "I remember—"

It seemed he wasn't going to say anything further, but then he continued.

"I remember the day Maxwell was born," he continued, keeping his voice low. "I've handled artillery rifles, shotguns, hand grenades…you name it. But I can tell you, holding his little body in my arms when we brought him home that first night was the most nerve-wracking thing I've ever done."

"R—Maxwell felt the same way, when we brought Emma home," she said.

"You should call him by the name you're used to," Charles said, gently. "I can't quite bring myself to call him 'Ryan' just yet, but I'm working on that."

Anna thanked him, and wished whole-heartedly that Ryan could have been there to witness the moment.

"Emma has Ryan's black hair…and yours," she said.

Charles looked down at the baby he held.

"More grey than black, these days," he said, and wondered where the time had gone. "She has her mother's eyes…just as Ryan has Eve's shade. They're more silvery-grey than blue, really."

Again, Anna stared at him, drinking in the moment. He was not a man given to wasting words, nor volunteering conversation unless he could help it but, in the quiet space of his grandchild's nursery, he let down his guard.

"I always think Ryan's are the colour of the North Sea, in a storm," she said.

Charles smiled at that. "Yes, that's a good analogy," he agreed. "It suits his temperament, too, wouldn't you say?"

"Perhaps," she admitted. "His waters run deep, but they're mostly placid until something really angers him—usually injustice of some kind."

Charles thought about his son's strong moral yardstick, and was proud.

"Ryan has great self-control," he said. "I don't know whether he learned that from me, his mother, or his schooling, but I suppose it helps him with his work to be somewhat detached."

"Did that help you?"

He looked up, mildly embarrassed. "Me?"

"Yes, with your work. I can only imagine how stressful that might have been, at times. It must have helped to develop a sense of detachment."

Charles looked back down at the baby, who had now finished her milk and promptly fallen asleep in a 'milk coma'. Without having to be told, he raised her to his shoulder and began rubbing slow circles on her back as he thought of the assassination attempts, the security breaches, the fear he'd lived with almost every day that his work for Her Majesty's government would jeopardise his family's safety.

It had been a relief to turn his back on it all, and retire; except, now it seemed that the baton of fear had been passed to his son.

"I did what I had to do," he said, at length. "I was brought up to respect duty, obligation and a chain of command. There were protocols and strict security measures I had to abide by, or else risk catastrophic consequences, but it meant sacrificing moments such as these."

Would he do it all over again? Charles wondered.

An impossible question to answer.

Almost as difficult as the question now facing his son.

CHAPTER 15

Tuesday 8ᵗʰ December

The following morning, Ryan left Anna and the baby sleeping soundly and made his way downstairs well before dawn, expecting to find that he had the kitchen to himself.

However, on this occasion, he was not alone.

Charles had been up since four, unable to sleep. He didn't need to be an intelligent man to understand that Ryan's trip to Yorkshire had been significant. Quite rightly, Ryan hadn't disclosed any details of the incident he and Phillips had attended, but when Charles had seen the late-evening reporting of a murder at Crayke College and then taken the trouble to do a basic online search, it didn't take too much of a mental leap to understand the possibility of a connection between the ancient Benedictine monastery that had been founded by St. Cuthbert, many centuries ago, and the problem of Cuthbert's cross having been falsified in Durham. A murder in each place was an unlikely coincidence and, if there was a connection, it meant that Ryan had been right, all along.

The perpetrator was still at large.

"Dad? You're up early."

Ryan entered the kitchen and moved directly to the coffee machine.

"It's a nice time of day," Charles said. "When it's still dark outside and the rest of the world is sleeping, it gives one a chance to think."

There were few people who used the word 'one' as a personal descriptor, nowadays, Ryan thought, but it seemed to suit his father.

"How was your trip, yesterday?"

Ryan took a gulp of coffee before answering, then cast his eyes to the ceiling, where all was quiet. He thought briefly of trying to fob him off, but Charles Ryan was not a man who was easily fooled and, frankly, he respected his father too much to lie to him.

"There was another torture killing," he said, and relied upon his father's honour not to repeat the details of what he was about to disclose. If you couldn't trust a man who'd worked in military intelligence to keep a secret, there were few that you *could* trust. "A monk by the name of Father Jacob Jamieson. They found him dead at Crayke College, and North Yorkshire CID asked if we'd go and take a look to see if there were any similarities."

"And were there?"

"Yes," Ryan answered shortly. "But, most damning of all was the man's connection with St. Cuthbert. He was a leading authority, you see."

"Therefore, the question becomes, what was the man's connection with your case in Durham?" Charles surmised.

"Exactly," Ryan said, and finished his coffee in two gulps before re-filling his cup. "Would you like one?"

Charles shook his head.

"More worrying than the possibility of a connection is the fact that our perpetrator is active again," Ryan explained, though he hardly needed to. It was comforting to offload his fears to a man who, he knew, was likely to have lived through and survived much worse.

"And, you still believe this person—or group—has killed before, to protect themselves?"

Ryan gave a jerky nod. "More than once."

"If it's the same person, they'll find out you were in Yorkshire," Charles said. "There's a chance they'll come after you."

"Yes," Ryan said, tonelessly, staring out of the kitchen window at the blackened landscape outside.

Charles moved a step closer, his hand itching to rest on his son's shoulder.

"You know what needs to happen," he said, clasping his hands behind his back instead. "You need to divide the unit."

The unit, Ryan thought, with a sad smile. So prosaic a word to describe his family, and reason for being.

"I know," he said softly. "Anna and Emma should go back down to Devon with you and Mum. It's the best thing for them, now."

"Good," Charles said. "We can leave this afternoon."

"I need to speak to Anna about it, first. She'll take some persuading."

"It isn't about persuading—"

"You're right," Ryan said, a bit sharply. "It's a matter for *discussion*. Anna is my wife, and a free agent. I can do my utmost to convince her but, ultimately, the decision must be hers."

"It isn't a decision she's qualified to take—"

"Anna isn't some simpering little woman," Ryan said, and his eyes flashed a warning. "She's far more intelligent than either of us, and is perfectly capable of weighing up the risks of the situation."

Charles hissed out a breath and turned away to pace to the window.

"I'm well aware of what you've found, in Anna," he said, after a minute or two slipped by. "Anna is to you what your mother has been to me, all these years."

Ryan scrubbed a hand over his face and let it fall away again.

"It isn't that I haven't considered the danger," he said. "It's all I've thought about, for nine solid months. Devon or Northumberland—it makes no difference, except that you'd be further away for me to be able to help, if need be."

Charles looked into his son's tired eyes and finally understood.

"Safety in numbers? In that case, let me do something else for you. Let me arrange for some private security—I still have all my old contacts."

Ryan thought of the dark-suited men and women who'd followed them around when he'd been a boy, and barely held back a shiver. He'd hoped for a different life for his own family.

Yet, here they were.

"We can't live that way," he said. "There's still no specific threat, no prime suspect we're hunting. If we call in a security team now, there's no telling how long they'd need to be here, watching our every move."

Charles thought for a moment. "Where d'you keep your weapon, son?"

Ryan blinked.

"Your service revolver? Where do you keep it?"

It wasn't regulation for a firearms officer to keep a police-owned weapon at home, and Ryan wasn't much of a fan of guns at the best of times. However, that didn't mean he hadn't taken it upon himself to purchase and register a rifle, ostensibly for use on the land.

"Under lock and key," he replied.

Charles nodded. "Mine's in a locked box in the boot of my car. Meet me there in a few minutes, and we'll see how well you've kept your eye in."

The first shot rang out as the sun rose, its fiery rays bursting across the Coquet Valley like rivers of molten gold as the world awakened. Father and son had removed themselves from the house, walking far out of sight and range of another living soul, to set up a makeshift shooting gallery in one of the fields that formed part of Ryan's smallholding. Now, they stood side by side, two generations of Ryan men on a patch of ancient earth that had borne the heavy tread of soldiers' footsteps hundreds of years before.

Charles emptied another five rounds, secured his rifle and then walked the hundred yards to the tree where he'd carved a circle with a cross in the middle.

The cross now bore six neat holes.

Satisfied, he walked back to where his soon stood with a rifle in his hand, his tall body framed by the rising sun at his back. All his life, he'd wanted Max to be strong, to be self-sufficient...but now, as he stood there looking like all of those things, Charles realised he wanted something else, much more.

He wanted his son to be safe.

Keeping his head bowed until he was in command of himself once again, Charles covered the ground and went about the business of correcting Ryan's stance.

"How long's it been, since you fired a gun?"

"A couple of years," Ryan said, honestly. "I was planning to head down to the range, to keep my certificate up to date—"

"Doesn't matter," Charles said. "It's like riding a bicycle."

Ryan wasn't sure that was entirely the case, but he humoured his father and allowed his posture to be altered this way and that. Northumbria Police Constabulary preferred a Glock semi-automatic revolver as its service weapon of choice, but a rifle was a different kind of beast.

"Keep the butt of the weapon tucked into your shoulder," he said. "Elbow nice and flat. Aim about half an inch above the cross, to get a bullseye."

Ryan closed his mind to all else, unhooked the safety and rested his finger on the trigger of the bolt-action rifle. As he lowered his face to look through the sights there was not a sound other than the gentle whirring of insects in the brush, and the whisper of the wind as it whipped over the crusted earth.

Breathe, he told himself.

He pressed the trigger, and felt the thrust of the recoil hit his shoulder as the sound echoed around the valley and sent a small flock of birds squawking noisily into the sky.

"You're a quarter of an inch too low," his father murmured, raising a hand to shield his eyes against the sun.

Ryan raised an eyebrow.

"You can see that, from here?"

Charles gave him an enigmatic smile and, for a moment, it was as though he was looking in the mirror.

"You can't?" he shot back, and flashed a sudden smile. "Maybe you need to make an appointment at Specsavers."

Ryan paused in the act of reloading the rifle, wondering if he'd misheard.

"Did you just crack a joke?"

"Yes, son, I believe I did. Think you can take it?"

Ryan gave him a lopsided grin.

"I can take it, if you can—*grandad.*"

"That's 'His Excellency, The Former Ambassador, Grandad', to the likes of you."

It was only the truth, Ryan thought, and wondered what Phillips would do if he knew that was the formal title of an ambassador, which his father had been for seven years.

He'd probably transfer to the Diplomatic Service, that's what he'd do.

"Yeah, well, don't expect a tray of *Ferrero Rocher* any time soon."

Charles laughed richly, enjoying himself despite the circumstances.

"Get six straight bullseyes in the trunk of that tree, and I'll serve you a tray myself," he said.

"Is that a bet?"

"Mm hmm. I'll even start calling you 'Ryan'."

His son paused, saw that he was quite serious, and raised the rifle again.

"You're on."

Anna awakened from another nightmare and scrambled out of bed to check the baby, who slept soundly in her cot. Skin clammy, heart hammering, she watched her daughter's steady breathing for a few minutes, to calm herself, before sitting down shakily on the edge of the bed.

What is the matter with me? she wondered.

Was this post-natal depression?

She'd read about it, of course, so that she would be prepared for any eventuality, and it was true that some of what she was experiencing seemed to match the symptoms.

Bad sleep patterns

Night terrors

Weight loss

Inability to concentrate…

Yet, her mood in general remained as positive as it had always been. Despite any evidence to the contrary, Anna continued to believe the best in people, and felt overwhelming joy whenever she was with her daughter.

Well, except when Emma was screaming, she amended. *She'd have to be barmy, or a masochist, to feel joyful about that.*

Just then, she heard the front door open and close again with a soft click, followed by Ryan's quiet tread on the stairs. A moment later, he appeared around the edge of the door.

"Morning," he whispered, upon finding her awake. "Can I get you a coffee?"

She shook her head and tried to smile.

"No—no, thanks."

Worried now, Ryan stepped fully into the room, tiptoeing past the baby to sit next to his wife. He brushed a strand of hair away from her face and then lowered his head to brush his lips against hers, tenderly, carefully, before drawing her into his arms.

"Your skin is cold," she said, with her face pressed against his neck.

"I went for a walk with Dad," he replied. "We had a few practice rounds with the rifle."

Anna drew back to look into his eyes, finding them tired but clear. If anything, he seemed more alive, despite having been up at the crack of dawn, and she was glad to see it.

"How are you?" he pressed. "Did you have another nightmare?"

Anna nodded, wearily.

"It's getting to be every night," she said. "I'm exhausted with it."

Ryan thought carefully about how to word his next question, for it had been playing on his mind for the last month or so, since her nightmares began.

"You know, I was reading about how hormones can affect a woman's body post-partum," he said. "Apparently, sometimes, there can be a bit of a delayed reaction and—ah—they can feel a bit less like themselves…"

Anna smiled. "I know," she said. "I've thought about the possibility, myself, but I'm so grateful that you brought this up. It makes it easier for me to know that I can talk to you, even though you have so many other things going on. Thank you."

"You don't need to thank me, Anna. Loving you, caring for you…it's as easy as breathing."

Her lip wobbled a bit, but she reached for his cold hand and warmed it between her own.

"I don't think it's PND, but I'm keeping an eye on it," she said. "If it gets worse, I'll let you know."

Ryan brought her fingers to his lips. "I may have a lot on at work, but none of it compares with you and Emma," he said, deeply. "None of it, d'you hear? I'm never too busy to listen, Anna, and I want to help with the baby as much as I can."

Right on cue, his daughter let out her first plaintive wail of the morning, and Anna batted her eyelids at him.

"You can change the first nappy, in that case."

"I walked straight into that one."

"You sure did—nappies and wipes are in the changing bag."

CHAPTER 16

It would happen soon.

Mathieu Lareuse—street name, 'Rodin'—had spent another uncomfortable night in the cells at Pentonville Prison. Whilst the surroundings were hardly salubrious, it wasn't the standard of accommodation that had kept him from sleeping. Rather, it was the unsettling knowledge that he was going to be murdered.

Today or tomorrow—who could say?

The only thing he knew for certain was that it would happen, and it was likely to happen *soon*.

Lareuse had accepted his last commission on the understanding that he would take a little hiatus immediately afterwards, and he'd been true to his word on that score. He'd spent a very enjoyable three years living in Egypt, in an expansive villa directly overlooking the Nile, where he'd entertained a series of nubile young men on a casual basis. He'd sunbathed by day, and by night he had sailed his little *felucca* boat to one of the many hotel jetties for dinner or a nightcap. All with the comfortable knowledge that Egypt had no extradition treaty with the United Kingdom, nor with his native France.

Unfortunately, that lifestyle came with a cost, and he'd run short of the kind of money needed to fund the lifestyle to which he'd become accustomed.

He'd begun to think about re-entering the scene, when news reached him about Cuthbert's Cross having been stolen, then recovered again. He'd laughed himself silly, at first; then, he'd been angry at the prospect of having undersold himself, to some considerable degree. For, if the police had recovered a forged cross, checked it and believed it to be real, then he was even better at his craft than he thought he was.

He'd flown back to the UK soon afterwards, with the vague idea of extorting more money from his former client.

Then, he'd heard about what happened to old Eddie Faber.

Fabergé to some.

Tortured, brutally murdered—and for what? He had to have known about the cross or found out about it, but not from him nor any of his acquaintances. There was nothing his client valued more than privacy; they'd been explicit about that, from the start, and every stage of producing the replica had been done in the strictest of confidence.

But Faber had a discerning eye, and Lareuse could only think that the old duffer had spotted the switch by chance. He'd heard rumours about Eddie having turned into a police rat, and maybe that's why pieces of him were now rotting in some godforsaken cemetery, already forgotten by most who ever knew him.

Suddenly, it hadn't seemed so important to ask for more money. He could manage on what he had, and pick up odd jobs to tide him over, until another plum commission came along. At least he'd be alive, and not six feet under.

But Lareuse had barely gathered up his suitcase and passport—forged, of course—before a knock had come at the door. How the police had found him, he didn't know.

Unless...

Unless they were tipped off, and the plan was to off him while he was behind bars, with nowhere to run.

He'd been demanding protection for days, now. Any one of his fellow inmates could have been hired to finish him; even the prison officers could be on the payroll, for all he knew.

The pigs thought he was lying.

Why would they believe a man who refused to give them a decent reason for demanding solitary confinement, or special treatment? If he wanted any privileges, he needed to start sharing some useful information, they said. Otherwise, he was just peddling lies.

Just another lie, from the man who sold lies for a living.

But this was no lie.

Not this time.

In fact, for the first time in Mathieu Lareuse's thirty-one years, he was telling the absolute truth.

"Morrison won't like this, mind."

Phillips made this insightful remark while watching the slow, inexorable progress of the drinks trolley along the gangway of the train carriage, heading directly towards him laden with goodies.

Was that bacon he smelled, wafting from the dining cart?

Get thee behind me, Satan, he thought.

"She'll blow a gasket, when she gets wind we've overridden her direct order not to go to London."

"Maybe she'll like it better when we speak to Mathieu Lareuse and he confesses to making that forged cross," Ryan said mildly. "Besides, we'll only be gone for a few hours— she'll barely have time to miss us."

Phillips leaned back in his chair, shuffled around in an attempt to get comfortable on the scratchy material, then sat up straight again as the train slowed to a crawl across the railway bridge spanning the River Tyne. He peered through the window and counted five other bridges to the east, including the curved 'Millennium Bridge' which had been repaired following a terror incident not so long ago.

"Y'nah, I haven't felt the same about train travel since we had that bridge bomber," he admitted. "I always get a bit nervy when we cross the river."

Ryan looked at the long drop to the murky waters below, and was reminded of a different incident entirely; one that had happened years before, where a man accused of the Hacker's crimes had plunged to his own death.

Then, there was that nun who washed up on the riverbank…

Come to think of it, still waters ran bloody deep in the Tyne.

"Well, the consolation is, you get to have a day trip to London," he said, cheerfully. "I'll even buy you a peppermint tea, when the trolley arrives."

"You'll turn my head with talk like that."

A long klaxon reverberated through the corridors of Pentonville Prison, following which the doors to the cells opened to allow the inmates an hour of social time in the communal areas. There was a cacophony of sound as his fellow inmates filtered out, eager to go about their business…whatever that might have been.

Lareuse stared at the open doorway in horror, wishing he could drag the electronic mechanism shut again.

"Ain't you comin' out?"

One of the prison officers happened to stop outside, no doubt wondering why he wasn't eager to walk around.

He shook his head.

When the officer shrugged and moved on, Lareuse looked around the cell for something—anything—that could be used as a weapon. If he'd been more experienced in these matters, perhaps he'd have known what to do, but he'd been out of the game for more than three years and didn't know who to ask for protection on the inside.

Through the doorway of his open cell on the upper level of a quadrangle-shaped cell block, he could see a large clock which read a couple of minutes after ten.

He stared at it with wide, frightened eyes, and willed the hands to move faster.

When the second hand had passed 'twelve' another eighteen times, a shadow fell across the doorway.

"You the bloke they call 'Rodin'?"

Lareuse knew then that his time was up.

CHAPTER 17

London never changed, Ryan thought, and yet it never remained the same, either.

There was always some new skyscraper being built, to rival the last one and claim the 'tallest building' award— or a new road system being laid, to give the cabbies something to complain about. It was a vibrant, colourful and cosmopolitan place with a character of its own, home to super-rich oligarchs and the impecunious alike, both walking the same network of streets that baffled tourists on a regular basis. Wheeler-dealers, Del Boys, Wide Boys, Rude Boys, Royal Convoys…London had it all, and much more besides.

"It's got a special kind of smell, London," Phillips declared, when they stepped off the train at King's Cross. "A delicate aroma of exhaust fumes, river water, street food and…"

"Dog shit?" Ryan offered, and raised an eyebrow towards the floor, where Phillips had wandered into a pile, unwittingly.

The air turned blue as Frank hopped around for a minute, trying to clean it off with a tissue.

"Bloody filthy sods!" he raged.

Ryan made a sympathetic sound while his eyes scanned the crowds milling around them, looking out for a familiar face.

"Who'd you say we were meetin' again?"

"DCI Hassan," Ryan replied. "He was a DI in the same command unit when I was down here in London, although I didn't report directly to him. My DI at the time was Jennifer Lucas, if you remember."

"Least said about that, the better," Phillips replied, and pulled an expressive face. "God rest her, an' all."

Years earlier, Ryan had graduated from the police academy and taken his first job at Scotland Yard, moving up the ranks at breakneck speed until he'd joined their Homicide and Serious Crime Command. The unit was split into eighteen Murder Investigation Teams, nowadays; but, fifteen years earlier, when governmental budgets had been more generous, there had been over thirty teams tasked with investigating the most serious crimes in one of the largest cities in the world. Ryan had cut his teeth as a young detective in one such team based out of the Command's 'Central' unit, which covered most of the city centre. He'd reported to a Detective Inspector Jennifer Lucas who had, ultimately, changed the course of his life—for, had she not been the abusive woman she was, Ryan might not have taken the decision to carve out a better life at Northumbria CID. Had he not done so, he would never have met Anna—and the rest was history.

Still, he had many happy memories of his time down south, and one of them weaved his way through the lunchtime crowd towards them with an enormous smile on his chiselled face.

"Here he is," Ryan told Phillips, who followed his line of sight and simply gaped.

"You didn't tell me your mate was Idris Elba!" he whispered, in outrage. "Between the two of you, I must look like a bloody hobbit…"

Ryan chuckled, and moved forward with hand outstretched to greet his old comrade.

"John," he said, warmly. "It's good to see you."

Hassan looked at Ryan's hand, then brushed it away in favour of an expansive hug.

"C'mere, big guy! Max Finley-Ryan, in the flesh! Let me look at you," he said, and released him from the embrace to cast his warm brown eyes over the boy he'd known, who was now a man. "Still breakin' those hearts, my friend?"

"Not any more," Ryan said. "I married a wonderful woman, and I'm a father now."

"God almighty! Well, congratulations—*congratulations*!"

He turned to Phillips.

"This is my sergeant and very good friend, Frank Phillips," Ryan said, and the two men shook hands.

"Been keeping this boy in line, I hope?"

"Tryin' to, but it's a losin' battle," Phillips said, liking the man more and more. "We'll have to exchange notes, over a pint, sometime."

"Now you're talking my language," Hassan said, and clasped an arm around Phillips' shoulders, already the best of friends. "But first, it's a sunny day. Let's walk up the road here, towards Pentonville—it's not far. It'll give us time to talk, and you can tell me what this is all about."

"Lead on, Macduff."

―――――――――

Pentonville Prison was many things and, chiefly amongst them, a misnomer; for the Category B men's prison was not in Pentonville at all, but rather on the Caledonian Road, in the borough of Islington and a short walk from King's Cross station. Having housed a number of high-profile inmates since its inception in 1842, the prison had formerly enjoyed some vicarious fame, which had more latterly descended to infamy, since the publication of a recent, damning report that described its conditions as squalid, inhumane and overcrowded. Just as worrisome for the justice system was the prison's chronic staff shortage and seeming inability to prevent contraband from entering its walls—though new windows had gone some way to easing the situation, as had anti-drone netting to prevent the micro-machines from landing in the prison yard and offloading their wares.

It was, altogether, a grim place to spend a Tuesday lunchtime, but needs must.

"Here we are again," Hassan said, with irrepressible cheer. "Bet this brings back memories, eh, Ryan? How many jokers did we throw in here, I wonder?"

"Lost count," Ryan said, without rancour. It was not a source of pride to him to know that he'd been responsible for removing a person's liberty; it was more a question of justice, and of righting wrongs. He was neither lawmaker, policy-maker, politician nor penal reformer but, if he was, he might have suggested a different system of justice altogether. Since he wasn't, he was forced to operate within its existing parameters.

"How many have they got in here?" Phillips asked, as they made their way towards the entrance. "Six, seven hundred?"

"Try doubling that," Hassan said. "The prison was built to hold five hundred and twenty, but now you'd be lucky to keep the figure under twelve hundred. Is it any wonder the place is infested?"

On which ominous note, they began making their way through a series of security gates, a process which could sometimes take up to half an hour before they'd even set foot inside the main building.

They were nearing the final checkpoint when a deafening alarm began to sound.

"*What's happening*?" Hassan asked of the security guard, over the din. "Has there been an escape?"

The guard looked nonplussed. "That's the emergency alarm," she explained. "Probably another attack, or casualty. I'm afraid I can't let you go in."

Ryan felt an odd sort of prickle trail down the base of his spine, and he turned to his old friend.

"John, I need you to find out what's happened in there," he said, urgently. "I think it might be something to do with Lareuse."

"You're paranoid," Hassan said, and was only half joking. "It's probably nothing. Who would waste time over some forger? In here, it's gang warfare—"

"Please," Ryan repeated. "As a favour, to me."

Hassan held up both hands. "All right, all right," he said, and leaned forward to speak to the guard again. "Look, we've got an appointment to speak to one of the inmates and these officers have come all the way from Northumbria to do that. Any chance you could let us—"

"No," the woman said. "Sorry, sir, but you'll have to take it up with the Duty Governor. Rules are rules. I can't let anybody in now, because the place has been locked down. The only way you can go is back the way you came."

"So much for your reputation," Ryan said, under his breath. "Time was, you'd have charmed the birds from the trees."

"I'm older now," Hassan said. "I only charm birds that are already on the ground."

Before they could decide what best to do, he received a call on his mobile.

"Hassan? Yes—yes…how? No, it's all right. I'm already here. I'll secure the scene in advance of the CSIs arriving."

A moment later, he ended the call and looked between the pair of them.

"I'm sorry," he said, and all trace of humour had gone. "You won't be able to speak to Mathieu Lareuse now—he was found dead in his cell, only a few minutes ago."

"That was quick," Phillips muttered.

Hassan pressed his face to the reinforced glass of the security window once again.

"The reason for entry has changed," Hassan snapped. "DCI Hassan, DCI Ryan and DS Phillips, responding to a report just received by Scotland Yard. We understand one of your inmates has been murdered."

The security door buzzed open, and they rushed inside.

There was no need to construct a notion of 'Hell', Ryan thought, when there was already a perfectly good approximation, right here on Earth.

The interior of Pentonville Prison was every bit as unappealing as its reputation promised, but they weren't concerned with the décor. In the few minutes it had taken them to cross the courtyard from the security office, one emergency siren had stopped and another had started, this time to signal that a riot was underway. Officers had been mobilised to shut down the prison, wing by wing, and the atmosphere in the reception area of the main building was chaotic.

"Hey!" Hassan called out to a couple of the prison officers, who streaked past them dressed in full riot gear, on their way to B Wing. "Where's the Duty Governor?"

"Pro'ly hidin' in a bloody bunker!" one called back, over his shoulder. "You shouldn't be in 'ere! Get aht!"

Hassan swore, and turned to Ryan and Phillips with a worried expression.

"Look, man, I think there could be a full-on riot. This isn't the time—"

Ryan needed no further persuasion. They were not trained prison officers; they wore no protective clothing and were otherwise not equipped to be anything other than a burden to an already over-worked staff. He also had a wife and child to consider, and wasn't prepared to put himself in unnecessary danger, nor run the risk of leaving his wife without a husband and his daughter without a father.

Not for this.

They beat a hasty retreat, Hassan speaking quickly down his mobile phone to report the situation and put the rest of his team on notice that it would be a while before they could gain safe access to the crime scene. Eventually, they re-emerged onto Caledonian Road, which might have been a million miles away from the disordered violence they had just left.

Phillips blew out a gusty breath.

"I'm gettin' too old for all this excitement," he said, wondering why it seemed that, everywhere he went, he could smell bacon.

Must be crackin' up, he thought. Either that, or wasting away.

"I'm sorry you didn't get a chance to ask him about that case you're working on," Hassan said. "Pentonville is a tough place—these things do happen."

Ryan thought about what he could and could not tell his old friend. As far as Hassan was concerned, they were in town to interview Lareuse about his relationship with fellow forger, Edward Faber, whose death was already a matter of public record. Just another routine interview, to the outside world, but perhaps not to the person who had ordered Lareuse's death.

"They do happen," he agreed. "But, as you say, I wonder why anybody would want to kill a forger? They're the pen-pushers of the underworld; the computer geeks, not the muscle."

"Maybe he stole from one of them, or their boss," Hassan offered. "Lareuse was inside for historic dishonesty offences—wide-ranging ones, too. It seems he was quite creative with art and money, so maybe one or the other caught up with him."

"The riot will hold everything up, now," Phillips said, as they wandered back towards the train station. "Might not be much of a crime scene left, by the time you get in."

Hassan nodded, dispirited.

"The timing is interesting, isn't it?" Ryan said. "Some might say, very convenient."

"Rioting isn't exactly unheard of in Pentonville," Hassan said. "You've got overcrowded, unsanitary conditions, understaffing, drug, alcohol and mental health problems, all wrapped up in a group of angry, confined men. If they sense any weakness, like when a prison officer has to deal with an emergency, more often than not they'll try to capitalise on it."

Ryan could see the logic in what his friend was saying, but the doubt remained.

"There'll be questions to answer," Hassan went on to say, as he read a series of e-mails coming through to his mobile phone. "Lareuse's lawyer has just sent through some more demands—he obviously hasn't heard the news, yet; it's too soon."

"What demands?" Phillips asked.

"This and that, but most importantly, that his client wants to be transferred to solitary confinement because he's in fear for his life."

Hassan swore softly, and ran an agitated hand over his neck.

"Too late, man. We were too late."

CHAPTER 18

At precisely the same moment Ryan and Phillips were dodging a prison riot in London, MacKenzie was called upon to dodge a different kind of threat—the kind that came from *within*.

"Denise?"

Chief Constable Morrison caught her on the fly, as she was returning from lunch in the staff canteen.

She pasted a professional smile on her face and spun around like a marionette.

"Yes, ma'am?"

"I was looking for Ryan and Phillips. Have you seen them?"

MacKenzie took a casual sip of the tea she was gripping between her sweaty palms.

"Mm? No, I think they took a call…something to do with the Faber case," she replied. That last part was true, at least.

Morrison tutted. "Pity, I was hoping to have a word with them about a couple of things," she said. "If they come in, would you mind telling them to pop into my office?"

"Of course, no problem."

Morrison narrowed her eyes, having only just noticed how hot and bothered MacKenzie seemed to be.

She lowered her voice so they would not be overheard.

"Denise."

"Yes?"

"You really should have told me."

MacKenzie swore she felt her heart stop beating. "T— told you…what?"

Seconds ticked by.

"Peri-menopause is nothing to be embarrassed about," Morrison said, at length. "If you're struggling, you should ask your GP about hormone replacement, because it changed my life. Honestly, I was sweating like a pig on market day…"

MacKenzie didn't know whether to be offended at the imputation that she was old enough to be peri-menopausal—she wasn't even fifty, yet, for goodness' sake—or grateful that Morrison had misread her guilt sweats as being something more benign.

Gratitude won out.

"Thank you," she said gravely. "I'll keep it in mind."

As she walked off, Morrison smiled, and wondered when they would ever learn.

One down, two to go, she thought, and went in search of her next victim.

Ryan and Phillips left DCI Hassan to await his team outside Pentonville Prison, having first elicited promises that he would contact them if anything of interest turned up in his investigation, and furthermore that he would make himself available for a well-earned pint just as soon as they were able to take the time.

"Nice feller," Phillips said, once they were on their way back to King's Cross. "Shame it's been a bit of a wasted journey, though."

"I wouldn't say that," Ryan argued, and cut down to a pathway alongside Regent's Canal, which ran east to west behind the King's Cross complex. "Now, we *know* that Lareuse was involved in the making of the replica cross. That has to be the reason he's dead."

"Well, now, just hold your horses there, lad," Phillips said. "There's nothing to say he couldn't have been killed for another reason. Blokes like him have got their fingers in all kinds of pies—"

Pies, his mind whispered. *Steak and ale pies...*

"Not every pie involves the death of a senior murder detective, a monk and a forger, not forgetting a high-profile heist targeting a UNESCO World Heritage Site."

"Will everyone stop talkin' about *pies*?" Phillips burst out.

Ryan gave him a funny look. "You brought it up—"

"Aye, well...why are we headin' down this way, anyway?" Phillips asked, having only just realised they'd wandered off the beaten track. "Isn't it quicker to head down the main road?"

"Not to get to where we're going," Ryan said. "If we continue along here, we'll hit St. Pancras station, and one street over from that is the British Library."

Phillips sighed.

"You're wantin' a look at that gospel book, aren't you?"

"You read my mind."

"They're hot on protocols, these places," Phillips cautioned. "You can't just rock up; you've got to make an appointment."

"Lucky I made one for four o'clock, then, isn't it?"

Phillips pursed his lips. "Anyone ever tell you, you're narf a jammy bastard?"

"You have, daily, for the past ten years."

"Aye, well, I stand by it."

"Duly noted," Ryan grinned. "C'mon, it's up here, on the left."

Morrison ambushed Lowerson in the break room.

"Jack?"

He nearly choked on the Christmas gingerbread latte he'd been in the process of quaffing.

"Ma'am?"

She stalked towards him, eyeing her prey very much as a lion might have done on the plains of Africa.

"I was looking for Ryan or Phillips. Have you seen either of them?"

On the countertop, a message flashed up on his mobile phone which read, '*CC on the war path. Watch your back! Mac x*'

He snatched it up, before Morrison could read the offending text, and vowed to change his phone settings.

"Anything urgent?" she asked, innocently.

"N—no, not at all. Ah, you were asking me something?"

"Yes, Jack," she said, very patiently. "I was asking you where Ryan and Phillips are."

"I don't exactly know where they are…right now," he said, and told himself these things were all a matter of interpretation. It was perfectly true that he didn't know where they were at that precise moment.

Morrison waited five full seconds, to let him sweat a while.

"They wouldn't happen to be in London, would they?" she asked, silkily.

"London? Ah—"

Luckily for him, MacKenzie must have sent a Code Red warning to Yates, who bustled into the room at all speed.

"Oh! Jack, thank goodness, I've been looking for you everywhere. There's somebody on the desk line for you— they said it was important…and urgent!"

"Gosh," Morrison said, widening her eyes. "Important *and* urgent."

"I'd better take that," Lowerson said, and scarpered as fast as his legs would carry him.

In the awkward silence following his departure, Yates offered a shaky smile, and Morrison smiled in return.

The third zebra, she thought.

"Looks like it's just the two of us left standing, Melanie," she said.

Yates told herself not to crack. It was a bluff…she couldn't know for sure where Ryan and Phillips had gone.

Could she?

"Would you like a cup of tea?"

Yates frowned, wondering if it was a trap.

"No, thank you," she said, politely. "In fact, I'd better get back to my desk—"

Morrison looked her squarely in the eye.

"That's it," she snapped. "Enough of this nonsense. What time are they due back from London?"

"W—who, ma'am?"

Morrison stared at her for a long moment then, to their mutual surprise, began to laugh. Whatever she thought of Ryan at that moment, one thing was certain.

He could inspire loyalty unlike any other person she'd ever known.

"Oh, go on, bugger off," she told Yates, without any malice. "Before I change my mind."

CHAPTER 19

The British Library was an imposing, red-brick building of 1970s design, boasting a slanted roof and a piazza, of all things, as well as the largest library catalogue in the world, estimated to be somewhere in the region of two hundred million individual items—some dating all the way back to 2000 B.C.

Shortly before four o'clock, Ryan and Phillips made their way through the aforementioned piazza to the library's main entrance. Venturing inside, it became clear to them that the British Library was far more than a collection of books—it was a temple to reading.

"Well, look at that," Phillips whispered.

"Not bad," Ryan agreed, with his usual flair for understatement.

The foyer was wide and airy, with a floor of criss-crossed marble and white-painted columns which supported a geometric floorplan of reading rooms, storage, conference and exhibition spaces. In the centre of it all was a striking glass column known as the 'King's Library', which contained a collection of books amassed by the eighteenth-century monarch, George III.

"I hope you know where we're going," Phillips said. "A person could get lost in a place like this."

"I can think of worse fates." Ryan smiled. "But, as it happens, I do know where we're going. The St. Cuthbert Gospel is normally on display in the Sir John Ritblat Treasures Gallery, and the Head of Conservation has agreed to meet us there."

They passed through the turnstiles using the visitors' passes Ryan had already procured for them, and made their way to the Gallery, which was on the ground floor. It was an impressive space, with a permanent display of literary treasures including one of only four remaining copies of the Magna Carta, notes written by Leonardo da Vinci and an original manuscript of *Alice in Wonderland*. They took their time weaving through the displays, *umming* and *ahhing* over each wondrous item like a pair of schoolboys in a sweet shop, until they came to the case which held St. Cuthbert's Gospel.

Or, should have done.

"Where is it?" Ryan asked, tapping a finger against the glass countertop. "The placard says it's supposed to be here."

All that remained was the empty stand.

"This could be the right person to ask," Phillips said, nodding towards an official-looking woman in a bright red blazer who was heading straight for them.

"You must be the two detectives from the North East," she said, with a cheery, slightly crooked smile. "I'm Doctor Isabel Malone, Head of Conservation here at the Library."

Ryan shook the hand that was held out to him.

"Thank you for meeting us, Doctor Malone," he said. "We were hoping to see the gospel book, but it appears to be missing."

"Ah, yes, I'm sorry about that," she said, with a touch of embarrassment. "Unusually, we had a last-minute request to view the book from one of our leading academics in the area, and so we indulged him. I'm afraid his appointment has overrun a little…"

She checked the time on her watch and made a sound of irritation.

"My colleague is with him now, in one of the private reading rooms," she explained. "I'm sure they won't be much longer…"

Ryan felt the nerve endings in his body begin to jangle.

"You said this man was a leading academic," he said slowly. "Anyone we would know?"

"Well, I suppose if you have an interest in the life of St. Cuthbert, yes, you might have heard of Father Jacob."

Ryan and Phillips stared at her, and Malone's hand rose to clutch her throat, for it looked as though they'd seen a ghost.

"Is anything the matter?"

"Father Jacob Jamieson?" Phillips repeated. "The monk?"

She nodded, glancing warily between them. "That's right. Why? Is there a problem?"

"Where is he now?" Ryan demanded, his eyes already scanning the exhibition room for a man resembling the late Father Jacob.

"In one of our private rooms, viewing the book," she said, shakily.

"*Where*?" he repeated. "Which one?"

"I—it's the one just across the hall, directly outside," she stammered. "Room G12—"

Ryan set off at a run.

Ryan was fast, but whoever had been in Room G12 was faster.

He burst into the private reading room to find it empty, but for the unconscious body of a young woman who'd been dealt a series of violent blows around the back of her head.

Phillips and Malone were hot on his heels.

"Siobhan!" the woman cried, when she caught sight of the conservationist.

Then she noticed something which, to her, was much worse.

"Oh, my God! The book! St. Cuthbert's Gospel is gone!"

"*Call an ambulance!*" Ryan shouted, and shouldered past them both to run out into the corridor towards the exit turnstiles.

It took only seconds for him to emerge back into the marble foyer, and only a couple more to locate his quarry.

There, passing through the exit turnstiles, was a bald-headed man with a grey beard, dressed entirely in a long black habit.

"*Hey!*" Ryan shouted. "*Police!* Stop where you are!"

People passing in and out of the electronic turnstiles froze, and the foyer fell quiet.

The man in black turned to look at him, and it was as though Ryan was looking upon the face of a dead man.

Father Jacob?

The man smiled, and then ran.

CHAPTER 20

Ryan didn't hesitate.

He gave chase, propelling himself across the foyer to vault over the turnstiles, ignoring the distant cries of the security staff, all the while keeping his eyes firmly on the figure in black who was making rapid progress through the piazza on the other side of the main doors.

Stop!

Stop, police!

He ran outside and into the darkness, heart pounding as he tried to keep up with the figure who raced towards the protective crowds of Euston Road.

Determined, Ryan pushed his legs harder, sprinting full pelt through the piazza, passing beneath a shadowy sculpture of Sir Isaac Newton until he reached the pavement.

He searched left and right, examining the sea of passing faces, trying not to be distracted by the glare of headlights from the busy road.

"Shit," he muttered, turning a full circle.

Which way?

West led towards Euston Station and, beyond it, Regent's Park.

East led to King's Cross and St. Pancras, only minutes away on foot.

He went with his gut and veered east, running through the commuter crowds making their way home from work, eager to catch their train home.

Bypassing St. Pancras station, Ryan continued on to King's Cross, reasoning that, if their perpetrator was connected in any way with the cult of St. Cuthbert, he was most likely to be based in the North East and might be hoping to catch a train from there to Newcastle.

He might have been on the same train as them, earlier in the day.

Shoving that sickening thought aside, Ryan ignored a red pedestrian signal and, spotting a brief gap in traffic, bolted across the road towards the nearest entrance to the station concourse, horns blaring in his wake.

Inside King's Cross, the place was heaving with people; faceless suits, mothers with children and everyone else in between, all lugging suitcases or backpacks behind them. They milled in clusters across the enormous concourse with its high curved metal roof, and fancy new shopping area.

How times changed.

But there was no time to think of local regeneration now; all his attention was on the passing faces of the crowd, remembering all the while that the man he hunted could be armed and dangerous.

When a minute ticked by without any sighting, Ryan began to think he'd made the wrong call and should have veered west…

Then, he spotted it.

Just a flash of black material, which was barely distinguishable from a small crowd of children all dressed in Harry Potter robes they'd bought from the Platform 9 ¾ souvenir shop, across the way.

"Move aside!" he shouted. "*Move!*"

The crowds parted as he made for another set of turnstiles—this time, giving access to the platform area.

"Hey! Stop right there!"

An officer from British Transport Police hurried over as Ryan pushed his way to the front, knocking over a large suitcase in his haste to catch up with the man who was making for the 16:26 from King's Cross to Newcastle.

The time was 16:25.

Ryan felt the officer's hand snatch at his jacket, but tugged free of it and surged forward, hearing the fatalistic sound of a train guard's whistle on Platform 3.

A few more seconds, and the train would leave the station.

Rounding the head of the platform, he saw the figure board the train as the doors swished shut, and he let out a cry of frustration.

By the time he reached the doors, his frantic hammering on the 'open' button had no effect. He tried to wrench the doors open by force, but the automatic locking mechanism held firm.

"*Open those doors!*" he shouted. "*Police! Stop the train!*"

But it was already pulling out of the station.

Ryan had barely recovered when a couple of British Transport Police officers caught up with him.

"What the bloody 'ell was all that about?" one of them demanded. "You nearly knocked a woman off her feet, back there! It's not on, you know, that's common assault—"

Ryan tried to reach for his warrant card.

"Whoa there, mate! What've you got in your pocket?"

Both officers braced, ready to defend themselves against a knife attack.

Ryan raised his hands again in a non-threatening, palms-out position.

"I was going to reach for my *warrant card,*" he enunciated, through gritted teeth. "I'm CID, for God's sake—"

"A likely story—"

Just then, Ryan caught sight of Phillips jogging down the platform towards him.

"Detective...Sergeant...Phillips," he wheezed, coming to a jerky stop beside them. "Northumbria CID. This one's with me."

They checked his warrant card and nodded.

"All right, sir, if you're sure you can handle him. He's a lively one, mind you—and he made a grab for something in his pocket, a minute ago."

Ryan stared, dumbfounded.

"Some blokes just can't 'andle missin' a train," the other one said.

"I agree with you, son, but this one happens to be a DCI," Phillips said. "We're after a real criminal, and he's gettin' away on that train, while we're standin' round here chewin' the fat. Any chance you two could shake a leg and get in touch with the train manager? We need to stop that train."

The two officers looked amongst themselves, then at the two policemen.

"Right...bloody 'ell! Right..."

"*Now*," Ryan snarled. "We need to stop it, *now*."

"We can't do that! It'll be past Haringey, by now—"

"Howay, man, before I shove my boot up your arse!" Phillips roared, and it was enough to have the two of them scarpering towards the Controller's office.

Chief Constable Morrison had spent much of the afternoon working on her anger management techniques. She'd sipped herbal tea, listened to ten minutes of a meditation podcast, and even tried something called an 'Empty Chair Technique' to think through what she might say to Ryan, if he were there in the room.

She was congratulating herself on the success of all her efforts, even thinking idly about enrolling on one of those artsy retreats somewhere in the forest or by the sea, when a call came through on her desk phone.

"Ma'am? Somebody from King's Cross Station for you. Says she's some kind of railway controller…"

"What? Did she say what it was about?"

"She says there's a couple of your officers demanding she stops a train, but she needs high level authorisation to do that, especially as it's not local Met Police and the matter's urgent."

A couple of my officers, Morrison thought. *I might have known…*

"Put her on."

A moment later, the voice of an extremely harassed-sounding railway controller sounded down the line.

"Ah-hah," Morrison said. "Ah-hah. I see. Can you put the gentleman on the line, please?"

A second later, Ryan came on the phone.

"I wouldn't have believed it, if I hadn't heard with my own ears," she growled. "Especially as I distinctly recall our conversation during which I told you, very clearly, not to travel to London to interview Mathieu Lareuse."

"Look, you've a right to be angry, but can we take a rain check on the lecture? I've got an assailant on the run, and he boarded the 16:26 to Newcastle. That was almost ten minutes ago, and I need these jokers to stop the train and turn it around, so we can make the arrest. Will you help?"

"Just a minute," Morrison snapped. "What you mean 'an assailant'? There's local police to deal with local issues, Ryan—"

"This isn't just any assailant," he said, growing increasingly impatient. "This one was dressed as a dead man—the monk, who died at Crayke College—and managed to gain access to the British Library, where he knocked a young woman unconscious and stole another priceless artefact. He has St. Cuthbert's Gospel, and he's getting away with it. We need to stop him before it's too late—we need to *stop that train* before it reaches its next calling point."

Morrison was silent for long seconds, weighing up the risks on either side, and knew she would regret the decision she was about to make.

"All right, Ryan. I'll authorise it, but you better be right about this."

"Thank you," he said, with relief. "I won't forget this."

"Neither will I," she grumbled, before the line went dead.

CHAPTER 21

Ryan, Phillips and a number of police officers from the local Serious Crime Command were gathered at the head of the platform as the 16:26 rolled back into King's Cross Station, under the pretence of there being a fault with the mechanics of the train. All passengers were told to remain in their seats, since the doors would not be opening and required repairs, which afforded a degree of cover while Ryan and his makeshift team made their way through each carriage, in turn.

They split into two teams, with Ryan and two officers beginning at the front of the train, while Phillips began at the back. Both were armed with a T-Key to open doors and cupboards on board, and protective clothing, on loan from the Met.

They made their way through the carriages systematically, checking every bathroom door and the face of every person seated or unseated on the train, but none resembled the late Father Jacob, and nobody was conveniently dressed in monk's garb.

"He's had time to change," Ryan muttered. "He probably stuffed the habit out of a bathroom window, during the time it took us to get the train back."

His face was a mask of anger, and instead of looking for a man who was already dead, he searched for a person who looked uncomfortable or out of place, perhaps perspiring heavily.

Unfortunately, that accounted for almost everybody, since the air conditioning was on the blink and hundreds of people were packed like sardines on a train going nowhere.

After a full forty minutes of painstaking searching, Ryan and Phillips met in the middle of the train.

"Nowt at my end," Phillips said. "I take it you haven't found him, either?"

Ryan shook his head and ran angry fingers through his hair, while his mind raced.

"Let's swap," he said. "I'll go over the ground you've covered, you go over mine."

Another half hour later, they stepped off the train and onto the platform, where they were watched through the windows by the angry, staring faces of passengers, who were now becoming irate at the delay to their schedule.

As was the Controller, who stormed towards them.

"Well?" she demanded. "Where's this dangerous criminal, then?"

"He's obviously jumped the train, or changed his disguise," Ryan said. "We acted too slowly."

"*We* did nothing slowly, mate," she threw back. "But it's us who'll get it in the neck for the train being held, that's for sure. You've messed up all my slots—there'll be delays across the network for the rest of the day now!"

Ryan opened his mouth to launch into all the many and varied reasons why disruption to train schedules didn't compare with violent murder, but Phillips laid a steadying hand on his arm.

"We appreciate that, and we're grateful for all you've done," he said, and gave her one of his best smiles. "We're sorry for the inconvenience."

That brought a reluctant smile.

"You're welcome," she said, in a more measured tone. "Safety has to come first, doesn't it?"

"Exactly," Ryan put in, and her smile fell again. "Which is why I'd like to put another call through to my superior to ask about searching the passengers' belongings."

Phillips slapped a palm to his face, because he already knew what the outcome of that conversation would be—but he also knew that Ryan had to try.

"Absolutely, categorically, out of the question," Morrison told him, a few minutes later.

"Ma'am, the gospel book must be on the train. There was no realistic opportunity for anybody to leave before it turned around. If our perp has changed his appearance, that's one thing, but he can't hide the book."

"First of all, Ryan, have you heard yourself? What's all this about suspects changing into different costumes, now?"

"It's happened before," he reminded her.

"Even so, you're wrong about not being able to hide that book. The point is, it could be anywhere on the train, inside any number of bags, slipped down the side of a chair or God only knows what. You're expecting me to authorise a full search of that magnitude whilst six hundred or so people twiddle their thumbs as you interfere with their private belongings—without a proper warrant?"

She was incredulous.

"I'm sorry, Ryan. I can't allow it. Stand down, and come home. If you're lucky, there might be a seat for you both on that train and, if you're luckier still, you'll have a job to come back to, tomorrow morning."

Ryan sighed, and looked across at the stationary passenger train.

He understood that Morrison was considering the impact of another failed search attempt, and the domino effect that would have on their public relations efforts, amongst other things. Nobody liked to be held up, especially not people at the end of a working day who were eager to get home.

"At least send a couple of officers to meet the train, in Newcastle," he begged her.

"And, if I do, who would they hope to see? Do you have a description of the perpetrator?"

Ryan only had a description of a dead man.

"Exactly," Morrison said, when the silence dragged on. "Do your homework, Ryan. Work with the Met to acquire the CCTV footage, get some eyewitness accounts… then come to me with demands about search and seizure warrants, and not before."

Ryan and Phillips spent some considerable time on site at the British Library liaising with the Met team, who were in attendance taking statements from material witnesses, and overseeing the forensic investigation into the theft of St. Cuthbert's Gospel. Finally, they boarded a train home at seven-thirty, world-weary and exhausted.

"Well," Phillips said, slumping back in his chair. "That was certainly an eventful day."

Ryan closed his eyes—not to sleep, but to think.

"You know what this calls for? A bacon butty," Phillips said, his mouth watering at the prospect. "Can I get you one?"

Ryan wasn't about to deny the man any carbohydrates at that juncture; they'd spent much of the day on foot, walking or running, and had barely eaten or drunk a thing.

"Make mine a ham and cheese toastie," he said, embracing the risk of a heart attack, in later life. "I'll get them, it's my turn."

"Nah, stay where you are. You look as if you might keel over," Phillips said.

Soon after, he returned with Ryan's food, a couple of bottles of water, a coffee and a peppermint tea.

"Where's yours?" Ryan asked.

Phillips held up a small, plastic-wrapped salad.

"I felt too guilty when I got to the counter," he confessed. "I went for the egg salad."

Ryan chewed the first bite of his toastie and tried not to look like he was enjoying it.

"I heard from Hassan, while you were gone," he said, between bites. "He had an update about Lareuse."

"What did he say?"

"There was a full-scale riot, after we left," Ryan replied. "Four prison officers injured, nine inmates hurt, too, but no other casualties. But that's not even the bad news."

"It gets worse?"

"Laueuse's body was damaged during the riot," Ryan said. "They didn't move him because the forensics team hadn't attended, and the electronic cell doors remained open throughout—apparently, they had a hell of a task trying to get all the prisoners contained."

"I bet," Phillips murmured, and took a reluctant bite of his egg salad, finding it depressingly un-meaty.

He liked animals, he really did, and agreed that the circumstances of killing them for food should be as humane as possible, whilst upholding the highest standards on all fronts. But there was no escaping his basic biology: Frank Phillips was a carnivore and, much as he tried to convince himself otherwise, boiled eggs just didn't cut it.

"The whole crime scene was compromised," Ryan said. "That's not counting the obvious fact that Lareuse's cell was hardly The Ritz—the standards of cleanliness were already atrocious, so there would've been multiple historic samples to wade through and make sense of. The chances of the CSIs being able to find meaningful evidence that could be relied upon in court have drastically reduced, as have our chances of finding out who was paid to do the hit."

He watched Phillips eating his eggs disconsolately, looked down at the remaining half of his toastie, and decided he was full.

"Finish mine, if you want," Ryan said casually. "I couldn't eat, after all."

Phillips' face perked up. "Y'sure?"

Ryan smiled, and pushed it across the table.

"Have it while it's still hot."

"What about CCTV?" Phillips asked, and sank his teeth into the first bite. "Oh, that's the Food of the Gods, that is!"

Ryan grinned.

"Hassan's requested the footage but, wouldn't you know it? The camera circuit on B Wing was down for a period of three hours, today."

"Wonders never cease," Phillips muttered.

"Quite. Hassan says they've got Lareuse's mobile phone and a few other personal items, so they'll start going through that today, and they've already got an order to access his UK bank account—not that there'll be much in that; he'll have squirreled it away in a Swiss account. They've found a key amongst his gear, presumably to a lock-up of some kind, but there's no telling where that might be."

"Aye, that'll be tricky to find, in a city this size," Phillips agreed.

"If it's even in London, at all."

They fell into a brief silence, watching their own reflections in the window which was little more than a black mirror against the darkness outside.

"We might have more luck at the library," Phillips said. "They've already sent us the CCTV footage from today and it's good quality, too. We can get one of the techie fellers to enhance it and try to get a photofit."

"If by 'techie fellers' you mean a member of our esteemed Digital Forensics Unit, then yes, I'm sure we could, but it won't be us doing that—the case belongs to the Met. They shared that footage with us as a favour, but we'll need Morrison to broker it for us if we want to work jointly."

"D'you think she will?" Phillips asked.

Ryan shrugged. "She's angry now, and rightly so. It was a calculated risk we took, coming here today, and things haven't exactly gone to plan. However, events have proven certain things beyond a shadow of a doubt."

"There's still a possibility that Lareuse was killed for other reasons," Phillips warned him. "You can't rely on that in support of our theories."

"I know. I was thinking more of the theft at the library, and the attack on that girl. In the first place, Jacob Jamieson is lying in a mortuary in Yorkshire, so he couldn't have been running around King's Cross. The security team at the library have already confirmed that the perp gained access using

Jamieson's Researcher Pass, and that he swiped in through the turnstiles at 15:28 for a three-thirty appointment with Dr Malone. How else could he have procured Jamieson's pass, if he didn't take it from the man himself?"

Phillips nodded.

"I've already contacted DCI Patel," Ryan continued. "I told her that a man posing as Father Jacob gained entry to the Library using his pass, or a copy of it, to attack a woman and steal the gospel book. She's come back to confirm that they've searched his belongings at Crayke and there's no sign of a British Library pass amongst them."

"He can't have been killed just for his pass," Phillips muttered.

"No," Ryan agreed. "I think that was a question of convenience. Whoever used Jamieson's pass had to act quickly before his name was made public, otherwise they ran the risk of somebody querying his identity, after seeing the news of Father Jacob's death. At the moment, all they've reported is the death of a monk at Crayke College; Patel deliberately ordered a media embargo on the details being released until they'd had a chance to try to track down his next of kin. Unfortunately, somebody took advantage of the window of opportunity."

"So, if they didn't kill him for a bit of plastic—then what?"

"As we said when we looked at that poor man's body, Father Jacob was tortured for a reason. We didn't know what that reason was, until today, but I think it has to do with the gospel book."

"Might just be a collector," Phillips argued. "Somebody who wants to acquire everything to do with St. Cuthbert, including anything he might have had inside his coffin, which is why the pectoral cross was taken, as well. It might not be anything more than that."

Ryan ran a hand over his mouth, considering.

"I agree, we're dealing with a collector," he said eventually. "But the timing is significant, here, don't you think? They orchestrated the switch of that pectoral cross three years ago, and arranged an elaborate heist to steal their own copy, rather than risk discovery. That takes a lot of planning and investment. Today, the same person walked into the national library of the UK, alone, dressed up as a dead monk but otherwise without protection, with the specific goal to steal that book. Choosing to pose as Jacob Jamieson was a risky strategy and took very little time or money investment. He ran the risk of capture—which is something we very nearly achieved, today."

He set aside bitter disappointment on that score.

"It feels like an escalation," Phillips said, brushing toast crumbs from his jumper. "I wonder what's driving them to take risks."

"That's the question, Frank. Something about that book was important—not just historically, but to those who believe in St. Cuthbert's cult."

He looked his friend in the eye.

"We need to find out what that something is."

CHAPTER 22

Ryan arrived home shortly after eleven, and felt his heart thud against his chest when he caught sight of a tall, well-built figure silhouetted in the porch light wielding a gun.

Charles lowered the rifle and secured the safety.

"Not exactly the warmest welcome," he said. "But you can't be too careful."

To Ryan's surprise, he leaned in to give him a manly, one-armed hug.

"Glad to see you back in one piece," his father said gruffly. "The little one's fast asleep, and Anna and your mum are in the living room."

Ryan stepped inside the house and felt a blast of heat warm his icy cheeks.

Home.

"Go on through and see your wife," Charles said, once Ryan had toed off his boots and hung up his winter coat. "I'll bring you a bowl of soup."

Ryan couldn't have said why that, of all things, was enough to breach his defences, but it was.

"Thank you," he managed.

"Don't mention it," Charles said quietly, before moving off towards the kitchen.

Ryan found two of the three most important females in his life sitting in the cosy living room, with the log fire burning. It was a festive scene, with a garland of ivy and mistletoe draped over the mantlepiece and Nat King Cole playing quietly from a speaker hidden behind the sofa.

"You're back," Anna said, and rose to her feet to return his kiss.

"Hi," he said, simply, and drew her in for a close embrace. "How are you?"

"Better," she assured him. "Emma's had a lovely day. We went for a walk by the river, then practised our crawling, didn't we grandma?"

"We did, indeed. Another month or so, and there'll be no stopping her," Eve replied, and patted her son's cheek as he leaned down to kiss her.

"Hello, darling," she said. "How was your day?"

Ryan settled himself on the sofa beside Anna, who rested her head on his shoulder, and thought of how to describe his day.

"Busy," he decided. "Productive."

"Oh?" Anna said, lifting her head again. "What can you tell us about it?"

He appreciated her being mindful of the confidential nature of his job and, for his part, were it not for the threat posed to his family, he wouldn't have liked to bring any of the darkness home with him. Here was happiness and light, love and family, and it was his mission to keep it that way.

But there *was* a threat, so long as the situation remained unresolved, and they had a right to know the full extent.

His father came into the room and set down a small tray of soup and buttered bread, which he placed on a side table beside his son before joining Eve on the opposite sofa.

"Thanks," Ryan said, and left it to cool. "I haven't talked too much about this, over the past few months, because I haven't wanted to worry anybody, unduly. You know what happened to DCI Tebbutt, from Durham Area Command?"

There were sober nods around the room.

"She was killed because of what she came to know about Cuthbert's cross, as was the man who spotted the forgery—Edward Faber. We kept things quiet to give us some time to investigate, a bit of breathing room, if you like. But now, that time is up."

They waited for him to explain.

"Until now, there's always been the potential that somebody out there would find out that we knew about the forgery, that we were investigating them, and would seek to silence me or perhaps other members of my team…maybe my family, too. Today, that threat became more of a reality, because I saw his face, and he saw mine."

There was not a sound in the room other than the crackling of the fire, until Anna spoke again.

"What does that mean?" she asked, quietly.

"It means that our cover is blown," he replied, and took her hand between his own. "If this person we're looking for harboured even a shadow of a doubt about whether we knew about the forgery, seeing me today was enough to confirm it. More so, since they ran, and I gave chase."

"You were chasing a thief," Eve argued. "Any police officer would have done the same."

"A local officer, yes, but a murder detective from the North East? It raises questions, such as what I was doing down there, and why; the only answer can be that I was investigating other relics belonging to Cuthbert, which I wouldn't bother to do, if the real cross had been returned to Durham Cathedral."

"Ah, yes, I see," Eve whispered. "Now, you don't have the benefit of their doubt."

"Exactly, but the good news is that I have some useful leads to follow now, which is more than we had this time a couple of days ago."

"Where did you see this man?" Charles asked.

Ryan suddenly realised that they hadn't heard, because it wouldn't have been reported, yet.

"At the British Library," he said. "I went there with Frank to see the St. Cuthbert Gospel, which is usually on display. By an odd quirk of fate, we came across a robbery in progress—a man dressed as the monk who died at Crayke

College on Sunday night gained access to the gospel book using the dead man's access pass, then attacked a young woman before making off with it."

"Was she all right?" Eve asked, not caring so much about the book as the person. Anna smiled privately, understanding where Ryan had learned compassion and his unwavering belief in *people* over *things*.

"She'll be all right," Ryan assured her. "She took a nasty blow around the head, but she'll recover."

Physically, at least.

"So, you intercepted him?" Charles guessed.

"Not quite," Ryan said, with some disappointment. "By the time we discovered what had happened, he'd reached the main doors. I chased him as far as King's Cross, where he boarded a train. We managed to stop the train and search it, but he seemed to have vanished."

Charles made a murmuring sound in his throat.

"I've asked for the footage on the train, so I can track the man's movements and find out how he did it, but that will take a day or so, possibly, which is time we don't have when a perp is clearly escalating their behaviour. That makes two incidents in two days, if we're right."

"I have some old notes on the St. Cuthbert Gospel," Anna said. "I could look them out for you, if that would help?"

Ryan thought of how lucky he was.

"That would be enormously helpful," he said. "The extent of my knowledge is a potted summary from Lowerson and what I read on the display placard—something about it having been made locally by monks in Jarrow and Monkwearmouth as an offering to Cuthbert, who was already dead by that time. It was always intended to be placed inside his coffin, as a kind of amulet."

Anna nodded. "Not a bad start," she smiled. "I'll tidy up my notes tomorrow, when Madam isn't demanding my attention."

Ryan grinned at the thought.

"It's a pity we can't look at the book, now," he said. "I think there has to be something in it that would explain why the monk died; I only wish I knew what it was."

"Well, you know, the British Library scans all its pieces into a digital archive," Anna said. "The images are very high quality, so you can actually scroll through the pages of the gospel as if you had the real thing in front of you."

Ryan framed her face in both of his hands and delivered a smacking kiss.

"Let me know if you're ever looking for a job," he said, with renewed optimism. "I'd hire you on the spot."

"You couldn't afford me," she joked. "But, since I like you so much, I'll have a scroll through the digital copy tomorrow and let you know if anything stands out."

"We'll help with the baby," Eve volunteered, happily. There was nothing she loved more than spending time with the newest member of the Ryan family. "Won't we, Charles?"

"Try and stop us," he said.

Talk turned to other things and, as the fire began to die and his parents excused themselves for the night, Ryan was left alone for a few precious minutes with his wife.

"I missed you, today," he said.

"I missed you, too," she said, softly, and brushed her lips against his. "I could tell there was more you wanted to say, just now, but didn't. If you need to talk about it, I'm here to listen; it cuts both ways, you know."

Ryan pulled her close and rubbed his cheek against her hair.

"The closer we get, the more dangerous it becomes," he said, as they watched flames lick at the remains of a log, its light casting flickering shadows against the wall. "I don't want to but, if it comes to it, you may have to take Emma somewhere safe, maybe down to Devon with my parents."

Anna's arms tightened around his chest, and she breathed in the scent of him, hardly able to imagine being parted when they'd so recently become new parents.

However much it hurt her to think of it, it must have hurt him even more to suggest it.

She told herself not to make things even harder.

"We'll do whatever's necessary to keep our family safe," she said, and hoped it wouldn't come to that.

Finally, the key rested in their hands.

It had been overwhelming, seeing it there in the reading room of the library. Such a little book, its pages faded and worn, but they could feel the power radiating from it in waves.

Cuthbert's power.

Now, their power.

They brought the book to their face, sniffing the goatskin binding, touching the tip of their tongue to the glue, rubbing it against their skin in a manner that might have been sexual, for some. But they were not concerned with pleasures of the flesh. Like Cuthbert, they were far above that now, however their thoughts might have strayed in the past.

Indeed, impotence was a blessing.

They chanted old rites and prayers as the book skimmed their naked body, and the sound of crashing North Sea waves surrounded them, pumped through hidden speakers in the wall. They'd have liked to have been on Inner Farne, Cuthbert's sanctuary and the place where he'd passed on to a higher realm, but that was not possible.

Not everyone understood such greatness, but there was a chosen few who did. They were the true believers…the true guardians of Cuthbert's way of life, and only they, through him, could benefit from his miraculous power.

From time immemorial, Cuthbert had rested with his relics; items destined to be buried with him for all eternity, invested with fragments of his strength. Through the ages they had been separated, scattered around the country to sit in glass boxes, until their power began to wane. Only when made whole again, could Cuthbert's strength be restored.

They'd made the mistake of thinking the cross and other trinkets were sufficient, but that was before they'd found out the disgusting, demoralising, *deceitful* truth that the 'new' church—one of Henry's creation—had flogged to the masses.

The very thought was enough to bring on an attack, and their body began to shake, convulsing and sweating as they rolled around the stone floor.

Through it all, they laughed, and felt no pain.

CHAPTER 23

Ryan awoke the next morning with renewed purpose, thanks in large part to the fact his daughter had slept soundly through the night, not uttering so much as a peep before six-thirty. Naturally, he and Anna took full credit for this wonderful development, as all new parents did on the occasion of their child doing something perfectly normal, no matter how infrequent.

Fuelled by an extra couple of hours' shut-eye, he strode through the doors of Northumbria Police Headquarters with the air of a man who was ready to face the world again—a state of affairs that was immediately called into question, when the Chief Constable's personal assistant cornered him as soon as he entered the building.

"Sorry to piss on your bonfire, but Morrison wants to see you, straight away," she said, with her usual refinement.

"*And* she says to tell you, she can't be bought by posh coffee, either."

The woman looked pointedly at the cardboard cups he held in his hands.

"I guess I'll have to drink them both," he said, with a bland smile. "I'll be there in a minute."

She stalked off, in a manner vaguely reminiscent of Nosferatu.

In the minute it took him to walk from one end of the corridor to the other, Ryan considered all the different excuses he could make for having overridden her orders, as well as all the justifications.

But he discarded them all, in favour of one simple message.

"I'm sorry," he said, without reservation.

Morrison eyed the coffee he held in his hand, and told herself to stay strong.

"I've heard that before, Ryan. Every time you flout my orders, you're sorry."

"It's true, I'm always sorry to have to do it."

She stared at him. "Is that supposed to be funny?"

"No, ma'am. It's supposed to be honest."

"Ryan, do you respect my authority?"

"Always," he said, without pause. "But, on occasion, I disagree with your application of it."

"You had the chance to be superintendent." She reminded him about the position that was still vacant despite an extensive recruitment exercise. "That would give you more clout, if that's what you're after—"

Ryan frowned. "Do you think that matters to me, at this point in my career? We've known each other a long time."

She sighed, and shook her head.

"No, I don't think you're led by ego—or, at least, no more than the next person—and I don't think you'd thank me for giving you another promotion," she said, quite accurately. "You could handle a more senior position with your eyes closed, but the day-to-day wouldn't suit you because you like working on the front line, don't you?"

He inclined his head.

"Cards on the table, Ryan," she said, indicating that he should sit. "I spent most of last night being angry at you, but then I had a kind of revelation, this morning. I realised something, which is that I've been away from front line work for too long. It makes it harder for me to make judgment calls on risk, which you're better placed to be doing, because you've got a proven track record. That's your forte, and it's an asset to the constabulary."

Ryan was taken aback by the turn of the conversation.

"Thank you," he said, cautiously. "I apologise, again, if my actions were insubordinate."

She laughed. "You've *always* been insubordinate. It's a defining characteristic—"

"That much is true," he said. "You can ask my mother."

"A very tolerant woman, no doubt," she said, with a smile. "The thing is, I applied for this job because I'm good at juggling police and politics; that's my strength."

"You're an excellent chief constable," Ryan said, and meant it.

"Thank you," she replied. "All the same, I feel I've been looking at things from the wrong perspective, and that's because your reporting to me was only ever supposed to be an interim procedure, until a new DCS could be appointed. Not that it hasn't worked, or that you're all that difficult to manage—"

"I'm obviously not trying hard enough."

There was a half-second pause, then she laughed, relaxing back in her chair.

"This is why you've got the longevity," she said. "You've never lost your humour, despite all the sadness surrounding the work we do."

"It's easy to stay upbeat, when you're surrounded by a great team of people, and you've got someone who loves you."

Morrison nodded.

"You can say that again. Not one of them cracked, while you were moonlighting in London—that's a mark of loyalty."

"I hope it's not misplaced," Ryan said. "I accept full responsibility for the decision-making in Operation Bertie—"

She waved a hand.

"Ryan, if I was going to dish out reprimands, I would have done it by now. I know it's you leading that team, but I also know you're not surrounded by a herd of sheep; if they didn't believe you had good cause to act in the way that you did, they wouldn't have gone along with it. That's the reason I'm not suspending you, today."

"Thank you," he said, as meekly as he could.

Morrison jutted her chin in the direction of the coffee cups he'd placed on the desktop.

"Are they just for show?"

He shook his head, and gestured for her to help herself.

"Thanks," she said, taking the first life-affirming sip. "The thing is, Ryan, for the vast majority of cases, you just keep your head down and get on with it, racking up closed case after closed case and generally doing exactly what you're supposed to do, which is to make us all look good."

Ryan smiled.

"But, every now and then, an unusual case comes along, such as the one we're dealing with now—Operation Bertie. It's less straightforward and carries much more risk to the department, including demands on its budget, as you know. From my side of the desk, I want it done with, finished, forgotten. In fact, I wanted that six months ago."

"Me too," he reminded her. "But for slightly different reasons."

"I want to see justice done," she said, with a tone to her voice. "But there are times when I have to make hard decisions; ones my heart may not agree with—but my head must have the final ruling."

"I understand that," Ryan said.

"Which brings me back around to my point, earlier. Really, we need to appoint a new superintendent to oversee the department, so I don't have to start taking blood pressure tablets."

"Still no suitable candidates?" he enquired.

"You know bloody well that you're our first choice for DCS," she muttered. "But you won't do it."

Ryan nodded, then he remembered an idea he'd had a while ago.

"I have a suggestion, if I may."

"I'm all ears."

CHAPTER 24

At ten o'clock, Ryan called a departmental briefing in the largest conference room at Police Headquarters with a full complement of CID staff, including Morrison, who had been persuaded to re-open Operation Bertie.

"All right, settle down," he said, once they were all assembled. "There's coffee and croissants at the back—don't get used to it."

There was a ripple of laughter and a scrape of chairs as people made a last-minute grab.

"I know some of you will be wondering why you're here," he continued, once the chatter died down and he had their full attention. "Jack? Hit the lights, would you?"

When Lowerson turned the lights off, Ryan fired up the projector screen.

"You're here to mark the formal re-opening of Operation Bertie, which, for the past nine months, has been a covert investigation into the theft of St. Cuthbert's pectoral cross and the murders of DCI Joan Tebbutt and Edward

Faber. He was a well-known forger and informant to our colleagues in the Durham constabulary, with whom we'll be co-operating and sharing information, as necessary. This is now a cross-constabulary exercise, and I expect the highest standards of cooperation, going forwards."

One of the younger members of his team stuck their hand in the air.

"Sir? I don't understand—I thought the cross had been recovered?"

There were murmurs of assent around the room.

"A cross was indeed recovered, but it wasn't the original."

He proceeded to set out their theory surrounding the replica cross, and the role it played in the deaths of Tebbutt and Faber.

"The key word here is *discovery*," Ryan said, and leaned back against a desk at the front of the room, hands braced on either side. "Whoever perpetrated these crimes did so to prevent discovery of the replica and, I believe, more importantly, discovery of the reasons why the original was taken in the first place."

He pressed his clicker, and a picture of St. Cuthbert's shrine in Durham came up on the screen behind him.

"For any of you heathens who don't know, this is Saint Cuthbert's final resting place in Durham Cathedral," he said, pointing at the image. "The bloke was a monk and a bishop a thousand years ago but, after he died, a cult developed around him because it was said his body hadn't decayed, which was hailed as a miracle."

He turned back to the room.

"Apparently, miracles were big business back then, because everyone with an ailment came to worship at the shrine and be 'cured'. They brought offerings and, if they happened to be wealthy or noble, you can imagine that racked up. It also brought a lot of prestige for the Catholic Church and the monks who guarded Cuthbert's body, and that's not something easily relinquished. However, it was all change after the Reformation, and the cult surrounding Cuthbert gradually declined in popularity—but that's not to say it died out, altogether."

He took a swig of coffee.

"That concludes the history lesson for today," he said, and there was another flutter of laughter around the room. "All of this is relevant because we believe there may be a person, or group, who still buy into this cult—more so than the average devout church-goer, who *de facto* believes in miracles, if they believe the word of the Bible to the letter."

He shrugged.

"Live and let live, but don't harm anybody else, that's what we say around here, isn't it? The problem is, we've got person or persons unknown running amok, fuelled by their convictions. It's hard to reason with a belief, at the best of times, but when you're dealing with an organised, well-financed operation, it becomes a real problem."

He brought up an image of Mathieu Lareuse, taken from his charge sheet less than a week ago.

"This is Mathieu Lareuse, street name, 'Rodin'—"

"Why 'Rodin', sir?" somebody asked.

"Probably, after the French sculptor," Phillips said, surprising them all. "What? I listen to Radio Four."

"Whatever the reason might have been, the name suited him," Ryan continued. "He was a French national with British citizenship, who worked in galleries around London for a couple of years—until it became clear he was selling forgeries on a regular basis, many of which he'd manufactured himself. He earned himself a name on the underground circuits as being one of the best in the business."

He clicked the next slide, which showed the forged pectoral cross, taken by Tom Faulkner, who was the senior CSI attached to their department.

"Lareuse was found dead in his cell in Pentonville Prison yesterday afternoon," Ryan said. "We believe the reason is that he was responsible for creating this replica cross, which is the one we recovered back in March and which has been returned to the exhibition space at Durham Cathedral."

They all sat up a little straighter.

"The decision was taken to allow the deception to continue, to give us a chance to figure out why anybody would want to steal something they knew to be fake—"

"How did they know it was fake?" somebody asked, and Ryan could only be glad he wasn't surrounded by morons.

"Timing," he replied, shortly. "We believe Edward Faber discovered his competitor's handiwork, perhaps by chance, and told his old contact from Durham CID—

who happened to be DCI Joan Tebbutt, who'd previously worked in the Fraud Unit. Unfortunately, somebody must have got wind of Faber's discovery because, the next thing, he winds up being tortured and killed. We believe that Faber admitted to informing Tebbutt, to try to save himself, but he was already a dead man. Thanks to him, so was she."

Ryan hitched a hip onto the edge of the desk.

"The point is, Faber's death took place prior to the Durham heist, and there's no other plausible explanation. We know that the late DC Justine Winter was involved in both murders, prior to taking her own life."

"Why'd she do it?" one of them asked. "Why would she turn?"

"Money," another one sneered.

"There's no present evidence to suggest money was a motivating factor," Ryan said. "However, we do believe there may be some connection between Justine's actions and Cuthbert's so-called 'cult'. She has a brother who is seriously ill, and for whom we believe she might have been persuaded to try and procure a miracle."

There were a few disbelieving laughs around the room, and Ryan could hardly blame them.

"I know it's a difficult mental leap," he said. "I'm not a religious person myself, nor do I have a loved one who is terminally ill or suffering from a debilitating, degenerative disease. But, if I did, I have to ask myself what I wouldn't do, to try to make them better."

That silenced any further outbursts, because it was only the truth. There was very little that people wouldn't do for those they loved; and, in some cases, that included committing murder.

"The idea of making sacrifices to one's chosen deity isn't new," he continued. "It's a practice that's been followed around the world for centuries—probably, millennia. It's harder to accept it happening in our modern, civilised society, because we'd like to believe we're past all that, and more evolved."

Ryan clicked onto the next image, which was a picture DCI Patel had shared with him, and showed the crime scene at Crayke College with the late Father Jacob front and centre.

There were horrified intakes of breath.

"Not a pretty sight, I'm sure you'll agree," Ryan said, and clicked onto a blank screen to give their eyes a break. "The deceased is Father Jacob Jamieson, a former monk and housemaster at Crayke College, in North Yorkshire. Prior to his conversion, he was a history teacher for a number of years and was a renowned authority on the life and times of St. Cuthbert."

Ryan paused to polish off his coffee before continuing— talking of murder was thirsty work.

"Father Jacob was found tortured and murdered in a cider mill on Monday morning, which is on the Crayke grounds and is owned and operated by the monastery. As you can see from that picture, his death was slow and painful, and unnecessarily dramatic, in the end."

"What did he do?" one of the intelligence analysts called out. "Fiddle with some of the kids?"

Ryan frowned darkly. "In the first instance, that's nothing to make light of," he snapped. "And, in the second, there's no evidence to suggest this man was anything other than a well-regarded member of his community, well-liked by his pupils."

He decided to address the elephant in the room, which was on all of their minds.

"Look, I know what people think of, when they think of the Catholic Church and young choirboys, or whatever, but we need to remain professional and clear-sighted when making decisions about matters than can affect those who are still living. Yes, there has been a lot of cause for concern as to safeguarding practices on a global scale, which is a source of great sadness and regret for all involved—especially those who were victims of predatory crimes. However, when approaching a case, we need to consider each individual set of facts on their own merits, and be sure not to tarnish all with the same brush. Am I understood?"

There were nods around the room.

"Good. Coming back to Father Jacob, there was nothing obvious to help us understand what might have motivated his death, other than a general connection to St. Cuthbert," Ryan said. "When we visited the scene, at the invitation of the SIO, it was on the basis that Jamieson's death might have had some connection with the death of Edward Faber—whose murder is the only other recent torture case on the shared police database. Whilst Phillips and myself agree there are definite similarities, we were unable to disclose to the SIO the full details of Operation Bertie, and of how both Faber and Jamieson's deaths are connected to the theft of Cuthbert's cross. Now that the Chief Constable has authorised the decision to re-open this matter, there is no need for further secrecy, and we will communicate and cooperate with North Yorkshire CID at the earliest opportunity."

Ryan clicked again and, this time, a picture of a small, red gospel book came onto the projector screen.

"This is a gospel book of St. John," he told them. "More commonly known as the 'St. Cuthbert Gospel', on account of it having spent the best part of eight hundred years inside the man's coffin, resting beside him. It carries cultural and literary significance but, for our purposes, it's important because, yesterday afternoon, a man posing as the late Father Jacob stole this piece from the British Library, causing grievous bodily harm to one of their conservationists in the process. They evaded the police and made for King's Cross, where we believe they were able to conceal themselves on board a train bound for the North. We expect CCTV footage to come through today but, at this stage, we suspect that Father Jacob was tortured and killed for information in his possession, and we suspect that information relates in some way to the gospel book."

"You mean, because it's one of Cuthbert's relics?" one of the PCs asked.

"Possibly, but if we were dealing with a group of people whose only intent was to gather up all of Cuthbert's relics,

I'd query the timing; we believe the cross was switched for a replica three years ago, whilst renovation works were underway in the exhibition galleries at Durham Cathedral, and a lot of careful time and effort was put into that operation. When the British Library reacquired the gospel book from Stonyhurst College, in Lancashire, they made an agreement with Durham Cathedral that it would be displayed in London and Durham—if they planned to steal it, why not do so while it was more accessible, in Durham? Why wait three more years, and take it in highly risky, opportunistic circumstances?"

He lifted a shoulder.

"It's more likely the information from Father Jacob was new, and important, and created an urgent imperative to steal the gospel book as quickly as possible."

"Did you say the book used to be at Stonyhurst?" Yates asked.

Ryan nodded, and looked to Lowerson, who nodded his confirmation.

"Yes—why? Have you thought of something?"

"Potentially," she said, scrolling quickly through her phone. "When I read the BBC news report about Jamieson's death this morning, there was a quote from one of his old teaching colleagues, from back in the day…here we go. It says they taught together at Stonyhurst for fifteen years, which means he would have been there while they still had the gospel book."

Ryan smiled. "Now, that is an interesting coincidence, and adds further weight to our theory about the book carrying some special significance, beyond the obvious fact of its historic importance."

He turned to look up at the image of the book and wondered how a collection of written words could wield so much power.

CHAPTER 25

While Charles and Eve took their granddaughter for a stroll in her pram, Anna dusted off her laptop and settled down to the business of researching St. Cuthbert's Gospel. As a senior lecturer at Durham University, her specialism was in early pagan history in the North East of England, rather than early Christian history— but no historian looking to understand the regional landscape could understand one without the other, and it was impossible not to know something of the facts and traditions surrounding its patron saint. Besides, Anna grew up on the remote island of Lindisfarne, where Cuthbert had been a bishop in the late seventh century, and near to the tiny island of Inner Farne, where he had spent much of his time as a hermit and where he'd eventually died.

Automatically, she reached for her hair, intending to tie it back from her face, before remembering she'd been forced to cut most of it off.

Funny, she thought. It was only hair, and would grow back, but how she'd cried about it in the privacy of her own company. A trivial and superficial thing to be concerned about, perhaps, yet so much a part of her identity for so many years, and what she expected to see when she looked in the mirror.

Now, she had a short pixie crop, which some might say suited her.

It was certainly more practical, but…

Really, the problem was that she hadn't had the freedom to choose whether or not to cut her hair; the hospital had been forced to make that decision in order to facilitate an operation to stem a blood clot on her brain. In those circumstances, she'd have gone Full Britney if necessary, but that didn't mean she was happy about it.

"Get a grip," she muttered to herself. "It's only hair."

Anna turned her mind to reading through her old notes surrounding the cult of Cuthbert, and refreshed her memory about the journey Cuthbert's body had taken following his death in 687AD. According to the Venerable Bede's *Life of St. Cuthbert*, the saint's body was transported the short boat ride from Inner Farne to Lindisfarne, where it was buried on the same day. Eleven years later, his sarcophagus was opened and the body found to be completely preserved, which kickstarted the cult whereby people attributed miracles to his intercession or to intercessory prayer near his remains. Then, when the Vikings took the monastery at Lindisfarne in 875, the monks were forced to flee with Cuthbert's body, which they carried around with them for seven years. The reason generally given for this was a desire to evade capture, but it was also the ninth century's equivalent of a rock star touring the North East, blazing a trail of miraculous power wherever the monks went and leaving countless churches named after Cuthbert in their wake.

After seven years, the body stayed for around a hundred years at St. Cuthbert's Church in Chester-le-Street, whereupon yet another Viking invasion forced the monks to hit the road again and transport his body to Ripon, in Yorkshire. Interestingly, Crayke Abbey was reputedly one of the saint's resting places, while in that part of the world, and that must have been something the late Father Jacob Jamieson would have known about. Finally, the monks' coffin cart got stuck in some mud near the riverbend at Durham, and legend has it this was the saint's way of letting his guardians know that's where he wanted to stay put. They set up camp at the top of the hill and built a simple 'White Church', which was the first predecessor to the enormous cathedral that now stood in its place.

Over the centuries, all manner of things were buried with Cuthbert, including the body of Bede, King Oswald's head and other gruesome keepsakes, like some sort of macabre travelling circus.

Amongst those things was a red leather gospel book, painstakingly created for him by the monks at Jarrow.

Anna read a brief history of the book, marvelling at the survival of a tiny book through the course of centuries, until one day in 2012 the British Library paid Stonyhurst College a princely sum to acquire the book so that it might be cared for and admired by anyone who wished to see it. Now, a person had stolen it, unable to see beyond their own beliefs and desires to appreciate the selfishness of their actions, and it was far from certain whether the little gospel book would survive the next stage in its journey.

Feeling an acute sense of loss, she accessed the digital archive copy of the gospel, which was accessible through the British Library's website, and sipped at a cup of tea while she flicked through the pages.

At some point during the second hour, she heard the family return and Anna stepped away from the computer to be with her daughter, but not before noticing something unusual.

Perhaps it was nothing, she told herself.

On the other hand…

While breastfeeding Emma with one strong, secure arm, she used her other free hand to go back to the beginning and scroll through the digital pages of the book, zooming right in so she could see the very grains of parchment up close.

So easy to miss, Anna thought. *Unless you were looking for it.*

She smiled down at her daughter, who was falling asleep in her arms after enjoying a belly-full of milk.

"I think your daddy is going to be very pleased, when I tell him what we've found," she whispered, and placed a soft kiss to Emma's forehead.

Back at Northumbria Police Headquarters, Ryan was in the process of managing the logistics of a wide-ranging investigation that crossed over four different command areas, and counting.

"I want regular lines of communication between our team here, North Yorkshire CID, Durham CID and the Met," he said, and divvied up the tasks to one of the liaison officers. "If there are any updates on the investigation into Father Jacob or Mathieu Lareuse's death, I want to hear about it. Understood?"

This was met by a vigorous nod of the head.

"Now that we have some recent activity to work with, we can use it to our advantage," Ryan said. "Jack? Melanie? Previously, I know you said it was difficult to try to interview or extract information from the list of people who had access to Cuthbert's cross during the renovation works, three years ago. I want you to go back over that list now and interview everyone, one-by-one, beginning with those who can't account for their whereabouts on Sunday evening or Monday morning, and all day yesterday."

"Consider it done," Lowerson said, while Yates made a swift note.

"Better still, cross-check them again, looking for any with a recent history of severe illness, or a close family member with a severe illness, or any recently deceased family members. We're looking for people who are vulnerable to the idea of a miracle being their only hope— so let's look for people who might be in need of a miracle."

"We'll get straight on it, this afternoon," Yates promised.

"Good. Mac? I need you to pick up where we left off with those hospital records," he said. "I want to know who Justine Winter and her brother would have seen on a regular basis at their regular appointments, as well as any support groups they attended. Interview the brother, if you can, and find out who they spoke to, or who his sister might have spoken of, more often than anyone else. There's nothing in her work e-mail account, or even on her private e-mail accounts, so we need to come at this from another direction."

"Leave it with me," MacKenzie said, in her soft Irish burr.

"Phillips? I need the CCTV footage from all of the crime scenes, and a photofit. I want to know who the hell got on that train, yesterday, and how we missed them."

"Nee bother," he said, with a smile. "By the way, we've had an update through from Hassan, in London. He says they've managed to find Lareuse's lock-up, on the Isle of Dogs. Apparently, he'd hardly used his UK current account in three years, then, all of a sudden, he's buying lunch and dinner within five hundred yards of some storage place called, *Storr-Eez*."

"Muppet," Lowerson said.

"You can say that again," Phillips agreed. "Apparently, it's like a treasure trove inside, because Lareuse used it as his workshop. Left all his tools and everything. Anyhow, given all the stuff around Cuthbert, Hassan got in touch to say he'd found something that might be of interest."

"Oh? What's that?"

"Well, they've only had time to do a quick search, so they might come across even more, but they've found a stack of pictures of Cuthbert's Cross. Close-ups, and all that."

"You mean, the kind a high-class forger might use to produce a copy?"

"Exactly that kind of thing," Phillips agreed, with a smug smile.

It was circumstantial, but still an important connection. More importantly, it confirmed Ryan's theory about Lareuse's involvement, and it was always a relief to know that he wasn't losing his edge despite the endless rounds of 'Old MacDonald'.

He looked around their faces, glad to see the energy running high amongst his team, because they'd certainly need it.

"All right," he said. "Let's get to work!"

CHAPTER 26

Durham was magical at all times of the year, but especially in winter, when frost clung to the roofs and chimney-tops of the stone cottages that lined its cobbled streets, and the uppermost spires of the cathedral were shrouded in mist so it seemed to be touching the clouds.

"Can you imagine what people must have thought, in the old days?" Lowerson said, as they walked along the pathway beside the river, at the foot of the cathedral. "If you were a lowly peasant, living in a hut somewhere, imagine coming to Durham and seeing that! It'd be easy to believe it was God's house, wouldn't it? You'd be in awe of it all."

"I'm still in awe," Yates confessed.

They took a moment to enjoy the sight of a swan and her cygnets swimming gracefully downstream, breathing in the damp air with its earthy scent.

"I can see why Anna enjoyed living here," Lowerson remarked. "It's peaceful."

"And beautiful," Yates added. "But too close to the Cathedral, for my taste."

"Really?"

She shrugged, a bit self-consciously.

"You already know that my parents struggled when my sister died, and their personalities completely changed. It's hard for me to describe how they used to be and it's been so long now, I wonder whether I'm remembering correctly or if it's just wishful thinking. Anyway, they can be quite antisocial…well, you've met them, so you know."

Lowerson couldn't disagree. The handful of times he'd met Melanie's parents had been painfully awkward, and peppered with barbed comments around the fact they were 'living in sin'. He happened to like their sinful life, with their lovely new home and their feral kitten, Mel's good taste and his flair for taking out the bins. If that was 'sin', then he was most definitely a sinner, and proud of it.

But it was not so easy for Mel to laugh off these things.

"Losing a child is bound to have a terrible impact," he said, kindly. "People cope with grief in different ways."

"Well, my parents found a lot of solace in the Bible," she said, staring out across the river. "Overnight, they went from being agnostic people who never stepped foot inside a church, except to attend weddings or funerals, to becoming missionaries. They're over in China, now, trying to convert people."

Personally, Jack could never see the attraction of travelling to distant lands with the express purpose of bashing other people's belief systems, whilst simultaneously trying to flog your own—all under the banner of 'do-goodery', of course. So long as you built a well or something, while you were out there, being condescending towards others didn't seem to be so frowned upon.

But he said none of that.

"I suppose, if you really buy into the dogma, you genuinely believe you're doing God's work," he said. "From their perspective, they probably think they're two of God's most loyal servants."

"Just like the person we're looking for," Yates said, and then laughed. "I'm actually quite glad my parents are in another country—at least we can eliminate them from the suspect list."

"Yeah, there's only room for one of us to have a murdering parent, in this relationship," he said.

"There's a sentence you don't hear every day."

Laughing, they turned and made their way up a steep hill leading from the river to the cathedral, emerging onto a pretty grass quadrangle known as 'Palace Green'. There was a Christmas Market set up to run throughout December, its stalls selling everything from toffee apples to eggnog, hot toddies, mulled wine and more. The atmosphere was festive, and the scent of caramel and roasted nuts carried on the air.

"D'you think we've got time to stop?" Lowerson wondered, as they wandered past a stall advertising pulled pork sandwiches.

"Maybe on the way back," Yates said. "We need to try to get through this list, and there's no time to waste."

He knew she was right. They'd spent more than an hour after the briefing earlier that morning ringing around the people on their list but, when it came to contractors who might have helped with the scaffolding, plasterwork, display casing or any other element of the renovation works at Durham Cathedral, it seemed the numbers just grew and grew. Partly, because some of those workers were transient, part-timers or sub-contractors, and, partly, because the company hiring them hadn't kept adequate records about their staff—presumably, because they didn't imagine they'd ever be called upon to provide information pertaining to the theft of a priceless national treasure.

Following Ryan's instructions, they'd been able to eliminate a good portion of the list over the telephone, merely by making enquiries about their whereabouts on Sunday evening, and the previous day. Taking that into account, the list became much more manageable, and they decided to begin speaking to the most 'high-profile' people who could not account for their movements, or provide a sufficient alibi.

"Cathedral or university?" Yates asked.

"Ladies' choice," Lowerson said.

"In that case, let's go for the cathedral first," she replied. "I might not like organised religion, but I can appreciate a solid bit of architecture, when I see it."

"Amen to that," he said, and followed her towards the north door of the cathedral.

Inside, they saw that very little had changed since the last time they had stepped inside the cathedral's hallowed walls.

The atmosphere inside was reverent, evoking an instant feeling of peace and serenity, for even the most disordered of minds. Its high columns and arches were a triumph of stonemasonry, the likes of which was unlikely to be replicated in any modern building in their lifetime.

"I heard a story about there being a deliberate mistake on one of these columns," Lowerson whispered. "Apparently, an apprentice was let loose with a chisel, one day, and chiselled the wrong design."

"Maybe it was their equivalent of graffiti," Yates said. "They wanted to leave their personal mark and be remembered."

"People get funny ideas about legacy, don't they?" Jack mused. "Personally, I'm not bothered about making a mark on the world; I'll be happy if my friends and family remember me as being a decent person."

She curved an arm around his waist.

"I promise, if you ever get rid of that Playstation, I'll remember you that way," she said, with a wicked laugh.

"Can I help you, detectives?"

They were interrupted by the stealthy arrival of the cathedral's chief operating officer, a man by the name of

Derek Pettigrew, who was tasked with the day-to-day running of the site. He was somewhere in his mid-forties, with a well-tended beard and a rapidly receding hairline he was evidently trying to disguise. They had met him during their investigation of the robbery, back in March, and he remembered them on sight.

"Mr Pettigrew," Lowerson said, slipping his professional mask back into place. "Thank you for the call, earlier today, and for agreeing to meet us."

"I hardly have a choice, in the circumstances," he said, without any social niceties. "As you may imagine, all of us here at the cathedral, including the Dean, were shocked and disappointed to learn from your Chief Constable this morning that the cross recovered last March is not, in fact, the original. What I don't understand is how such an oversight could have occurred."

"Is there somewhere we could discuss this in private?"

The cathedral was thronged with people, some who were there to worship, others who were there to admire the architecture, and none of whom needed to overhear their conversation.

"Of course," Pettigrew said, and lowered his voice instantly. "Let's use my office."

He led them to a panelled side door marked, 'PRIVATE', and, beyond it, through another panelled corridor to a door at the very end. Inside, the room itself was unremarkable, with its whitewashed walls and bog-standard desk furniture, but the view was something else.

"I don't know how you manage to work in here," Yates said, and walked over to the window to look out at a panoramic view to the west, with the river running far below.

"I am very fortunate," he agreed, coolly. "Please, do sit down."

They fell into two under-stuffed chairs that dipped at the base, which meant that their knees were slightly higher than their waists.

"We understand the cathedral undertook some renovation works to the exhibition space, roughly three years ago," Yates said, edging forward a bit to try to get comfortable. "Is that correct?"

"Yes, indeed," Pettigrew replied. "Our Monk's Dormitory and Great Kitchen were renovated to create exhibition space for the treasures of St. Cuthbert, amongst other things. It was a large project, spread over a number of years. May I ask why that's relevant?"

"We have reason to believe the original cross might have been substituted for a replica during the renovation period," Yates replied.

"Impossible," Pettigrew snapped, slicing his hand through the air like a knife. "We had a full security team on site at all times, and the artefacts remained in sealed display cases, under lock and key, before they were transferred to their new display area. I don't see how it would have been possible."

"Did you have the pieces authenticated, before the project was signed off?" Lowerson asked.

Pettigrew looked uncomfortable.

"There was no need," he said. "The pieces had already been authenticated and, to the best of our knowledge, nothing had changed. Besides, we had restoration and conservation experts on site. There's very little chance that so many people could have made such a drastic oversight."

He included himself in that number, but wasn't about to say as much.

"Can we have the names of those individuals, please?" Yates asked, flipping open her notebook to compare them with those already listed.

"I—I'd have to check to be certain, but the restoration firm was called Finest Restorations and the gentleman leading the team was a chap called William Chatterley, I seem to recall. He's local to the area, because I see him in here from time to time. There was a postdoctoral student cataloguing the project as part of some research he was doing, a young man by the name of Andrew Duggan-West. He still volunteers with us, at weekends, when he isn't doing a show."

"A show?"

"He enjoys amateur theatre, I understand."

"I see," Yates said, and prepared to bite the bullet. "My next question is a delicate one, Mr Pettigrew, but I'd like to reassure you that it's an entirely normal part of our investigation."

He nodded, warily.

"The question I'd like to ask is: could you please tell us your whereabouts on the evening of Sunday 6th December, and again yesterday daytime?"

He didn't blink.

"I have no secrets," he said, folding his arms. "On Sunday evening, I was at home, like any other sane person in this country. Yesterday, I was unwell, and had the day off sick."

Lowerson and Yates displayed twin expressions of sympathy.

"I'm sorry to hear that," Lowerson said. "Nothing serious, I hope?"

"Not any more, I'm very pleased to say. I'm in remission after undergoing a round of chemotherapy," he said. "Unfortunately, I still suffer from topical sickness and tiredness, from time to time, which I'm told will improve."

"We're very glad to hear it," Lowerson said. "Are you with the cancer centre at the University Hospital?"

"Yes, that's right."

That was easy enough to check, they thought, and the man had been forthcoming with his explanation, so far, which went in his favour.

Set against that, the upshot was that, for the significant time periods, Derek Pettigrew claimed to be at home.

"Do you live alone, Mr Pettigrew?"

His face became shuttered.

"Why is this relevant to the theft of the cross?" he asked. "What does my whereabouts this past week have to do with the cross having gone missing three years ago, if you're right on that score?"

"We're not in a position to discuss active lines of enquiry," Lowerson replied. "We would, however, be extremely grateful for your cooperation."

Pettigrew lifted his chin.

"Much as I am happy to assist in your investigation, there are elements of my private life that are..." He cast around for the right word. "Ah...*private.*"

He looked between the pair of them, seeking reassurance.

"The thing is, my partner—Michael—lives separately... ah—"

They thought they understood the problem.

"Michael is married?" Yates asked, keeping her voice carefully neutral.

Pettigrew nodded.

"I would much rather keep his name out of this. He hasn't told his family..."

"Nonetheless, I'm afraid we will need to verify your whereabouts as part of our wider investigation," Lowerson said, firmly. "We will not share the information unless it has to become a matter of public record at a later stage."

It was the best reassurance he could give.

Pettigrew nodded miserably, and reeled off a name.

CHAPTER 27

There were countless support groups, cancer centres, private counselling offices and other services that worked alongside the hospitals and GP surgeries in the North East which, even when narrowing the geographic area to Durham and its surrounds, presented a logistical challenge to Ryan and his team. The objective was to try to uncover the means by which Justine Winter first came into contact with a person or group who managed to convince her that the only way to help her ailing brother was to seek a miracle. An extensive dive into Winter's personal history elucidated a sad, lonely sort of life; not at all what one might have expected of a woman her age. However, Justine had acted as both mother and father to her younger brother, responsibility having been thrust upon her at an early age following the death of her mother from breast cancer. Her father had, by all accounts, not been much to speak of. Her brother, Danny suffered from early-onset motor neurone disease, extremely rare in children, as well as severe learning difficulties, and

Justine had been his carer—as well as working a stressful, part-time in Durham CID. Outside of work, Danny was her only focus in life, and their regular hospital appointments one of the few social engagements she attended.

Having built up a picture of Justine's life, they were able to narrow the list of support groups she attended and other potential meeting points to three possibilities: an MND support group which met on Tuesday evenings; a general support group which met on Wednesdays; and, anyone she might have happened to come across on a Monday, when she accompanied her brother to his weekly appointments with a neurologist and a neurophysiologist. It had been a difficult task to elicit the names of attendees for each group, but armed now with a warrant to compel disclosure, MacKenzie had come to speak with the hospital staff directly. In her long experience, it was often the case that you learned interesting little titbits in conversation that could otherwise be missed.

"I know the circumstances aren't exactly romantic, but it's a rare treat being out and about with you, my love."

Since Ryan was tied up with other tasks back at Police Headquarters, Phillips had decided to accompany his wife for the afternoon, and the two of them pulled into the car park of the University Hospital in Durham like a pair of teenagers on their first date.

"I could say the same," she said, leaning across to bestow a kiss on his upturned face. "It isn't Florence, that's for sure, but I'll still take a wintry day in Durham, so long as it's with you."

Phillips puckered up for another kiss, but she held him off.

"Since you're in such a good mood, there's something I need to tell you."

His heart skipped a beat, as all manner of worst-case scenarios flooded his mind.

Denise was ill.

Samantha was ill.

She'd heard he ate that leftover ham-and-cheese toastie, the day before...

"Samantha told me she has a boyfriend."

Much worse than he could ever have imagined, Phillips thought, dumbstruck.

"Frank? Now, don't overreact—"

"D—don't overreact?" he burst out. "The lass is barely ten years old, and she's courtin' already? What year are we livin' in—1500? She needs to be at least...twenty-one before there's any talk of boyfriends!"

MacKenzie sighed, and let him rant.

"In my day, the kids were still climbin' trees at that age! What's his name?" he suddenly demanded.

"Now, Frank, don't go thinking you can check up on the poor boy. He's only ten, you know."

"I only want to ask him about his intentions," Phillips muttered, and folded his arms across his chest.

"Frank, I don't think you really understand what ten-year-olds mean when they say 'boyfriend'," MacKenzie said gently. "All it means is that she's picked her current favourite—probably the one who wears the coolest trainers—and they're walking around the playground holding hands for a while, while the others giggle about it. At worst, there's probably a peck on the lips, quickly wiped clean, to everyone's disgust."

"Aye, that's how it starts," Phillips grumbled.

"Yes," she said. "It *is* how it starts, Frank, for all normal kids. Years of innocent handholding, of crushes on pop stars and, when she gets older, there'll be a perfectly ridiculous pre-teen obsession with some TV character who's a vampire at a high school in America. She'll do her hair in all kinds of ways and, because she's a redhead—and I speak from experience—she'll go through the inevitable phase of wanting to chop it all off or dye it brown, after some muppet calls her a 'ginger'."

"Only a ginger can call another ginger, 'ginger'," Phillips acknowledged. "I hope she doesn't change, Denise. I don't think I could stand it."

"Of course you could—and you will," she said. "We signed up to be parents, Frank, and, for the most part, Sam makes a hard job seem easy. She can do many things, but she can't promise not to grow up."

Phillips looked out across the car park, remembering the first time he and Samantha had met.

"She'll always be my little girl," he said. "No matter how big she gets, I'll love every hair on her head—even if she changes the colour of it."

MacKenzie took his face in her hands and gave him a long, lingering kiss.

"I'll remind you of what you've just said, in a couple of years," she said. "Come on, let's go and see what we can find out from the General Support Group."

"Aye, we can ask them if they accept fathers tryin' to cope with their daughters growin' up too fast," he mumbled, as they headed across the car park towards the main entrance.

"If they don't, you can always start up a special support group. Ryan can be your second member."

"I think we have one of those, already," he said. "Lifetime membership."

MacKenzie smiled, and wondered what on earth one would do without the other.

Hopefully, they'd never have to find out.

Following their discussion with Derek Pettigrew, Yates and Lowerson made their way back through the nave of the Cathedral and along towards the exhibition galleries, stopping beside an unmarked door, this time with a coded entry box.

"This is the security office," Lowerson said, and rapped his knuckles on the outside.

They remembered the Head of Security, Mike Nevis, as a skinny, balding man, whose face bore a hollow look, giving the overall impression of one who spent far too much time indoors reading the latest news on how to combat cybercrime. He'd been in his post throughout the renovations to the exhibition galleries and would undoubtedly have been able to gain access to the displays, particularly since he knew how to manipulate a system he was in charge of running.

However, the man who opened the door to the security office was at least ten years younger than Nevis, and easily fifty pounds heavier. He had been seated on a plush-looking ergonomic wing-backed chair at the head of an enormous desk arranged in a zigzag formation, allowing him to view several screens at once.

Judging by the way his mobile phone had been propped upright and its screen paused halfway through an episode of *Keeping up with the Kardashians,* he'd been otherwise engaged.

"This area's private," he said. "If you're lookin' for the loos, they're further along—"

"DC Yates and DC Lowerson, Northumbria Police," Melanie said. "We were looking for Mike Nevis."

The man—who turned out to be David "Call me Davey" Huxley—looked between them and then back at his phone.

"Never mind about that," Lowerson said. "Where's Mike?"

"He's on annual leave, this week," he replied. "Not due back on shift until Monday."

"Did he say what he'd be doing?" Yates asked.

Huxley just stared, and she tried a different question.

"Was he planning to go abroad, or visit family, perhaps?"

He was sweating profusely, rivulets running down the sides of his temples.

"I don't know—probably. He didn't say."

Lowerson and Yates exchanged a glance.

"How long have you worked here, Davey?"

"About six weeks," he said. "I'm still in my probation period."

"I see. Look, we're not bothered if you're using the cathedral's internet connection to watch Kim and Khloe on your phone," Lowerson said. "What we really want to know is Mike's home address. Do you have it?"

The man brightened, visibly.

"I know he's over somewhere in Dalton-le-Dale, but I can't remember the street. Derek will know."

"All right, Davey. Thanks for your help," Yates said, and then pointed towards one of the screens at his back. "You might want to look at Screen 4; somebody just swiped a box of biscuits from the gift shop."

They left Huxley scrambling about for his radio and made their way back through the cloisters towards the exit.

"What did we find out about Mike Nevis, in terms of personal history?" Lowerson asked, once they stepped back outside.

Yates consulted her notebook.

"Divorced, one kid, aged nineteen; no previous record. Tried to enlist in the army, then the police academy, but rejected both times," she said. "That's pretty much all we know."

"Wonder why he was rejected," Lowerson said.

"Let's ask him, later, but first, on to our next stop on the Magical Mystery Tour of Durham."

"The university?"

"Via the pulled pork stand," she said.

"Did I ever tell you, you're a *wonderful* woman?"

"Actions speak louder than words," she said, with a glint in her eye. "Why don't you show me later?"

CHAPTER 28

The University Hospital of North Durham looked much the same as any other modern building of its era; made of concrete and brick, it was blocky, uniform and was intended to serve, rather than inspire.

"Justine came here with Danny every Monday morning," MacKenzie said. "He had a couple of regular appointments to see his neurologist and neurophysiologist."

"Poor kid." Phillips tutted. "And, now, after what's happened to his sister...how old is he?"

"Eighteen," MacKenzie replied. "At least Justine had the foresight to make sure he would be looked after. If you remember, she had a comprehensive life insurance policy that wasn't rendered void by suicide, and he's the sole beneficiary. I think they managed to find a place for him at a specialist care facility, though I can't imagine that was an easy task; Danny has MND, and all that goes with that, but he has learning difficulties on top."

"Makes you feel grateful, doesn't it?" Phillips said. "We're so lucky not to have those worries. I s'pose I'm guilty of forgettin' how hard it must be for other folk, at times."

"You're always a thoughtful person," his wife assured him. "It's impossible to be perfect."

"You make it look easy."

MacKenzie stopped dead and turned to him, reaching out a hand to straighten his preposterous tie—which consisted of a pattern of tiny reindeer faces, each with a red, sequinned nose.

"That was very smooth," she said. "You can be a charming devil, when you want to be."

"It's often been said."

She curved a hand around the tie and tugged him a bit closer, right there in the car park.

"I won't tolerate flirting in the office place," she said, with mock severity. "Luckily, we're not in the office, right now."

She yanked him forward to administer a thorough kiss.

"That's for being wonderful," she said. "Come on, sergeant. We haven't got all day."

"Yes, ma'am."

There was a certain smell associated with hospitals.

A combination of bleach-based cleaning products, canteen food and something more subtle, like meat gone bad. Both MacKenzie and Phillips had spent some considerable time in and out of hospitals, and the smell never improved.

They made their way to the reception desk, where they were directed towards the Neurology department.

"I thought we could have a word with Danny's specialist, on the off-chance he heard or saw anything unusual during his meetings with Danny and Justine," MacKenzie said, as they made their way through the hospital corridors.

Phillips nodded, and deliberately slowed the pace so that MacKenzie's leg would not be put under too much pressure. Three years earlier, she'd suffered terrible injuries, leaving her with deep scar tissue that could often be painful, especially if she over-exerted the muscles in her leg, as she often did. Incapacity did not come naturally to a woman like Denise, who could do almost anything she put her mind to.

There had been times when he'd seen her cry tears of pure frustration, and times during the first few months after the attack when she'd been so depressed, he'd worried she'd never come back to him—and, he supposed, she hadn't. It was not the same Denise he awakened to each morning; just as he was not the same Frank as the one he'd been aged twenty, before he'd known anything about love and loss. Life changed you, for better or for worse, and it was a question of rolling with the punches, where you could. He'd fallen in love with a strong, independent woman, and he still loved that woman, for she was even stronger than before.

She was a survivor.

Then, there had been his first wife, Laura, who'd succumbed to cancer back in 2010. She'd been his first love and, God's truth, he'd never looked at anyone else while she'd been alive. He was a loyal man, not driven by the kind of ego that led some to seek their thrills where they could. No, he'd been happy and satisfied with what he had at home, and it had come as a terrible shock when they'd learned the news of her illness. He'd tried to help her fight the disease and, for two years, they'd held off the inevitable, fighting the insidious illness eating away at her from the inside. He'd taken time off work to nurse her; bathing Laura's poor, wasted body, wiping her clean, making sure she had her pain medication, drying her tears and listening to her occasional anger about the futility of it all. He'd wheeled her along corridors much like the one he was walking now, smelling the same *bloody* smell, until all he'd been able to do was hold her, rocking her against his chest until she slept and never woke up again.

"—Frank?"

He shook himself and reached across to take MacKenzie's hand.

"I was just rememberin'," he said quietly. "All this talk of miracles has got me thinkin', I s'pose. Maybe Ryan was right—who's to say what any of us would any of us do, if we were desperate enough? If someone had come along during those final few months when Laura was dyin', and they'd told me there was any chance of a miracle...I'd like to think I'd have seen through them and that I'd have told them to bugger off and darken somebody else's door, but who's to say? Plenty of people turn to religion in their darkest moments, and believin' in miracles isn't far off."

MacKenzie nodded. "I can only imagine what you went through," she said, softly. "I saw pieces of it, when you'd come into the office looking so sad. I didn't know it at the time, but I think I started falling for you all the way back then, when I had no business to. I couldn't help admiring the way you looked after Laura, right to the very end. I thought to myself, to be loved like that would be a grand thing."

Phillips brought her hand to his lips.

"I'd do the same again, in a heartbeat," he said, deeply. "No matter what the future holds for either of us, I'll be here beside you for as long as I can, my love."

MacKenzie felt the warmth of his words seep through her body, and felt as rich as a queen.

"I can't agree with what Justine Winter did," she said, keeping her voice low. "There's no justification for killing Tebbutt, or being a party to what was done to Edward Faber; it was inhuman. But, when I consider the demands on her mind, the stress of her situation and all the emotions that must have been swirling, I can find a bit of pity in my heart. Perhaps it's pity for the life she might have had, if she'd had a bit more support at home, or for the little girl who lost her mother, her father and couldn't save her brother. She must have been so lonely that she lost sight of herself."

Phillips nodded.

"If I've said it once, I've said it a thousand times. Life isn't all black and white. We can hate what she did, and still feel sorry about the fact she went off her chump."

MacKenzie felt laughter bubble up in her throat. "Frank?"

"What's that, love?"

"Never change."

CHAPTER 29

After an abortive attempt to locate Andrew Duggan-West in his college rooms, they finally caught up with him at the university's Student Theatre, which was based from the Assembly Rooms on North Bailey, a street running directly parallel to Palace Green and within spitting distance of the cathedral. The theatre itself was over one hundred and fifty years old, but it had been modernised during the intervening years to create a performing arts space for the bright young things who came through its doors and was now a trendy arts venue boasting comedy, drama, dance and more.

Lowerson and Yates made their way inside and, finding the foyer empty, carried on through to the auditorium, following the sound of crashing seas and wailing voices through a door marked, 'STALLS'.

"Now, would I give a thousand furlongs of sea for an acre of barren ground, long heath, brown furze, anything. The wills above be done! But I would fain die a dry death..."

They listened to a young man who had been dressed to look older, complete with false beard and sixteenth-century seafarer's costume, prance about the stage, gesticulating wildly.

"Wonder what he's tryin' to do," Lowerson whispered.

"I think he must be Gonzalo, from Shakespeare's *The Tempest*," Yates whispered back.

"I know that—I was wondering whether he was trying to murder it…"

She gave him a sharp jab in the ribs.

"I haven't seen you treading any boards, lately," she said.

Shh!

A young man in his mid or late twenties shushed them, and then, with an irritable clap of his hands, called the rehearsal to a halt.

"*Stop*! Everybody stop!" he called out, and the actors came to an abrupt halt, peering through the glare of the stage lights to see what had caused the disruption.

"Uh-oh," Lowerson said, and wondered if they could make a speedy getaway.

The young man moved swiftly along the row of red velvet seats and the two detectives braced themselves to receive the brunt of an artistic temperament.

"It's the height of rudeness to interrupt a dress rehearsal," he raged. "Even worse to talk through it. Who the hell do you think you are?"

They might have felt suitably chastised, were it not for the distracting nature of his apparel—dressed in tight black jeans, a billowing white shirt and leather blazer, complete with a silk headscarf and black fedora hat, they might have been talking to a Cap'n Jack Sparrow lookalike.

Lowerson was tempted to ask him where all the rum had gone.

"We're very sorry to have disturbed your rehearsal," Yates said, reaching for her warrant card. "Unfortunately, it can't be helped. DC Yates and DC Lowerson, Northumbria CID. We're here to speak to Andrew Duggan-West. Can you tell us if he's here, please?"

The young man went very pale.

"I—I'm he. Him. I mean, that's me."

Yates smiled, indulgently.

"Do you have five or ten minutes to spare us, please?"

"Ah—can't it wait? No, no, I suppose not," he muttered. "Just a sec, let me wrap this up and I'll be with you."

Lowerson and Yates made themselves comfortable on a couple of theatre seats, and watched him hurry off down the aisle to disband the company, at least for the present.

A moment later, he returned, and the sound effects reel was turned off.

"What did you think of it?" he asked, unwisely.

Lowerson scrambled about for something to say that wasn't scathing but, thankfully, Yates came to his rescue.

"The Bard is always great material to work with, isn't it?"

This non-answer seemed to appease him, for Andrew broke into a wide smile and nodded vigorously.

"I always say, 'less is more' when interpreting Shakespeare," he said, without any irony whatsoever. "In fact—"

They judged it a wise moment to forestall a lengthy discussion on the topic of Shakespearean interpretation.

"Thank you again for making time for us, Mr Duggan-West," Lowerson interjected. "We appreciate your time is precious, so we'll come straight to the point. We're investigating a number of serious crimes pertaining to the relics of St. Cuthbert and, in the course of our investigations, your name has come up in relation to the renovation works that were undertaken at the Cathedral three years ago. Do you know why that might be?"

Andrew raised his eyebrows—or would have done if he'd had any, for they had been shaved off and all that remained was the vague shadow of where they might once have been.

"Well, I suppose it's to do with my research about the Deanery," he said, settling down to an in-depth chat. "I read History of Art at undergraduate level, and I went on to write my postgraduate thesis about the twelfth century frescoes of St. Cuthbert and King Oswald in the cathedral. My postdoctoral research was an extension of that, really; exploring the pomp and pageantry of the Dean's residence from around the twelfth century, which was much more impressive than was traditionally the case. Originally, the prior would have had a bed in the communal monks' dormitory, you see. No more and no less than the rest of his brothers, in accordance with the Rule of St. Benedict. But, after the mid-1200s, the Dean must have decided that he preferred his own residence and, judging from some of the fifteenth century frescoes we uncovered beneath years of ordinary emulsion, successive deans had even more lavish notions."

"So, how long did you spend on site, during the renovation period?" Yates asked him.

"Ooh, must've been around two months—but not every day, of course. I had written permission from the Dean to access the site with some notice to the contractors and conservationists, so I could observe their work uncovering the frescoes and see what they unearthed. My subject is all about interpreting the meaning behind works of art, and the use of frescoes at the cathedral is so interesting."

Despite himself, Lowerson was interested.

"What were your conclusions?" he wondered.

"Oh, mostly what you'd expect," he said, with an artistic wave of his wrist. "Art representing life, and as a visual reminder to visitors of the power of the Prince Bishops in Durham…"

He seemed to come out of himself, remembering his audience.

"I'm sorry, it's easy to fall down a rabbit hole when you get onto your favourite subject," he said. "Was there anything else you needed to know?"

"Do you happen to remember anything unusual, during your time on site? Anyone who showed an unusual interest in St. Cuthbert, or his cross, for example?"

Andrew's eyes shone, and he leaned forward.

"Is this to do with the theft of the cross, earlier this year? It was all so…*dramatic*."

"I'm afraid we can't discuss active lines of enquiry, at the moment," Lowerson said.

"Of course, of course…well, I'm sorry to say, I didn't notice anything unusual…nobody trying to break into the display cases with a swag bag, or anything like that!"

He paused for a laugh and, when none was forthcoming, carried on.

"Almost all the people working on the project were already big fans of Cuthbert, and considered it an honour to be working on restoring the cathedral to its best—I was just happy to be a visitor during the process, and to have seen how some of the work is done. The restoration of those wall frescoes was meticulous."

"Yes, we heard some of the conservation work was undertaken by a company called Finest Restorations. Is that correct?"

"That's right." He nodded. "It's run by a chap called Will Chatterley, but he's really a one-man band. He's an absolute master when it comes to restoring fine art; really, he could have been an artist, himself."

"Do you know him well?"

"No, but he let me shadow him for a few days while he was working on the frescoes, which was very decent of him."

"Just a couple more questions, if I may," Yates said, with a smile. "Have you been rehearsing all week?"

He let out a gusty sigh.

"Yes, the play opens on Friday, so we've been refining things little by little."

"Well, thank you very much for your time." She passed him a card with the incident room details listed on the reverse. "If you think of anything else—here's the number to call."

Andrew bade them a cheery farewell and, as he sauntered off, Lowerson passed one final critic's comment for the day.

"Now, *that* was a performance."

CHAPTER 30

After a friendly but, ultimately, unfruitful discussion with Danny Winter's neurologist at University Hospital, MacKenzie and Phillips decided to make one last stop on their way back to Newcastle, where they were due to collect Samantha from an after-school club at five o'clock.

Vennel's Café was a hidden gem of a place, tucked in beside other shops in the centre of the city—its historic walls spread over three floors packed with fireplaces draped in garlands and old sewing tables decked out in festive tablecloths, which gave an overall impression of stepping back in time when you crossed the threshold.

It was a test of willpower for Phillips, whose eyes slid towards the displays of scones and cakes with helpless longing.

"Stay strong," MacKenzie said, patting his arm. "You can do it."

He might have made a small whimpering sound—he couldn't be sure—but before he could embarrass himself by leaping across the counter to attack a tray of freshly baked rolls, they hurried upstairs to the first floor where, they were told, the general carer's support group was now being run by volunteers on a Wednesday afternoon.

They spotted a group of around eight or nine people seated on the far side of the room beside a small Christmas tree, sipping mugs of coffee and hot chocolate. Tables had been pushed together to form one large one, and men and women of differing ages were gathered around it, nodding and sometimes laughing at something another person had said.

They felt bad interrupting their meeting, especially as it was a vital lifeline to those carers who might otherwise feel isolated during the rest of the week, but it was imperative that they tried to learn who had managed to compromise Justine Winter.

"I'm sorry to interrupt you," MacKenzie said, and the conversation stopped immediately. "I'm DI MacKenzie, and this is DS Phillips. We're from Northumbria CID."

"Oh, my God, it must be about Robbie!" one woman cried, leaping up from her chair as if to run from the room. "What's happened to him?"

MacKenzie held up both of her hands.

"We're not here regarding any of your loved ones," she said quietly. "We're here because we were hoping you might be able to help us get to the bottom of an investigation we're running into the death of Justine Winter who, we understand, was a former member of your support group."

The woman sat down again, obviously relieved.

"Poor, poor Justine," she said. "We were all so shocked, when we heard the news that she'd taken her own life…and about…well, what she'd done to that police officer. We could hardly believe it, could we?"

There were murmured negatives, right on cue.

"Do you mind if we join you, for a few minutes?" Phillips asked.

"Please do," another woman replied, whose name turned out to be Kim. "How can we help you?"

Phillips pulled up two more chairs for himself and MacKenzie, and they joined them around the table. There seemed to be a mix of carers and their loved ones who were unwell, as well as survivors. The group was run by a man called Fred who volunteered his time on a weekly basis to organise and facilitate the sessions. He was, himself, a cancer survivor and knew what it was to live with that fear hanging over his head.

"Just clouds every moment of your day," he said, to nods of agreement around the table. "Hard to think of anything else, but the world keeps turning."

"How did Justine find caring for her brother?" MacKenzie asked.

"I think, mostly, she felt guilty," Kim remarked. "As most carers do, at some stage or another. It's hard to be fit and healthy, while you're caring for someone in the opposite situation. You feel guilty for being in good health, and often wish you could turn the tables."

"I wouldn't want that," her husband said clearly, although his voice shook with the effort of enunciating his words. "I want you to go on living."

"Oh, Mark…"

She pressed her lips to his temple, and reached over to hold his hand.

"I think she'd found God, or something of that kind," the first woman said, and introduced herself as Martha. "She was talking a lot about it, those last few times she came along."

"Justine stopped coming around February time," Fred explained.

"Was that unusual?" Phillips asked.

"Not in general," Fred said. "People do come and go; sometimes, they've taken what they need from the group and go away feeling stronger, which is exactly what we'd want for our friends."

"In Justine's case, I wonder whether she dropped out because she was spiralling a bit," Martha said, and Kim nodded her agreement. "She'd had some bad news about Danny, if I remember correctly."

"Oh? Do you remember what it was?" MacKenzie asked.

"I think he'd been trialling a new drug that was supposed to make a big difference but, as with all these things, so much comes down to chance and, unfortunately, it just didn't work for Danny," Martha said, and reached across to wipe her son's chin with a gentle hand. "I think Justine had placed all her hopes on that drug working and, when it didn't…"

MacKenzie knew the rest.

"I understand," she said, softly. "Let me ask you another question. Did Justine ever talk about St. Cuthbert, or the idea of miracles?"

They looked amongst themselves.

"I'm sure, at some stage or another, all of us have wished for a miracle," Fred said, with a smile. "Justine was no different, but I can't say I recall her talking about miracles in any *meaningful* way."

"Actually," Martha said, and frowned, as if trying to remember. "I seem to remember her asking me whether I believed in miracles."

"When was this?" Phillips asked, while he held the hand of the elderly man beside him, who smiled as he rubbed the papery skin gently between his calloused hands, warming the joints to ease the old man's pain.

"Must've been around the time the drugs failed, this time last year."

"Quite a long time ago," Phillips said, and thought that made sense. If somebody had a mind to indoctrinate a vulnerable young woman, they'd have to lay the groundwork slowly and carefully, especially if she happened to be a police officer.

"Justine had been to see faith healers, clairvoyants…the lot," Martha continued. "I think she'd have tried anything, if it might have helped."

"I just can't understand why she killed that poor woman," Kim said, and her eyes welled up with tears. "I'm sorry if the woman was your friend but, well, for a while, Justine was ours. All I remember about her was a sweet, kind girl who always tried her best. I can't understand it at all."

"We're tryin' to get to the bottom of it," Phillips said, passing her a paper napkin so she could dab at her eyes. "We want to make sure this sort of thing doesn't happen again."

"Maybe we could have done more," Martha said, half to herself. "She must have been struggling, so badly."

"You did all you could," MacKenzie said. "We are each responsible for the actions we take, although, in this case, we happen to think Justine had a little help along the way."

"You mean, somebody might have encouraged her to… to do that?"

MacKenzie nodded. "Have any of you been approached by anybody who tried to convince you to start praying at St. Cuthbert's Shrine, or who claimed to have performed miracles?"

They looked amongst themselves, and shook their heads, but then Kim's husband, Mark, uttered a single, painful word.

"Phil."

"What's that, love?"

"Phil. Bill."

Kim looked blank, and then the memory came back to her.

"Oh, my goodness, yes!" she cried, giving her husband a kiss on the cheek. "Well remembered."

She turned to MacKenzie and Phillips, eager to share the information, if it could be helpful.

"About two years ago, when Mark was first diagnosed, I used to head down to the hospital canteen for half an hour while he was having his physio," she said. "Now, the physio comes to us but, back then, we drove in, didn't we?"

Mark bobbed his head.

"Anyway, I'd seen this chap a couple of times in the canteen and, this one time, he came over and sat beside me—completely uninvited, I might add," she said, with a squeeze of her husband's hand. "He started chatting and, to be honest, he seemed harmless enough, so I didn't mind humouring him. But then, he said he'd seen me a couple of times with my husband, who looked to have had some bad news. Now, back then, you have to understand, it was all very new, and I was feeling quite raw about everything."

"Of course," MacKenzie said. "Who could blame you?"

"Well, I think he must have spotted me and thought that I looked like an easy target, because he started on about whether I believed in miracles and, if I didn't, then I would by the time I'd heard his story."

"What was his story?" Phillips asked, very casually. If you showed too much interest, a witness could clam up and forget the juicy bits, he'd often found.

"Now, let me think," Kim said, raising a hand to her forehead. "I think he said he'd been diagnosed with terminal cancer sometime before that, and the doctors had no hope for him. He'd turned to God and had got in the habit of praying at Cuthbert's Shrine over at the Cathedral, because it was a peaceful place to be while he prepared himself for the end. Well, at this point, I felt sorry for him, I really did, especially as he was still wearing a toupee and it was slippin' right off his head..."

There was a slight detour in conversation while several other members of the group exchanged their opinions about where to get a good quality wig, if you needed one, and how much better they were than in days gone by.

"Anyway," Kim said, returning to her story. "After he'd been prayin' for a couple of weeks, he went back to his oncologist and they said the tumour had stopped growing. Just like that! Well, I felt pleased for him, but I had my eye on the time and he was goin' on a bit, so I was only half-listenin' to the rest of his story, but he might have said something about it lightnin' having struck twice, and that he knew how to summon a miracle, if I needed one."

"What did you make of that?" Phillips asked.

"Whey, I thought the poor sod had gone barmy," she said, and the whole table laughed. "I mean, I was happy that his tumour had stopped growing, if it had, and I told him so. But I worked for twenty years as a nurse, and I know there are all kinds of reasons why a tumour might suddenly stop growin' and we don't know the half of them. Still, I thought, if he wants to believe it was a miracle, where's the harm? Then he started talking about secret codes, runes—all sorts! I drew the line when he started trying to convert me, and I said I had to get going."

A lucky escape, MacKenzie thought.

"Do you remember his name? How he looked?"

"He was definitely over thirty," she said, but didn't sound so sure. "Mark thinks he was called Bill or Phil—but it might have been something really ordinary, like Mike, or Kevin, you know? I'm sorry, I just can't remember, and I'd be pretending, if I did."

"It's all right, you've been wonderful, remembering as much as you have."

"Here, listen, you don't think this feller got to Justine, maybe?" Kim asked, having suddenly realised what could— and probably *had*—happened. "If he was hangin' round the canteen, she could have seen him when she was in there visitin' with Danny."

MacKenzie took down as many details as she could extract, and Phillips tried a few tactics of his own to try to help the woman remember what the mystery man looked like, but it had been more than two years since she'd seen him.

They stayed a bit longer for a cup of tea, enjoying the company, and then left the group to their cake and scones.

Outside, the sun was heading rapidly towards the horizon, and it was time for them to collect their little girl.

"At least we know where he likes to hunt," MacKenzie said. "He chooses vulnerable people, especially those who could be useful to him, and tries to convert them."

"How was Kim useful to him?"

MacKenzie turned her phone to face him, and he saw a professional profile of Kim's husband, Mark, who was evidently a very wealthy man.

"It might not always be a question of money, but he's not ignorant to its uses," MacKenzie surmised. "That's an interesting insight."

"I'll get in touch with the hospital and see if they have any CCTV coverage down in the canteen, or in the main areas. It'll be a job for the analysts, but we might hit lucky."

"There's all kinds of power, isn't there, Frank? There I was, thinking gangs were the problem, but you've got people out there suggesting suicide pacts, preying on people's weaknesses, exploiting them for their own gain... and then, there's the fanatics."

"I ask myself, why can't people just kill their spouses and bury them in the back garden, like the good old days?"

"I'm so glad you didn't say that when the Adoption Panel interviewed us."

"So am I, love. I think the humour might have been lost on them."

CHAPTER 31

After two late nights in a row, Ryan was determined to make it home in time for his baby girl's bath time at six-thirty. Despite there being a hundred more calls to make, reports to write and staff to manage as Operation Bertie restarted, he left the office on the dot of five and stepped through his front door as the clock chimed six.

"Hi there!"

Anna's face lit up as she came down the hall, baby in arms.

"I thought I heard your car," she said, and tipped her face up for a kiss before turning the baby towards him, so he could lift Emma high above his head and make her giggle.

Watching them together, Anna experienced a strange emotion, deep in her belly. It felt peaceful to know that, should anything ever happen to her, Emma would be safe with this lovely man.

Nothing was going to happen to her, Anna thought. *Why think like that?*

"Are you hungry?" she asked him, brightly.

"I can make something," he said, and nuzzled Emma's tummy to make her laugh again.

Ryan had always been one of those rare creatures who didn't expect others to do things for him, especially not things he could do perfectly well himself—unless, of course, they really wanted to.

"I think your dad is planning to grill some steaks," she said. "Your mum thinks I'm getting too thin, so she's been trying to feed me up."

Ryan tucked Emma against his chest and looked at his wife—properly looked, removing the 'love goggles' he wore every day.

"Perhaps you've lost a bit of weight, but that's bound to happen when you're running around after this little one and probably forgetting to eat."

Anna nodded. "I'm sure that's it," she agreed. "But, as I told your mum, if I have to stuff my face with steak and chips, followed by a slab of coffee cake, then I guess I'll have to force myself—for the good of my health."

"That's the spirit," Ryan agreed, and flashed a devastating smile that, even after all these years, could still make her stomach flip over.

Then, she caught an odd look in his eye, and knew there was something he needed to tell her. But, not now.

If they needed to speak of dark things, they would do it far away from their daughter's ears.

"Let's give her a bath," she said, huskily. "Then, we'll have some dinner. There'll be time to talk, once Emma's asleep."

"All right," he said, and leaned across to press a kiss to her temple. "I love you."

"I know. I love you too."

Ryan's parents seemed to have sensed something about his manner, too, for they seemed as eager as she was to enjoy every moment of their dinner together, where there was no shop talk whatsoever. However, once the plates were cleaned away and small talk dried up, Ryan knew it was past time to address the thought that was uppermost in his mind.

But, still, he delayed.

"Did you have any time to look out those notes about the gospel book?" he asked his wife.

Anna grasped the topic like a lifeline. "Yes, I did," she said, and rose from her chair to reach for a slim folder she'd printed off, earlier that day. "A copy of all this is saved on my laptop, too."

Ryan flipped open the first page and felt a shudder of recognition.

The image was a colour print of a painting entitled, 'The Death of the Venerable Bede' by an artist called William Bell Scott, painted in 1857. It showed the dead man, Bede, lying on the floor of a study or workroom within the walls of a grand monastery, one full of books and interesting treasures. In the painting, Bede is surrounded by five other monks, one of whom is kissing the crown of his head.

On the window ledge in the background, there were four multi-coloured bottles, and to the left of the body was a rustic worktable slanted inward, on top of which rested a long white feather.

In Bede's lap there was a small red book containing the gospel of St. John.

"I saw this," he said quietly. "Or parts of this—at the scene at Crayke College."

"What do you mean?" his mother asked, leaning forward to look over his shoulder.

"The killer had tried to recreate this painting, or parts of it," Ryan said. "They left four bottles on the window ledge of the cider mill, where Father Jacob was found, and a long white feather perched exactly like this on the edge of a worktable, not far from the body."

He paused, feeling vaguely ill. "I can't say the body was left in the same condition."

"I'm sorry," Anna said. "I had no idea—I included that picture because it's quite famous, and shows the gospel book in Bede's lap. It was made at the same monastery where he spent most of his life, down in Jarrow."

"No, don't be sorry," Ryan said, flipping through more pages. "The more information we have, the better."

"Knowledge is power," his father murmured.

"Exactly. The more insight I have into this person's mind, the better chance I have of catching him."

"You think it's a male, then?" Charles asked.

Ryan gave up all pretence of confidentiality and nodded.

"It feels male," he said. "The association with Cuthbert, the physicality of the person I saw at the British Library... it fits."

"From a historical perspective, anyone who knows about Cuthbert would also know he was reputed to have disliked women because he saw them as distractions."

"Quite right," Charles chimed in, and received a playful nudge from his wife.

"There's a long black marble line across the floor which traditionally barred women from crossing into the nave," Anna said. "Anyone who wanted to devote themselves to the cult of Cuthbert would know about this and, frankly, speaking as a woman, it's a stumbling block."

Ryan grinned, and looked back at the folder, thinking of all the time she'd taken that day to try to help him.

"Thank you for doing all this, I—what's this?"

He pulled out the last page of the folder, which consisted of a single sentence which read:

If Cuthbert ye seek, look atop the highest throne

"Ah," Anna said, with a gleam in her eye. "This is the interesting bit."

She reached for the folder and extracted forty sheets of paper, each showing a printed image of a different page from the St. Cuthbert Gospel, not in chronological order as they appeared in the gospel book, but numbered with a red pen in the top right corner of each page. Moving aside their coffee cups, Anna laid out the pages for her family to see, then sat back down again.

"Notice anything?" she asked.

They studied the images, but nothing was immediately apparent, except to Charles.

"These dots," he said, tracing a finger over what, at first, appeared to be no more than a tiny fleck or a photographic blip beneath certain letters.

"I wonder why I didn't see it," Ryan said, and could have kicked himself. "I might have known ol' hawk-eye would have spotted it."

"Old habits die hard," Charles shrugged. "Is this the message it spells out?"

Anna nodded. "When I was going through the full digital version of the gospel book, I hardly noticed these little pin-pricks and, to be honest, I wouldn't have noticed them at all, if I hadn't been looking for something unusual in the first place," she said. "Anybody flicking through those pages would probably miss it—there's only a single dot beneath a single letter on different pages throughout the book, and they had even been jumbled into an anagram. It took me a minute to unscramble the letters."

Ryan smiled, and wondered how long it would have taken him to perform the same task—days, probably.

"Whoever did this was smart, and they were obviously very familiar with the specific details of this book," Anna said. "For instance, it already has pinholes on parts of its pages, but those relate to its binding, nothing more. Whoever concealed their message in this way knew it would be a fairly safe bet that anybody casually looking through the book wouldn't consider the new pinholes to be significant—unless they were already looking for something of significance."

"Especially as the book is written in Latin," Eve said. "It's only once you put individual letters together that it makes any sense, in English."

"Exactly." Anna nodded.

"What do you think it means?" Ryan asked, trying to understand what it was about that single sentence that had been so important as to motivate someone to kill. "That Cuthbert's spirit has ascended to heaven, or something like that?"

"Possibly," Anna said. "I've been thinking about it all day, and I feel like something's tugging at the edge of my mind. It'll come to me, probably after a good night's sleep."

Ryan smiled, and rose from his chair to walk around and kiss her.

"What was that for?" she asked.

"For looking into all of this," he said. "I want you to know how much I appreciate it—how much I appreciate all of you."

He looked between them, and knew the time had come to say what he hoped he would never have to say.

They moved into the living room, where all was cosy and warm.

Charles and Eve settled themselves on one of the sofas, whilst Ryan and Anna took the opposite one, tidying away some of Emma's leftover toys into a basket as they went.

They took the time to stoke the fire and turn the lights down low, before Ryan broached the subject he had been avoiding all evening.

"Things have changed, over the past few days," he began, and reached over to link his fingers with Anna's. "Previously, there was a nebulous threat from a person who was careful and quiet, organised and ruthless. In the last two days, that person's behaviour has escalated. Two people have died in as many days, and another artefact has been taken, causing serious injuries to another person in the process."

Charles reached down to lay his hand over his wife's, in silent support. They had lost one child to a madman already; they would not be losing another.

"What can we do?" he asked. "Tell us, and we'll do it."

Ryan nodded, and turned to his wife.

"Anna—before, it made sense to maintain a status quo. It looked the least suspicious, and there was safety in numbers. But now that Operation Bertie is no longer covert, this person knows they're being hunted and that I won't stop until I find them. That leaves them with two choices, as far as I can see."

"Run and hide, or stay and fight," Charles muttered.

Ryan nodded.

"If they come for me, they'll come for my whole family. If they want something from me, they'll try to use my family as leverage, and I can't allow it."

He rubbed the pad of his thumb over the soft skin of Anna's hand.

"I think it's time you and Emma went down to Devon," he said, and turned to his parents. "*All* of you. Just for a while, until this is resolved."

It killed him to say it, to send away those he loved most, but it was the best and only way to protect them.

"But—you said it wouldn't matter where we were, if this person really wanted to find us," Anna said.

"I still believe that," he said, frankly. "But there's no need to make things easy for them."

"I could travel down to Devon with the girls, then come back to help you," his father offered.

Ryan shook his head.

"I appreciate the thought, Dad, but I'm relying on you to stay and look out for everyone down south," he said. "I want you to call in your old security team and turn Summersley into a fortress."

He referred to the family home, set in hundreds of acres of land in the Devonshire hills.

"There's nobody else I'd trust with my family's life," he added.

Charles looked him in the eye. "You can trust me."

"For how long?" Anna asked, keeping her emotions in check as best she could. "How long will we be apart?"

Ryan looked down at their joined hands, thought of the sleeping baby upstairs, and tried to stay strong.

"I don't know," he said, honestly. "I'll try to finish this as quickly as I can, Anna, so we can all be together again."

"What about you?" Eve asked, and her voice trembled. "Who'll be looking after you?"

"I'm a big boy," he said, with the ghost of a smile. "I'll look after myself."

Eve was hardly satisfied with that.

"We could arrange some security for Ryan, too," she said to her husband, who nodded his agreement.

"We'll cross that bridge when we come to it," Ryan told them. "For now, I want to know all of you will be somewhere safe, far away from anything remotely to do with any of this. Will you do that for me?"

This last question he aimed at Anna, whose brown eyes shone with unshed tears.

"Yes," she whispered. "For the sake of our family, and to give you the space you need to work without worrying about any of us, yes, I'll go to Devon."

"Thank you," he said, and held her as she snuggled closer and laid her head against his chest. "It's for the best."

She knew that he was saying it to convince himself, as much as her.

"I know," she reassured him. "But knowing doesn't make the doing any easier."

Across the room, Eve and Charles exchanged a glance.

"We'll leave you two in peace," his mother said. "We'll get on the road first thing tomorrow."

Eve brushed a maternal hand over Ryan's head as she passed, then leaned down to kiss his brow, blinking away the tears that threatened to fall.

"Goodnight," she whispered, and left them both to say their long goodbye.

It took him a couple of days to crack the anagram, which was lowering for him to admit.

But it was easily explained.

He would hardly be a worthy recipient of Cuthbert's Code if he was able to understand its mysteries straight away, and nor would Father Jacob have been a worthy guardian if his message had been obvious to all who read it.

Only the most loyal followers could see it, and understand it.

Once he'd understood the message, he knew immediately where to look for the next clue, and it had taken all of his restraint not to go there immediately and claim what was rightfully his.

But he could not.

That would be foolish, for the place was under constant surveillance and its unique placement made it almost impossible to access without being discovered.

He needed a proxy.

Somebody with the intelligence, the means, the power and the incentive to do his bidding.

He knew just the man.

Reaching for the prosthetic mask he kept in a glass case, laid out on a satin pillow, he lifted it to his face and looked at himself in the mirror, smiling like the madman he was.

He was Cuthbert's holy heir.

He was the vessel for his power.

He reached for one of a stack of unused burner mobiles and placed a call to one of his most useful contacts. When the arrangements had been made, he fell to his knees and prayed.

CHAPTER 32

Thursday, 10th December

The only person who slept through the night was Emma, who awakened fresh as a daisy and blissfully ignorant of any sad undercurrents in the household. Through her child's eyes, she saw her father's face appear above her cot, looked into his loving blue gaze and kicked her arms and legs in excitement, ready to be held in his strong arms. She breathed in his smell, as she laid her small head in the crook of his neck and heard the rumble of his voice as he sang a shaky rendition of 'Water of Tyne' on their way downstairs. Then she smiled for her mother, who followed after them with eyes that were bloodshot, for reasons she couldn't understand.

"I'm going to miss you, little one," Ryan told her. "Don't forget me, will you?"

He turned to Anna, and held out his free arm, which curved around her to form a tight circle, just the three of them.

"I'll come and get you, the minute this is done," he promised, kissing the top of both of their heads. "If you see anything unusual, anything that concerns you, don't stop, don't wait—you just run. Understand?"

Anna nodded, and knew that her tears would soak through his shirt.

"Be careful," she said, and took the baby from him. "Don't worry about us, focus your attention to bringing him in."

Ryan looked at the pair of them, turned and made for the door, before turning and walking swiftly back to claim Anna's mouth in a searing kiss, as if it was their last. Afterwards, he cupped the baby's head in his hand, kissed the top of it, and turned to leave.

His mother met him at the front door.

"You don't need to worry," she said, with admirable control. "We'll look after them for you, but you must promise me something in return."

"Anything," he said.

"Look after yourself," she said. "You're all I have left."

Ryan enveloped his mother in his arms and breathed in her scent, which was worth a million memories.

"I promise," he said. "Drive quickly, but safely."

She nodded, and raised her hand to wave as he walked swiftly down the drive towards his car, where Charles was waiting to see him off.

"Just been checking the tyres," he said, for something to say. "Your front ones needed a bit of air, so I…"

Ryan pulled him in for a hard hug, and held his father for longer than was strictly necessary.

"There now," Charles said, with a catch to his voice. "We'll be fine, and so will you."

"It's for the best, isn't it?"

"You know it is."

Ryan nodded, and pulled away, scrubbing a hand across his face.

"If you see anything, hear anything—"

"I'll know what to do," Charles assured him, and then took his son's shoulders in a light grip, standing eye-to-eye. "Listen to me now, Ryan."

It was the first time he'd used the name, and Ryan stood up a little taller because of it.

"Wondered when you'd use that name," he said. "I won our bet, after all."

"Yes, you did." Charles smiled. "Six straight bullseyes, that I counted. But it's the seventh one that counts, son. That's the one you don't see coming, the one that comes at you when you least expect it, and it's not always a bullet."

He paused, his eyes demanding attention.

"You watch your back—that's an order."

Ryan gave a brief nod, and looked back towards the house.

"Get as far away as you can, as quickly as you can."

"We'll be on the road within thirty minutes," Charles replied, and shook his son's hand. "Go and do what you do best."

The best laid plans of mice and men often go awry.

The car was packed and they were ready to go, but for a final nappy change. Unfortunately, as luck would have it, Anna realised they'd run out of nappies. How that could have happened, she didn't know—but it had.

"I'll head down to the shops," Charles offered, checking the time on his watch.

Twenty past eight.

The corner shop would be open, as it always was in the early mornings, and it would only delay them by ten minutes at the most.

He'd take the car, to speed things up.

"I'll be back in five minutes," he said, casting an eye around the empty landscape.

Not another person or car in sight.

Good.

"Lock the doors," he said, for good measure.

When he heard Eve bolt the door, Charles walked swiftly to his car—now packed to the rafters with baby gear—and fired up the engine.

A moment later, and he was on the road.

A thought struck Anna as she was checking her office for any stray nappies that could be used to refresh what was beginning to smell like a toxic explosion inside her daughter's Christmas onesie. Her attention diverted, she shifted Emma to her other hip and reached for one of the textbooks on her bookcase, flipping through the pages until she found the image and the reference she was looking for.

…atop the highest throne…

"That must be it," she said to herself, and Emma made a humming noise in agreement. "We'll ring your daddy from the road and let him know but, for now, I'll leave the page open here."

Downstairs, Eve walked through the various rooms to check all the lights had been switched off, giving herself something to do while they waited for Charles to return.

As she stepped out of the living room and back into the hallway, she caught a flicker of movement through one of the glazed side panels on either side of the front door.

There was no time to react.

Wood splintered as a battering ram broke through its sturdy locks, and the door flew open on its hinges to reveal four masked men, dressed entirely in black.

Eve had always wondered how she would react in a fight or flight scenario, and that day she had her answer.

She fought.

"*ANNA!*" she screamed to warn the girl, and made a grab for the vase of flowers on the hallway table.

Two of them came for her, dark, faceless figures who saw her not as a person, but as a number.

She swung at them—a glancing blow that missed its mark.

Seconds later, she hit the floor, knocked down by a single, brutal blow to her face.

Anna heard Eve's warning shout, and knew immediately.

They had come.

Adrenaline surged through her body, and she heard the quick tread of footsteps climbing the stairs. There were four rooms to search before they reached her study, and she needed to make sure they didn't get that far.

Thinking quickly, she knew there was only one thing to do.

Hands shaking, she fumbled for the emergency dummy she kept in the pocket of her jacket, and slid it into Emma's mouth.

"Shh," she said, and walked quickly to the tall storage cupboards they used for spare jackets and coats.

Down the corridor, she heard the crash and bang of cupboards being searched.

Struggling out of her coat, knowing it would have her comforting scent, she spread it as a makeshift bed and laid the baby on top of it.

"Shh, baby girl, shh," she said, tapping a finger to her lips.

With one last, loving look, she closed the cupboard door and hurried out of the room and into the corridor, in time to intercept the two men who were on the cusp of searching the final room on that floor.

Anna held her arms aloft, in a gesture of surrender.

The two men might have admired her grit, if they had the capacity to feel any empathy at all.

Her wrists were tied behind her back, her mouth was gagged, and a dark hood placed over her head.

"Stay smart, and nobody needs to get hurt," one of them said, in a voice entirely without emotion. "Now, walk."

CHAPTER 33

Charles was on his way back up the hill towards the house when the van came hurtling in the opposite direction, and he knew instantly what had happened.

What he had allowed to happen.

Viciously shoving aside his feelings, he swerved towards the front of the van, trying to force it into the hedge, but its driver anticipated the move and increased his speed even further to avoid it.

Charles turned quickly to catch the number plate of the van, but it was smeared with mud, in a trick as old as the hills.

He gunned the engine of his vehicle and reversed with precision and speed back down the hill, but he was too late; the van had already disappeared.

Beside himself with guilt and grief, Charles raced back up the hill, swerving into the driveway with a squeal of tyres. He threw open the car door and made a grab for the weapon he had in the back, covering the ground at speed.

He saw the door hanging limply on its broken hinges and, beyond it, his wife, the mother of his children, lying face down on the hard, stone floor.

"Eve," he whispered.

He was with her in seconds, placing two fingers on the side of her neck as felt for a pulse.

Weak, but still there.

He turned her, and let out a gasp of pain as he caught sight of her face, bloodied and torn.

Ruthlessly banking down all the hurt and the anger that threatened to overwhelm him, Charles reached for his mobile phone with unsteady hands.

He called the ambulance, first.

Once he had been assured they were on their way, he was on the cusp of making the difficult call to his son, when a sound stopped him.

The distant sound of a baby's cry.

Ears cocked, half thinking he'd imagined it, Charles listened intently.

There it was again.

"Emma," he said, with a sob.

He placed a coat over Eve, to keep her warm, and then took the stairs two at a time, searching every room, following the sound of her cries. Finally, he reached Anna's study, where the cries came loudly from the direction of a tall built-in cupboard in the corner.

Charles crossed the room in three long strides and snatched open the door, to find his granddaughter's face staring up at him. She'd been crying, but not too long, if he was any judge, and his trained eye spotted Anna's coat tucked around her, as well as the dummy lying discarded beside it.

She'd done her very best, protecting her child.

Overcome, Charles lifted Emma into his arms and held her close, blinking away tears.

"Grandad's got you, darling. Shh, now, don't cry. Grandad's here."

———

Ryan was nearing the junction that would take him off the A1 southbound and onto the A19 dual carriageway towards the east end of the city of Newcastle, where Northumbria Police Headquarters was now based, on Middle Engine Lane in an area known as Wallsend. It was a journey he took most days on roads he knew like the back of his hand.

He was approaching a roundabout, when the call came through from his father.

I'm sorry...

Anna has been taken...

Ryan said very little; he couldn't have found the words to express what he felt in that moment.

He could only act.

His body took over, shifting the car into another lane and then accelerating around the roundabout to return to the A1 and retrace his journey, this time at the kind of speed he'd been trained to use in emergency scenarios, such as this.

He switched on his blue lights, and rang the office.

Back at his desk, Phillips answered on the first ring. "DS Phillips."

"They've taken Anna."

Phillips thought he had misheard. "What? What was that?"

"Anna. They've taken her."

Ryan undertook a vehicle doing seventy, and returned to the fast lane. The landscape whipped past him in a blur of blue and green, but he saw nothing except Anna's face when he'd left her this morning.

He'd left her...

"When?" Phillips demanded. "Where?"

"The house, less than ten minutes ago," Ryan said, in a horrible, toneless voice he barely recognised. "Send help."

Phillips was already keying in the order to the Control Room to dispatch squad cars, and planned to contact the forensics team as soon as he'd spoken to Morrison.

But, first, he needed to be sure Ryan wouldn't drive himself off the road.

He needed to keep him very, very calm.

"Where are you now," he asked, in an even, unthreatening voice.

"Morpeth junction. A1, northbound."

"Good. All right. Do you feel competent to drive? If not, you need to pull over."

"I need to get there. Time is slipping away."

"I've got squad cars on the way, and an ambulance, if one hasn't been dispatched already," Phillips said.

Across the bank of desks, Lowerson and Yates had fallen silent, listening intently to the one-sided conversation with growing alarm. When MacKenzie entered the room with cups of vending machine coffee, Yates held up a hand to warn her something was amiss, and she hurried across to take a seat beside Frank.

Spotting her, he wrote a single word on his notepad, and circled it twice.

'MORRISON'.

Rising again, she hurried from the room to fetch their Chief Constable, hardly knowing what to tell her, except it was a matter of extreme urgency, judging by the pale, horrified expression on her husband's face.

There could be only one reason for that, and she could hardly bear to speak it aloud.

"Ryan, give me an update. Where are you now? What speed are you doing, son?"

"Passing Longwitton," he said, in a voice that was barely audible. "Sixty or seventy."

"All right, I need you to slow that down, you're going through a village. I know you don't want to cause any accidents. I've just been told that the ambulance has arrived, for your mum."

Ryan heard the words from far away, as if he were swimming underwater, but some part of him recognised the good sense in what his friend had said, and he eased his foot off the accelerator.

"She's gone, Frank. They've taken her; she's gone."

Phillips closed his eyes, knowing this particular nightmare only too well.

"We'll get her back, you just wait and see. Keep that speed under forty for the rest of the way, now."

"All right, Frank," Ryan said, and kept his friend on the line until he reached Elsdon.

CHAPTER 34

Ryan arrived home soon after the ambulance, bringing his car to a jerky stop beside it. He walked unsteadily to the front door, trance-like, not quite in command of himself in that moment, so great was the shock of her loss.

He stepped through the broken doorway to find his mother being tended to by a couple of paramedics, her face covered with blood which had spattered across the wall. His father stood a short way away, holding Emma in his arms while she fed from a warm bottle of milk.

Even in the midst of it all, he had looked after the child.

Spotting Ryan, his father's face crumpled, and tears began to fall.

"I'm sorry," he said. "I failed you, son."

Ryan shook his head and stepped inside the house, moving like an automaton.

"Nobody touches this doorway," he said, in a faraway voice. "Nobody touches anything, until the forensics team arrive."

"Ryan?"

He held up a hand for quiet, and moved closer to speak to his mother, who was conscious again.

Seeing the damage done to her face, he flinched and closed his eyes for a moment, turning away. Bearing down, Ryan turned back again, and became the murder detective, his face shuttered against the pain of a loss so great, it could not be quantified.

"What did you see?" he asked. "Mum? What did you see?"

A description, he thought. *I need a description.*

"Son, now isn't the time—"

"There is no more time," Ryan said, simply.

"Black masks," Eve mumbled, lifting a hand to shove her oxygen mask out of the way, ignoring the protests from the paramedics at her side. "Tried to warn Anna, but…they were too quick. Four of them, all men. Shorter than you, taller than Anna. I'm sorry. I'm so sorry—"

Ryan knelt beside her and clasped her shaking hand.

"Thank you," he whispered. "Rest now, Mum. Let the doctors look after you."

"But, what about—"

He stood up again, and signalled that the paramedics should move in. Both men watched as Eve was strapped to a stretcher and lifted outside, where she was taken to the ambulance.

"You should go with her, Dad," Ryan said.

"I can't leave you like this," Charles said, scrubbing a hand over his swollen eyes. "Not like this."

"She needs you," Ryan said softly, and held his arms out for the baby.

Charles looked down at the child, then at his son, and wondered if she might be the one to help him, as a kind of talisman to ward off more of the evil that had already tainted their lives.

He transferred Emma into her father's arms and took his son's advice, knowing that Eve would be suffering from shock and needed him beside her.

He'd never felt more torn.

Then, a kind of miracle happened.

Charles looked back to see Emma reach up her little hand to touch her father's face, and something thawed inside him, breaching the defences Ryan had erected in order to make the journey home. He held her close, rocking her as they waited for his team to arrive.

Before he left, Charles needed to tell Ryan one more thing.

"Anna was the one who protected her," he said. "Not me. Not us. It was Anna who hid her inside the cupboard in the study, so they wouldn't find her. She wrapped Emma inside her coat, so she wouldn't catch cold."

Ryan didn't turn around.

He couldn't.

"It wasn't your fault," he said, because he felt it was important. "It was mine."

Charles shook his head. "No—"

"The ambulance is waiting, Dad."

"I'll be back as soon as I can," Charles said, and turned away, having aged ten years in the space of an hour.

"Say that again, Frank."

"The bastards have taken Anna," Phillips said, as he reached for his coat. "Fifteen minutes ago, from their house in Elsdon."

Morrison prided herself on being one of the coolest customers around, but this was too much, even for her.

She turned away to stare blindly out of the window, trying to imagine what Ryan must have been feeling in that moment, but failing.

"Control—?"

"Squad cars are on the way," Phillips told her. "Ambulance has been and gone, and the docs are taking care of Ryan's mum, who suffered facial injuries and is probably concussed."

"The baby?"

"Safe and well," Phillips replied. "I spoke directly with Ryan's father, Charles, who wants me to get up there as quick as I can. I hope you don't mind, ma'am, but I authorised the CSIs to attend the scene—"

"Don't insult me, Frank. I'm authorising a full search. Anything and everything you need."

That Ryan needs, Morrison amended, privately. It was the least she could do for him.

"Thank you," Phillips said. "I'm going to make my way up there now, so he's not left alone for too long."

Morrison drew herself up to her full height, sufficiently in command of her emotions to turn around again. "Lowerson, Yates? I want you both firing on full cylinders to push ahead and find this son of a bitch. Call in all the help you need from neighbouring command units, and freeze all other non-urgent business. I want APW's for all vehicles matching the description of the van and I want CCTV from all ANPR and other cameras in the vicinity."

Lowerson and Yates nodded, their eyes over-bright with unspoken emotion.

"Yes, ma'am."

"MacKenzie? You go with Frank, and stay there as long as you need to. Pass over anything useful to Jack and Mel, and be with your friend."

Denise nodded, and gained a new level of respect for the woman standing before her.

As they turned to leave, Morrison threw a final remark over her shoulder.

"Man the phones," she said. "They've taken her for a reason, and we'll find out what that reason is, soon enough."

CHAPTER 35

"What do I say to him? What can I tell him, to make this better?"

MacKenzie looked across at Phillips from the driver's seat of their car, and then back at the road.

"What did he say to you, when I was taken?" she asked him, softly.

Phillips' chin wobbled, and he turned to look out at the passing landscape.

"He told me we'd find you, together."

"He was right."

Phillips nodded, swallowing tears. "We were dealing with a different kind of animal, back then. We knew what the Hacker was, and that was terrifying, but there was a level of understanding. This is a walk into the unknown."

"Then, we'll learn," she said, firmly. "We'll do whatever it takes, because that's what he did for us, Frank."

She sucked in a tremulous breath.

"If we think, *even for a moment*, that Anna won't survive this—or, if we let Ryan believe that—she's as good as dead. Do you understand me, Frank? She's alive, and she's going to stay that way."

Anna was her friend, and MacKenzie wasn't about to lose the woman who'd been a sister to her, for the past five years.

"She's alive," Phillips repeated.

"That's right. We're nearly there, so put your game face on."

Phillips would later recall his wife's unshakable conviction, and think of it as a defining moment in the hours that followed.

Forty minutes after leaving Police Headquarters, they climbed the hill leading up to Ryan and Anna's home, where they found Tom Faulkner had arrived just ahead of them with several members of his team. The Senior CSI was already in the process of tucking his hair into a hairnet before tipping up the elasticated hood on his polypropylene suit. A squad car was parked nearby, its officers already inside taking statements from Ryan and his parents— his mother having refused, point blank, to remain at the hospital in the nearby town of Rothbury.

They exchanged a brief word with Faulkner, whose sad brown eyes stared through the gap in his mask, then donned shoe coverings upon entering their friend's home, where they had shared dinner and countless good times in the past, and which was now a crime scene.

They made their way through to the kitchen, following the sound of voices in hushed conversation.

"…officers are going door-to-door now, sir…"

The local bobby trailed off as they entered the room.

"Give us a minute, son," Phillips told him, and gave him a grateful pat on the back, as he left.

Ryan's eyes were wide, swirling pools of misery in his ashen face.

"Frank," he said, brokenly. "They took her, Frank. They took my Anna."

Phillips half-ran across the room to pull his friend into a hard embrace and didn't care who the hell saw it. He let Ryan cry, the great, shuddering sobs of a soul in torment, and said not a word.

MacKenzie bore down and moved across the room to take a seat beside Ryan's father, who held the baby in his arms and watched his son with such terrible grief, it tore at her heart.

"Let me take her, for a minute," she said gently, so as not to startle him.

He seemed reluctant to let go of his granddaughter, but saw the sense of it.

"I need to check that Eve is all right," he said. "She needed a couple of stitches above her eye, but she refused any further treatment because she wanted to be near Ryan. She wouldn't desert him; she said she couldn't live with herself, if she did."

MacKenzie nodded. "Look after her," she said. "There are no rights or wrongs here, Charles. Caring for your wife is the right thing to do now. We're here to help, and we'll stay for as long as necessary."

She'd already put a call through to the mother of Samantha's closest schoolfriend to arrange childcare cover for the immediate future.

"Thank you," he said, rising from his chair. He hovered there for a moment, seeming lost and unsure, and started to move towards the stairs.

"Dad," Ryan said, in a thick voice. "What now?"

Charles Ryan wanted to enfold his son in his arms, as Phillips had done. He wanted to be the one to dry his tears and tell him all would be right, but that was far from certain. He was a man with backbone, of substance built over the course of seventy years or more of living—and if it had taught him anything, it was that, in moments such as these, there was a time to fold and a time to fight.

Now, it was time to fight.

He corrected his stance, so he was no longer the world-weary old man who had failed his family. He was a veteran, and a former diplomat, and would behave as such—if not for himself, or even for Ryan, but for the woman who had shown the presence of mind to protect her child, even in her darkest moment.

"What now?" he said, sharply. "Now, we bring her back home, using all means necessary. On your feet now, son."

Phillips opened his mouth to say something, but MacKenzie shook her head.

His father's words seemed to penetrate, re-igniting the fire in Ryan's belly, and he rose up from the table to stand tall.

"That's better," Charles said. "Now, gather the intelligence and formulate your strategy, as only you know how. Anna is relying on it."

With those words hanging in the air, Charles turned and went in search of his wife, who was relying on *him* at that moment.

Ryan looked at his friends, then at the sleeping bundle in MacKenzie's arms.

"Anna hid Emma in the cupboard in her study," he said, forcing himself to think logically. "When I left this morning, the plan was for them to leave within half an hour. The car was already packed, but Dad tells me they'd run out of nappies, which is why he went down to the shop. It would only have taken five minutes, but they timed it just right—that can't have been deliberate, since they had no way of knowing he'd be leaving then. However, they could have waited until I left."

Phillips cleared his throat. "Aye, that seems logical. What else?"

Ryan paced around a bit, running his hands back and forth over his dark hair, actively fighting the panic that threatened to choke him.

"It makes no sense for her to have been in the study," he said, and turned suddenly to stride across the room towards the stairs.

MacKenzie made a sweeping motion with her free hand, encouraging Phillips to follow after him.

"We'll have some girl time, eh, sweetie-pie?" she said to the baby, who was fast asleep in her arms. "Don't you worry, darlin', we'll find your mummy and bring her back."

She could have set the baby down in her cot, but MacKenzie stayed there in the quiet kitchen a while longer, listening to the comforting sound of Faulkner's team brushing and swabbing around the front door and in the hallway, searching for the tiny clues that would bring those thugs to justice, one day. She sang a soft, Irish lullaby to the baby girl and said a prayer for her mother, wherever she may have been.

Anna was sick twice in the back of the van, the motion having been so violent as to turn her stomach, while the gag she wore made it difficult to breathe or to prevent the acidic bile from pooling in her throat, suffocating her.

Heaving, gasping for breath, she lay in the foetal position on the floor of the van, surrounded by at least two others that she could smell.

She could see nothing at all, and could barely move, but she could hear and she could smell, so she used those faculties to make extensive notes in her mind. She counted 'elephants' between one road turning and the next, taking an educated guess at the average travelling speed of the vehicle and noting whenever the van turned left or right. Knowing the county as she did, Anna was fairly certain they'd travelled cross-country towards the Northumberland National Park, but even one misjudged turn could have completely skewed her sense of direction.

She smelled engine oil and sweat.

In the darkness of the van, a man's hand travelled up her thigh, and she kicked out, scuttling away to another corner, only to be thrown against the edge of the metal casing.

Male laughter echoed around the interior, and she thought of Ryan.

She would do whatever it took, to stay alive and return to her family.

Whatever it took.

CHAPTER 36

Yates and Lowerson indulged in a private, five-minute break at Police Headquarters, during which time they poured out the grief they felt for their friend, his wife and all their family. They cursed themselves for being slow-witted and lazy; for not working hard enough to prevent this from happening; for not seeing this action as the next logical step, even though it seemed to be entirely at odds with the perpetrator's previous *modus operandi*.

But it was too late for personal recriminations and regrets; all they could do now was *act*.

They re-emerged stronger, an emotional state that was sorely tested when they returned to the open-plan offices of CID to find every single available officer in the building crammed into the room.

"They want to help," Morrison said, from a desk she'd commandeered at the front of the room. "Without my asking them, they began to gather, asking how they could be of service. I've set them to work."

Another testament to the loyalty Ryan inspired in his staff, Morrison thought, and hoped the goodwill and added manpower would be enough.

"MacKenzie and Phillips picked up a new lead, yesterday," Yates told her. "An account of a man trying to peddle miracles to a vulnerable woman whose husband had recently been diagnosed with a degenerative disease. She described him as being at least thirty, well-spoken, well-dressed, wearing a toupee. This man told a story of how he'd beaten a brain tumour, twice, and credited that to St. Cuthbert having worked one of his miracles."

"Ring the oncology department," Morrison suggested.

"Already done," Lowerson was pleased to tell her. "They say the senior oncologist will be back in his office at nine."

Morrison checked the time on the big, plastic wall clock and nodded.

"Ten minutes," she said. "What else?"

"When we speak to the oncologist, we're hoping she'll be able to give us a name for this guy," Yates said. "It will make our work much easier, if she can. If she can't, which is also possible, we plan to visit more of the people on our list. If we have to flush him out by more old-fashioned methods, so be it."

Morrison nodded.

"There's an APW out for a white van matching the description Charles Ryan gave us but, without a plate, it's not going to help much. Word has gone out to highway patrol, and officers in all neighbouring command divisions are searching, as we speak. I'm assured they will leave no stone unturned."

None of them spoke of the fact this seemed to have been a professional job, which meant it was more likely the owners of the van in question would drive it straight to a lock-up and re-spray it or change the plates, which would make it almost impossible to find them.

"Anna doesn't have any communication devices on her, which means she was probably stripped of her mobile phone before she was taken."

Again, a professional detail.

"What do they want with her?" Yates wondered.

Morrison tapped the mobile phone which sat on the desktop beside her.

"We're waiting to hear," she replied. "I've ordered a media ban, until we know their demands. The last thing we want to do is antagonise whoever's holding our friend."

When they said nothing, she looked up and nodded.

"Yes," she said. "It's personal for me, too. Get to work."

Ryan side-stepped the CSIs who were sweeping through the first floor of his home, and made directly for his wife's study at the end of the hall. There wasn't much to it; just a wall of bookshelves, the window, a desk and chair, and another wall of cupboards. His eye was drawn to the corner cupboard, where the door was still open, and he moved across to look inside at the makeshift bed his wife had cobbled together for their daughter, under extreme stress and in fear for their lives.

If she could do that, then he could do this.

Reaching down, he picked up Anna's coat and held it to his face, closing his eyes to inhale the lingering scent of her that clung to the seams.

"Anything?" Phillips asked, from the doorway.

Ryan let the coat fall away, and scanned the surfaces of the room until his eye fell on one of her textbooks which was lying open on top of the desk. The page had a bookmark she must have bought from Durham Cathedral, sometime.

"Maybe," he replied, moving to the desk to get a better look.

The page showed a black and white image of the 'Bishop's Throne' in Durham Cathedral, the cathedra, or seat, of the bishop. Knowing his wife, there must be some reason why she'd highlighted this image, and he slid into her chair to scan the text beside it:

"*...Bishop Hatfield asked some of his monks to travel to the Vatican and measure the height of the Pope's throne. When they returned, he told them to make his throne one inch higher, so that it would be the highest throne in Christendom...*"

Ryan's lips twisted into a smile, and he looked across to where Phillips stood, waiting.

"She found the answer for me, Frank."

"The answer? To what?"

Ryan explained the significance of the gospel book, and the coded message it contained. Until then, they'd been in the dark about what it meant to 'look atop the highest throne', but now he knew exactly where to look—or rather, where the man who had his wife would be looking, for he was also in possession of the clue Father Jacob had left inside St. Cuthbert's Gospel.

"We need to know what's on top of that throne," Ryan said. "I want a team over there, right now."

Phillips nodded, and reached for his phone so he could put a call through to Morrison.

"We need a surveillance team watching that throne, at all times," Ryan added. "He'll want to know the answer, too, and we need to be waiting for him, if he's stupid enough to try."

"Let's hope he is," Phillips said, and raised the phone to his ear.

Ryan doubted it, but there was no harm in hoping.

Cancer services for those with an established diagnosis were centralised through the Northern Centre for Cancer Care, based out of the Royal Victoria Infirmary in Newcastle. It was a full-service clinical directorate, offering radiotherapy, palliative care, chemotherapy and complementary services and more, and its comprehensive care facilities confirmed their understanding of the perpetrator's reason for being at the canteen at the University Hospital of North Durham— namely, that he had no reason at all to be there, except to conduct a fishing exercise, targeting vulnerable people who may be prone to indoctrination.

Lowerson spoke with the Clinical Director of Oncology, Dr Chowdhury, on the dot of nine o'clock, and proceeded to have an illuminating conversation with the woman in charge of the largest cancer services facility in the North East. After Lowerson forcefully set out the ways in which she and her team were legally compelled to share medical information in order to facilitate the prevention, detection or prosecution of one or more serious crimes, she was disposed to be generous with the information at her disposal. Given that he had no specifics to give her, including either a name or date of birth, it was impossible for her to produce a medical record. However, based on the unique patient history this man had given to Kim, from the support group, Doctor Chowdhury promised to ask all of the staff in her directorate whether they remembered any such patient having been in their care.

As soon as he ended the call, Yates came to find him.

"Morrison's just heard from Frank," she said, hurriedly. "Before she was taken, Anna figured out the answer to a coded message she found inside the gospel book."

"Wait—what message?" he asked.

"Never mind that, now, there's no time to explain. Ryan needs us to go over to the cathedral, right now, and have a look on top of the Bishop's Throne."

Lowerson had never been shy of acting first and asking questions later, and made a grab for his coat.

"Any joy with the Clinical Director?" she asked, as they jogged downstairs and out into the staff car park.

"No, but she's asking around as a matter of urgency. I think we'll hear back from her, if anything comes through—she seemed to be on the ball."

"There are plenty more people on the list of potentials," Yates said, as she climbed into the driver's seat of her car. "Hopefully, if Chowdhury comes through for us, we won't have to go through that process of elimination."

"For Ryan's sake, I hope not," Lowerson said. "I can't imagine what he's going through, right now. They don't deserve this to happen—he and Anna have already been through enough."

"It seems to come with the territory," Yates said, sadly. "He's like Icarus, isn't he? If he flies too high, too close to the sun, he gets burned."

"Some people are born to fly high," he said, and thought that Ryan just wasn't suited to a life of comfortable mediocrity. "But you're right. The more cases he solves, the higher he flies, and the more of a target he becomes."

"Him, and his loved ones."

They were quiet for a moment as Yates manoeuvred them through the morning rush hour towards the Tyne Tunnel, which would take them beneath the river to Gateshead, and from there, on towards Durham.

"Mel, what if—"

"Don't say it, Jack. Don't even think it."

CHAPTER 37

The 'highest throne in all Christendom' had been built for one of the longest serving 'Prince Bishops' of Durham Cathedral, namely Thomas Hatfield, who held the office from 1345 until 1381. At that time in history, a Prince Bishop had nearly all the same powers in the 'County Palatine of Durham' as the King did in the rest of England, which made them all powerful in the important buffer region between 'civilised' England and the raucous, unpredictable land of Northumbria and the Borders, which was constantly at war with the Scots. In addition to all his ecclesiastical and secular powers, Bishop Hatfield was a vainglorious man who embarked upon an ambitious programme of architectural improvements, including the building of the Castle Keep in Durham and the erection of an ostentatious throne for himself, in order to remind others of his rightful place in the pecking order.

But, as Ryan had always maintained, death was an incredibly good leveller.

Nowadays, Hatfield was no longer seated upon his mighty throne but was little more than dust inside a tomb which sat at its base.

"Bit of a come down," Lowerson remarked.

He and Yates were accompanied by Derek Pettigrew, whose surprise at seeing them so soon after the previous day's interview was swiftly overtaken by his outraged rejection of their appeal to set up a ladder and climb to the top of the Bishop's Throne, to see what might be on top of it. It had taken a swift call from their Chief Constable to the Dean of the Cathedral, who allowed it on condition that he be present at all times.

Though he could have done without an audience, Lowerson found himself climbing a long ladder, which the head caretaker of the Cathedral had procured for them.

"Be careful," Yates called up to him.

"Now she tells me," he muttered, and made the mistake of looking back down to where four heads looked up at him, each displaying varying degrees of concern.

Don't swear in the House of God, he told himself, and pressed on until he drew level with the top of the throne.

Unfortunately, the top was not within sight, unless he happened to carry a long-handled periscope.

He made a quick cost-benefit analysis, and determined that the benefits outweighed the potential risks. Ryan needed his help, and there was no way he was leaving empty-handed.

To the Dean's horror, Lowerson made a grab for the top of the throne and found a toehold against one of its carved columns which allowed him to keep one foot on the ladder whilst leaning across to inspect the top. Yates checked again that the caretaker was still holding the ladder steady, and moved across to hold one side of it, not because he needed the help, but because it made her feel better knowing there were two people supporting him, rather than one.

"Can you see anything?" she called out.

Lowerson tried to push away thoughts of falling and concentrated on inspecting the wooden top of the throne. It was layered with hundreds of years of accumulated dust and grime, and he wrinkled his nose before brushing it off with his sleeve.

With one foot still on the ladder and another holding firm on the throne, he reached carefully for his mobile phone, which was in the back pocket of his trousers. With a slow, steady hand, he held it up high above the top of the throne and took a few pictures. A quick check told him he had captured the shot, and he slipped the phone back into his pocket.

Yates' breath caught somewhere in her chest when Jack's shoe seemed to get caught on the wooden carving of the throne, and he found himself straddled between that and the ladder. Thankfully, it came loose after some nifty footwork, and soon he had both feet back on the ladder.

There was a hushed silence as Lowerson made his way back to *terra firma*, and only then did he allow his knees to shake.

"What did you find?" Yates asked, while the Dean and Pettigrew waited expectantly, their faces revealing nothing of what they might have felt in that moment.

Lowerson brought up the images and scrolled through the few he'd taken to find the clearest shot. There, carved onto the top of the throne, was a message which read:

"Seek out the sanctuary of sandstone, held aloft by a single pillar, and find within a tribute to God's most faithful and true servant."

When they looked up, they found the others had disappeared, and all that remained was the hollow echo of their receding footsteps through the cloisters of the cathedral.

Back in Elsdon, Ryan's phone buzzed and he opened an email from Lowerson with an attached image of the message he'd discovered on top of the Bishop's Throne. He read the message twice, and was overcome with a sense of helplessness and anger.

"*Highest thrones* and *sandstone sanctuaries*...why are we wasting time, chasing after these riddles? It won't bring my wife back," he snarled, and thrust his phone away to pace around the kitchen like a caged tiger. "What about other leads, Frank? Have we heard anything—"

They were interrupted by the jingle of an incoming call on Ryan's phone, and he snatched it up again.

"Ryan."

There came the sound of soft laughter at the other end of the line. "I believe you've been looking for me, chief inspector."

Ryan put the call on speakerphone and gestured for Phillips to try to run a trace on the call, which he did using software downloaded to Ryan's laptop.

"Where's my wife?"

"Now, now, there's no need to worry. Mrs Ryan is perfectly well."

"Please, let me speak to her."

"No, I don't think so," the caller said. "Now, I imagine you'd like to know why I have her with me?"

"What do you want?"

"Such an important question," the caller agreed. "I'm glad you come straight to the point. I will be equally straightforward in setting out my terms, which are as follows."

Ryan made a grab for a pen and some paper. "Go on."

"I would like you to deliver Cuthbert's remains to me by nine o'clock this evening, at a meeting place of my choosing, which I will inform you of closer to the time."

Ryan was confused. "Cuthbert's remains? I don't have them to give you. They're buried beneath his shrine, at the cathedral—"

"*Lies! All lies!*" the caller shrieked. "You've been to the Bishop's Throne, so you must know what the code will reveal."

Code? Ryan thought.

"I don't understand," he said, quite honestly. "I'm not a historian, or a devoted follower of Cuthbert—I'm just a regular guy. I don't know anything about a Code of St. Cuthbert."

"You had better learn, then, hadn't you?"

"There's not enough time—"

"For an intelligent man such as yourself, nine hours should be ample time for you to recover the bones. One last thing, Ryan. There must be no other police involvement. If I spot a single police officer, your wife will die. If you fail to deliver on time, your wife will die."

Pure, white hot rage coursed through Ryan's body, but he held it in check and told himself to be careful, and tread softly.

"How do I know she isn't already dead?" he forced himself to ask.

"You don't," the caller said. "I suppose we'll have to trust each another to deliver the goods. Nine o'clock, Ryan. Don't be late."

The line went dead.

CHAPTER 38

Ryan, Phillips and MacKenzie were seated around the table in the kitchen at Elsdon, with Chief Constable Morrison connected via speakerphone.

"We can be discreet," she was saying. "Lowerson and Yates expect a call, imminently, from the Clinical Director of the Northern Cancer Centre with the name of the perp's oncologist. Once we speak to them, we'll have his name and address and, as soon as we do, we can execute a raid—"

Ryan considered the options as objectively as he was able. It had been a longstanding maxim of his never to negotiate with terrorists. Unfortunately, when his wife was involved, principles tended to fly out of the window.

"No," he said, clearly. "He said no police, and I won't risk it. He's dangerous, and sees people as a means to an end. He wouldn't think twice about killing her." Ryan tried not to let emotion cloud his judgment, but it was an impossible task.

"If you want my tuppenceworth, I say the lad's right," Phillips put in. "It's one thing sending in a couple of plain-clothed officers, keeping them well back. It's another thing to raid the man's house. His mentality is geared towards sacrifice and the idea of an afterlife—he won't mind offing himself, if his number is up, and there's a chance he'd take others down with him."

Morrison thought for a moment. "Mac? What's your take on this?"

MacKenzie handed the baby back to Ryan, who rubbed slow circles across his daughter's back and was hardly able to believe that he could feel instant joy in response to the sound of her gurgles, whilst also feeling such intense pain.

Before MacKenzie could give her opinion, Ryan's phone beeped to indicate another incoming call from Yates. He pressed a button to enable her to join their conversation.

"Mel, what have you got for me?"

"We heard back from the Clinical Director, who gave us the name of an oncologist who thinks he treated the man we've described. We spoke with Doctor Welsh just now, and he told us about a patient called Bill Chatterley he first treated back in 2017, whose prognosis was terminal. He had an enormous tumour growing on his brain but, to everyone's surprise, a few weeks later, they did a scan and found it had stopped growing—or even reduced in size."

"Which Bill attributed to a miracle," Ryan said.

"Yes, and the same thing happened a second time, two years later, in 2019. He was referred to Doctor Welsh again, who reiterated her prognosis based on what appeared to be irrefutable evidence—another large tumour had grown, this time in a different part of his brain, and it should have been enough to kill him. Instead, he recovered a second time, and Doctor Welsh thinks it reaffirmed Chatterley's belief that the reason for his recovery was the miraculous healing of St. Cuthbert and the fact he'd been praying at his shrine, religiously."

"This was back in early 2019 but, apparently, when the oncology team approached Chatterley to offer him a routine follow-up appointment, he presented with what Doctor Welsh described as 'very erratic behaviour'. He thought it might have been symptomatic of further tumour growth, but Chatterley refused to have any further treatment and Doctor Welsh hasn't seen him since."

"What do we know about Chatterley?" Ryan asked, urgently. "Do we have an address?"

"He's already known to us, in a manner of speaking. William—or Bill—Chatterley was on our list to visit, as a matter of fact. He's a specialist art restorer who runs his own firm, Finest Restorations, and was one of the key contractors in charge of uncovering the fifteenth-century frescoes in the Deanery at the cathedral, as well as restoring the murals of St. Cuthbert and King Oswald, in the Galilee Chapel, during the renovation works three years ago. He's a big deal in the world of art restoration."

Ryan wondered if that's how Chatterley came to know Mathieu Lareuse, who had worked in art galleries selling forged pieces of art until business allowed him to drop the pretence of a legitimate profession. If Lareuse had been an expert in mouldings and metalwork, Chatterley could have been a useful contact if you were looking to make a quick buck from forged paintings.

And it would explain the level of private income needed to fund thugs for hire. There was a busy trade in forged masterpieces, and a King's ransom to be made, if you knew the right people.

If any of that turned out to be true, the fact Lareuse wound up brutally murdered in his prison cell only went to prove that there was little honour amongst thieves.

"Where is he based?" Morrison asked.

"The medical records give an address in Shincliffe," Yates replied. "We could organise a raid within the hour."

"We were just discussing that possibility," Ryan said, keeping half an eye on Emma, who played happily with her jungle gym mat, which he'd spread on the floor nearby. "Mac, you were about to give us your thoughts."

MacKenzie ran through their options in her mind, trying valiantly not to think of what could be happening to her friend, with every passing minute they delayed.

"Chatterley says he wants Cuthbert's remains in exchange for Anna," she began. "Let's think about his motivations, for a moment, before we make any hasty decisions. Let's say this man really believes he recovered from two brain tumours thanks to a miracle, and the cult of St. Cuthbert. The fact of this happening twice, whilst he was praying to Cuthbert, reinforced his beliefs and played into his own false narrative."

"I can see that happening," Phillips said. "Only too easily."

"Let's also say his tumour returned but, this time, it doesn't go away, and he doesn't need a scan to tell him things are looking bad," MacKenzie said, imagining the disappointment. "He's getting the same old headaches, the same strange visual auras and all kinds of other side effects; maybe it's affecting his eyesight and therefore his ability to work, and above all else, it's affecting his thought patterns, making him unpredictable."

"So, Chatterley tells himself he needs to gather Cuthbert's relics close, because it's the only way to ensure he gets the full force of the healing powers—that's why he stole the pectoral cross, but it still isn't enough to stop the cancer spreading," Ryan said, following the logic.

"I think he truly, deeply believes in Cuthbert's powers to heal," MacKenzie said, after considering the trajectory of Chatterley's actions and behaviour. "When he thought a miracle had cured him, perhaps he had a genuine desire to share the news and help others, which is why he went around bashing his Bible and recruiting followers—like Winter. Later, when he realises that he's unwell again, and all that praying at Cuthbert's shrine wasn't working any more, he started to do some research further afield, and his motivations turned selfish. He's got a ticking time bomb, and a very real sense of desperation and urgency to gather up all the relics he possibly can, to save himself. The only problem is, he needs help. He has some contacts, but he needs more.

That's where the power of indoctrination comes in. Just look at Charles Manson, and what he was able to achieve."

"Power corrupts," Yates agreed, and thought of Bishop Hatfield and his enormous golden throne.

"Indeed, it does," MacKenzie said. "Then, there's the problem of Cuthbert's remains. Durham Cathedral are adamant his remains are buried in the Shrine, yet we know his coffin was opened numerous times over the centuries and the bones of other well-known people wound up being chucked inside. Researchers tested them and found a mixed bag, shall we say."

"Chatterley wouldn't be happy about that, would he?" Phillips remarked.

MacKenzie shook her head.

"I don't think so," she said. "I think he'd feel cheated."

"He became very irate on the phone, when I suggested Cuthbert's remains were in the shrine at the cathedral," Ryan put in, from where he was seated beside his daughter, who played happily with a squidgy teething toy in the shape of a giraffe.

"He obviously believes the real remains are buried elsewhere," Morrison chimed in, and they all jumped slightly, having forgotten she was still on the line until her disembodied voice rang out into the kitchen. "Why would he think that?"

Ryan remembered the notes Anna had prepared about Cuthbert and tried to recall something she'd jotted down about a 'Code'.

"On the telephone earlier, Chatterley mentioned there being some kind of 'code'. He thought the message we found in the gospel book and the one we found on top of the Bishop's Throne are all a part of it," he said. "Before she was— before Anna was taken, she left me a dossier of notes she'd found about St. Cuthbert, alongside some of the myths and legends that have sprung up around him, over the centuries. I seem to remember there being one about 'Cuthbert's Code.'"

"Here we are," Phillips said, a moment later, having done a quick internet search. "Says here, St. Cuthbert's Code protects the secret of Cuthbert's true burial site, and the secret is only known to a band of three—or twelve—monks at any one time, depending on who you believe. When one monk dies, the secret is passed to another, and the Code carries on through time. Legend has it, around the time of the Reformation, when Henry VIII was dissolving all the monasteries, Cuthbert's remains were swapped with those of a recently deceased monk, and that Cuthbert's body was taken somewhere else, for safekeeping."

"Chatterley actually believes this?" Morrison wondered.

"He's unhinged," Phillips pointed out. "He'd believe anything, if he thought it was going to bring about a miracle."

MacKenzie had been listening carefully to all of their theorizing, and had to admit it made good sense, seen from Chatterley's warped perspective.

The problem was knowing how to deal with someone who'd left reality behind.

Clearly, they couldn't rely on him seeing reason, any time soon.

"I think we should take a double-pronged approach," she said, decisively. "I think Ryan should at least be seen to be following these clues to Cuthbert's Code, if nothing else, because time's ticking away and this guy means business. Separately, I would suggest a short, sharp raid on his home address—if there's even the remotest possibility of Anna being there, we have to explore it."

Ryan nodded and, for the first time in his career, was glad somebody else was taking charge.

"The approach to his house must be flawless," he said. "We need a good cover story, so he doesn't get wind of a police presence until the very last moment."

"Done," Morrison said. "I'll expect an update within the hour. Oh, and Ryan?"

"Ma'am?"

"I'm sorry about all of it, truly sorry. Stay strong—we'll be beside you every step of the way, in spirit if not in person."

CHAPTER 39

The village of Shincliffe was an ancient, picturesque place, ten minutes south of Durham city centre. Originally built upon the site of a Mediaeval bridge spanning the River Wear, it was a farming community throughout the Middle Ages, its lands owned by the Prior of Durham Cathedral, and had developed into an affluent community for the well-heeled of Durham society.

At precisely half past one, three teams of police staff assembled at their designated checkpoints in a triangular formation on the outskirts of the sleepy little village, each supported by members of the specialist firearms unit. Their target address was Houghall Hall, a spectacular, seventeenth-century moated manor house on the other side of the river from Shincliffe, belonging to the elusive William Chatterley.

"Who says art doesn't pay, eh?" Lowerson remarked, from the back of an unmarked police van parked on the other side of the river, with clear views across to the Hall.

"I guess it depends if it's your own art, or knocked-off copies of somebody else's," Yates replied. "Either way, you can't take any of it with you."

"A sentiment that's particularly relevant to our friend, Chatterley," Lowerson agreed.

"Five minutes till the drop," Yates said, picking up her field glasses. "Any minute now, a delivery van will rock up to the front gates. Meanwhile, Team B will move in from the west, and we'll remain here to monitor activity from the north, and move in, if necessary."

"House looks pretty dead, to me," Lowerson said, running his glasses over the windows of the Hall. "No sign of life."

"*A's a go,*" came a crackling voice, which Yates acknowledged.

Seconds later, a van bearing the recognisable logo of a well-known delivery firm trundled up to the front gates. A driver, who happened to be one of the newer members of the Firearms Unit, rang the buzzer at the gate and waited.

Nothing.

He tried again, and even smiled for the security camera.

Still nothing.

With a shrug, he climbed back into his van and drove away, remaining in character for the benefit of anybody within.

"*B's a go,*" came another crackling voice, which Yates acknowledged.

They kept their glasses trained on the moat that wrapped around the old limestone Hall, until they spotted the shadowy figures of their colleagues advancing around the perimeter wall, where they forced entry through a side gate.

Lowerson and Yates listened through their earpieces as the team moved through an inner courtyard and into the Hall, shouting warnings as they went. They moved from room to room, until eventually the team leader spoke to them on his radio.

"The place is clear, over."

Lowerson and Yates couldn't prevent the wave of disappointment because, if Anna wasn't being held there, it meant they were right back to square one, and the responsibility now rested with Ryan to procure the bones of a saint from an unknown location, which had been a closely guarded secret for hundreds of years.

Less than eight hours until the deadline.

The clock was ticking.

Anna lay perfectly still in the boot of the car, just as she'd been told to.

Not that she could have moved very far; her ankles and wrists were bound together with hard wire cord, the uncomfortable position forcing her spine to curve, pulling the skin on her stomach painfully taut across the Caesarean scar.

How long had she been here?

It was impossible to say. Three, maybe four hours?

Inside, the air was cold but stifling, heavy with the stench of dried mud and something worse; something like dried blood, and faeces. She didn't think about what it could be.

She would not break.

She would not break.

She closed her eyes against the oppressive darkness of her surroundings and retreated to a place of safety, where men in black masks could not hurt her. Shivering uncontrollably, she listened to the crashing of the sea outside and wondered if she had been left there to die, never to watch her daughter grow into a woman.

Silent tears leaked from her eyes, but she kept saying the words.

I will not break.

I will not break.

Somewhere out there, she knew Ryan would be looking for her, and it gave her comfort. But, if their time was up and there would be no more tomorrows, she told herself to be grateful for all the time they'd spent together, and for all they had meant to one another.

It had been so much more than most.

"*I love you,*" she whispered into the confined space, and hoped her message would carry on the wind to find him.

I love you.

Ryan spun around, certain he'd heard Anna's voice just behind him, but there was nothing there except open countryside and the solitary outline of his car.

"Going mad," he muttered, and it wasn't far off the truth.

He felt wild with anger that was barely contained; but the anger was directed at himself, for he had known, one day, that something like this would happen. You couldn't work as he did, facing the darker side of humanity each day, and not bring any of that darkness home with you.

Today, the darkness had a name, but, next week, it would have another one.

Edwards, Walker, Moffa, Gregson, Freeman, Lucas, Singh, Chatterley...

So many names that swirled around the recesses of his mind, filtering to the surface from time to time, to remind him that evil would find him again, whether he looked for it or not.

It seemed poetic that he was seeking a sanctuary.

'Seek out the sanctuary of sandstone, held aloft by a single pillar...'

It had taken less time to decipher the location referred to in that part of the Code, because St. Cuthbert's Cave was a well-known local landmark. It nestled in the Kyloe Hills of North Northumberland, and was little more than an overhanging outcrop of flattened rock, framed by trees on all sides, with a limestone roof supported by a single stone pillar. 'Cuddy's Cave' was reputed to have given shelter to the monks of Lindisfarne, who carried Cuthbert's body there in 875 AD whilst fleeing the Vikings, and formed part of a modern-day walking route known as 'Cuthbert's Way', which ran for sixty-two miles between the Borders town of Melrose to the west and the island of Lindisfarne to the east.

It was unremarkable, Ryan supposed, as caves went; he'd seen far more impressive rock formations on his travels, over the years. However, there was a certain quiet feel to the place...what some might have called, a *spirituality*. He wasn't sure whether the atmosphere was projected by those who visited, or whether it was a quality inherent in the landscape, but he could understand why a person seeking solace would take themselves off to spend time at Cuddy's Cave to commune with themselves, their god and nature.

After parking his car, Ryan made his way to the top of a gentle hill, where he crossed over a gate and stile and then turned right, following a grassy pathway lined with gorse bushes with a forest on one side. Reaching the corner of the wood, he spied a gate and made his way towards it, keeping his head bowed to the wind, which whipped through the trees and sent the branches swaying, howling like a woman in torment.

He stopped again, closing his eyes as the breeze rushed against his face and, for a moment, it might have been Anna's fingers trailing through his hair; her voice calling to him across the valley.

Heart heavy with grief, Ryan hurried onward, ever conscious of the passage of time and of how every wasted moment could mean the difference between life and death.

Spotting Cuthbert's Cave to his left, Ryan broke into a jog, eager now to find the 'tribute' to the man hailed as

God's most faithful servant, according to the message inscribed on top of the Bishop's Throne.

The sun had already begun its long descent towards the edge of the world, and the light was beginning to fade, but he'd come prepared with a high-powered torch, which he used to guide his way as he approached the opening to the cave, and the pitch blackness within.

He stepped into the abyss, and went in search of a tribute.

Ryan stared at the wall, hands shaking slightly with an excess of adrenaline, which caused the bright light of the torch to flicker in the darkness.

Was this it?

Aside from the usual lovers' hearts and other graffiti left by those with very little concern for future generations, or indeed the laws of the land, there was only one other wall marking that could possibly be relevant to the message.

It was a tiny, intricate carving of what looked to be a coat of arms, above which read:

In deepest gratitude to our brother, who rests forevermore by St Mary's of Wooler, where once he used to play.

The frustration was acute.

There was no time for a wild goose chase, he thought, while his mind was flooded with nightmarish images of what Anna might be suffering, whilst he crouched inside an old cave, deep in the heart of Northumberland.

He lived his life by reference to logic and reason. He had no patience for conspiracy theories or fairy tales about castles in the sky; not when there were real problems in the world that required real solutions. Mostly, he kept his counsel, and let others live as they chose, so long as their flights of fancy weren't dangerous. But now, given the situation he found himself in, Ryan was forced to ask himself whether all those years of polite silence had indeed been a mark of tolerance, or whether he'd been one of the many enablers in the world. For, if fantasies were left uncorrected, they became fact to the person that made them and allowed them to fester and grow. Worse still, they could take on new life.

When others were endangered because of another's fantasy, that was something Ryan could not forgive.

He took a photo of the coat of arms and sent it to Phillips, with a question mark. He sent another message to Lowerson, asking for any information about St Mary's Church in Wooler. Then, he rose to his feet and took a final look around at the cave's basic surroundings, imagining a group of monks transporting their most famous saint over hill and vale, taking refuge on the land where they could.

It took all sorts.

CHAPTER 40

Inevitably, it was not long before news of Anna's abduction was leaked to the press.

They had hoped to maintain the press embargo for a few more hours—just long enough to give Ryan the time to do what he needed to do, without outside interference. Unfortunately, at the same moment he'd been photographing the coat of arms he'd found on the wall of St. Cuthbert's Cave, local news outlets had flung open the flood gates, unleashing their prized scoops upon the world, including the man they called "crazy".

When Morrison heard of it, she stormed into CID and laid down a marker.

"Everybody, stop."

She didn't need to raise her voice; she'd learned that a measured tone could strike plenty of fear into the hearts of any young, foolish officer who thought they could leak a story in the course of a highly sensitive investigation, where the perp would just as soon kill you as look at you—and he'd do it in the name of miracles.

"Listen to me, very carefully," she said, looking at each of them in turn, trying to sniff out the rat. "If I find out the name of the person who leaked the details of this investigation to the press, without my authorisation, thereby endangering the whole operation, I won't suspend that person. They will be summarily dismissed, without pay, and without references.

She paused to let that threat sink in.

"If, however, that person is brave enough to come and tell me what they did, I will settle for a reprimand. It's up to you," she told them. "But I want one thing to be understood. Within these walls, we are a team. We support one another's triumphs and commiserate with any failures. At no point do we endanger the lives of our colleagues with loose talk—and especially, not to the press."

Morrison's eye came to rest on a young PC from a different department, who looked as if she might burst into tears at any moment.

"My door is open," she said. "I hope you'll do the right thing."

Reprimands were all very well, but the deed was done, and none of them knew how Chatterley would react, considering he'd expressly said that police were not to be involved. Reading an article about himself that cited 'police sources' could be incendiary.

She only hoped Anna would not end up paying the price for another person's folly.

Ryan had just returned to his car when his phone began to ring. He expected it to be one of his team, telling him who the coat of arms belonged to, or some background information about St. Mary's Church in Wooler, but he did not recognise the number.

He prepared himself, and hoped the terms had not changed—or worse, that Chatterley had decided not to follow through on his side of the bargain.

"This is Ryan."

"Quite the little birdie, aren't you?"

Ryan was taken aback by the tone, which was markedly aggressive in comparison with how cordial Chatterley had been earlier in the day.

"What's happened?" he asked, coming straight to the point.

"*You broke our agreement!*" Chatterley shouted. "Did you seriously think I wouldn't be monitoring the news? I told you, clearly, there was to be *no police involvement*, and I explained what the consequences would be, should you choose to ignore that condition."

"I haven't ignored it," Ryan said, in a voice raw with emotion. "Please—I don't know what's happened, because I've been up in Holburn, following the next part of the Code, which is what you wanted. If the press has run a story about you, they haven't had it from me. I give you my word."

Chatterley was silent for a few seconds, and Ryan closed his eyes, swallowing hard.

"Five hours left, Ryan," he said, and the line went dead.

"Is there any news, Frank?"

Phillips heard the desperation in his friend's voice, and was sorry for it.

Sorrier still, that he didn't have good news to impart.

"No, lad, nothing yet. We've got Chatterley's house under surveillance, but he's not shown up and there's no car in the driveway. We ran a vehicle check against his address and there's nothing registered, which seems unlikely."

"But not unexpected," Ryan said, raising a hand to massage a throbbing headache in the base of his neck. "He's well connected, so it wouldn't be difficult for him to get an unregistered car from somewhere."

"Aye, and as for where he's hiding himself, Chatterley could have a second home, a rental place, or many a thing," Phillips said. "But, after he's got hold of what he wants, I don't think he's planning on coming back. He left everything at his house—clothes, paintings, the lot, but there's no sign of the artefacts, so he may have those with him."

"They're the last things he would leave behind," Ryan agreed.

Phillips thought about mentioning the basement area they'd uncovered during an initial search of Houghall

322

Hall, but decided against it, on compassionate grounds. The place had been kitted out as a kind of fantasy dungeon devoted to Cuthbert; a replica of Inner Farne, with giant murals of the sea, speakers and even a tiny stone hut, built to resemble Cuthbert's hermitage. There'd been wigs and masks—horrifying masks, made especially to resemble the face of the dead saint—and stacks of notebooks containing information about people he planned to 'convert'.

Ryan didn't need to know about any of that, or the extent of Chatterley's obsession; not when he was doing all he could to hold himself together and stay strong.

"What can you tell me about the coat of arms I found on the wall of the cave?"

"It belongs to the De Villiers family," Phillips said. "It's one of the most ancient names in the UK, dating back to Norman times, so I had a look at the College of Arms website and managed to find it in the 'Old and Illustrious' section."

At another time, he might have joked about there being no 'Phillips' listed in that section, but not today.

"What does the De Villiers family have to do with Cuthbert?" Ryan asked.

"I had a look through that folder Anna put together for you, and there was a link to a website about the monastic history of Britain. On there, you can see a list of all the names of the monks recorded as being a member of each monastery, the dates of their deaths and whatnot. It's a bit hit and miss, at times, but—"

"Was De Villiers on there?"

"He was," Phillips was pleased to say. "Edward De Villiers was a monk at the monastery in Durham his whole life. He died there in December 1537, which is also when King Henry VIII's Commissioners were said to have paid a visit to the Cathedral, *and...*"

"When, according to Cuthbert's Code, the saint's body was switched with that of a recently deceased monk."

"Bingo."

"What's the connection with Wooler?" Ryan wondered.

"From what I can gather, Edward De Villiers came from an aristocratic family and there's an old listing for a manor house owned by the family near to Wooler. St. Mary's Church would have been nearby—perhaps the De Villiers used it as their family chapel."

"So, if the legend is to be believed, rather than sending Edward De Villiers home to be buried with his family in Wooler, they may have switched the bodies, which means that it could be Cuthbert's remains buried in the De Villiers family crypt, and not Edward's?"

"It seems that way," Phillips said. "What are we going to do about it?"

Ryan was already on the road to Wooler, to see the grave site for himself.

"Chatterley wants the remains by nine o'clock," he said. "If it means getting my wife back, then I'll do whatever it takes, Frank."

CHAPTER 41

Wooler was a small town on the edge of the Northumberland National Park, often referred to as the "Gateway to the Cheviots" given its close proximity to the Cheviot Hills, which were a walkers' paradise with their waterfalls and gorges, peaks and troughs. The town itself was another calling point on the 'Cuthbert's Way' walking route, and attracted plenty of tourists who shared an appreciation of the Great Outdoors and of ancient landscapes. On another day, Ryan might have enjoyed the sight of the hills rising up towards the darkening sky, which was a melting pot of deep blues and lilacs as day turned into night. He might have smiled at the Christmas lights, which spanned the High Street of the town, or admired the tall Christmas tree that held pride of place in the town square.

But he thought none of these things—he thought only of Anna.

St. Mary's Church was situated in the centre of the town and, though a supermarket chain and other shops might not have been there when its foundation stone was laid, it retained a quaint charm, especially at that time of year. Phillips had told him that although the present church was built in 1764, the remains of stonework from the twelfth century had been uncovered some years earlier, and the churchyard contained a number of graves dating from the same time period.

It was almost six-thirty, by the time Ryan made his way into the churchyard, armed once again with a powerful torch to help him see in the velvety darkness. There had been no time to try to source a map of the graveyard, so Ryan scanned the area for the oldest looking stones and made a start there.

Unfortunately, the stonework was so old, it was impossible to read the wording, the facing having eroded over the centuries.

As he walked the rows, Ryan's foot met with something firmer than fertile grass. It was a rectangular slab of black marble, noticeably different in quality to some of the other corroded stones around it, and it caught Ryan's attention. Trailing plants and tufts of grass had grown between its cracks, and he propped the torch on the ground nearby, so he could kneel down and clear away the detritus to see the carving beneath, which read:

"Here lieth the remains of our most esteemed brother, Edward, whose sacrifice hath made him the most glorious of God's servants."

d. December 1537

Beneath the insignia was another coat of arms that, at first glance, appeared the same as the one Ryan had found on the wall at St. Cuthbert's Cave. However, this one had a key difference, which was the inclusion of a tiny pectoral cross, sitting in between the traditional fleur-de-lis.

Ryan looked at it for a long moment, and wondered if he should feel more excitement at the possibility of having found Cuthbert's last resting place.

But he couldn't muster the emotion, or anything like it.

Just then, his phone rang again, from a different number he didn't recognise.

"This is Ryan."

"How are you getting along in your quest? Well, I hope?"

"Very well indeed," Ryan said. "I've found what you've been looking for."

There was a quick intake of breath, and Ryan could feel the other man's excitement transmitting itself down the line.

It was sickening.

"Where should we meet?" Ryan asked.

"Nine o'clock, at the head of the causeway on Holy Island," Chatterley said.

"Land side or island side?"

"Island side. Don't be late, and remember my warnings, Ryan—I'm a man of my word."

The line went dead and Ryan smiled down at the gravestone, wondering whose bones really lay slumbering at his feet.

It hardly mattered, for his purposes.

Turning, Ryan headed back to his car and thought of what he kept in the boot, for emergencies.

That would do the trick.

Anna couldn't stop her teeth chattering.

She was frozen to the bone, her body shivering so badly it jarred the restraints on her hands and wrists, cutting into the delicate skin.

But she hardly felt it.

The wind had picked up outside the car, rolling in from the sea to rock the vehicle back and forth, seeping through the cracks and crevices to swirl around the woman who lay trapped inside, with no possibility of escape.

She'd spent hours trying to gnaw through the gag on her mouth, and had eventually made some progress there, nudging it past her chin so she could drag in enormous gulps of air and moisten her lips, which were cracked and bloody from a lack of water.

Anna had come to terms with the knowledge that her captor had no intention of coming back. She knew this, not only because he had never looked at her face or cared to see her as a person, but because she knew exactly where he'd left her—and the only possible reason for that would be to let her die.

She'd given up on shouting for help, after the first two hours. Nobody would be crossing the causeway by foot in these temperatures; they would be heading home by car, back to their cosy lives, never suspecting that the car they passed by had a person inside it.

Anna had no idea of the tide times for that day, but if there was one thing she knew for sure, it was that tides waited for nobody. They would roll in, sooner or later, bringing the might of the North Sea in midwinter to bear on the causeway.

When that happened, the waters would seep into the car, rising quickly to extinguish Anna Taylor-Ryan, forever.

CHAPTER 42

One of the strangest things about crime fiction, Ryan had always thought, was its insistence that every baddie must be in possession of above average intelligence, or even genius. With a couple of possible exceptions, most notably in the case of Keir Edwards, he'd always found the perpetrators of violent crimes to be depressingly average, without any charisma or glittering intelligence to speak of.

He suspected this would be the case with William Chatterley, when they finally came face-to-face.

Though he must have some creative skill as a painter and art restorer, it only took a bit of careful planning and a degree of specious charm to prey on the impressionable, or vulnerable. In his line of work, Ryan only came into contact with the victims and criminal associates who had found themselves entangled in the perpetrator's web, but he would have been interested to know how many others didn't become embroiled, and he suspected that number would be much higher.

In Chatterley's case, Ryan could hardly believe his luck that the man wanted to meet on an island he knew would become cut off from the mainland when the tides rolled in, shortly before nine o'clock. Unless he was planning to make a speedy getaway by boat—which was nigh impossible during December and at night, for the waters around the Farne Islands were treacherous—William would be stuck there with nowhere to go except down to the local nick, the next morning. There was another possibility, which was that he hoped to beat the tides after making the exchange and drive like the wind to get to the mainland.

Never advisable, considering how many vehicles were swept away from the causeway on an annual basis.

Ryan's headlights cut through the long, winding roads leading towards the causeway, and his stomach grew tighter with every passing mile. It was comforting to know that Lowerson and Yates would already be on the island by now, in plain clothes, while Phillips and MacKenzie remained in Elsdon, helping his parents to care for Emma while his mother recovered and, he dared say, his father recovered from the shock of it all, too. Despite all that, Ryan could not know for sure whether his wife was still alive, or whether Chatterley had subjected her to the same fate as so many others, until he was able to hold her in his arms again and see with his own eyes that she was safe and unharmed. There was an unpredictability to Chatterley's behaviour, something already noted by his former oncologist, and that was a source of grave concern to Ryan. Predictability was a desirable thing, despite what people said, because it allowed you to plan with confidence. In the case of William Chatterley, his delusions—some of which may have been caused by the cancerous tumour in his brain—made him an unknown quantity, and Ryan would not be able to relax until it was all over.

He saw the causeway looming up ahead, and checked the time on his dashboard.

Eight forty-five.

The causeway was due to close in ten minutes, and he could see the ripple of the tide as it rose inexorably higher, creeping across the causeway inch by inch, until it would be completely immersed. Ryan knew he had to cross now, or miss his chance.

Accelerating through the shallow puddles that were starting to form, Ryan focused on the road ahead, which was becoming less distinct as the water rose up around it. Presently, he came to the middle of the causeway, where the road widened so it could be used as a passing place, or a place for people to park at low tide to get out and take pictures, dip their toes in the sand, or walk across the 'Pilgrim's Way'. To his surprise, he spotted the outline of a parked car in one of the passing places, which would be submerged in another ten minutes, if he was any judge.

Though he was eager to find his wife, and conscious of not being late, Ryan's sense of decency won out, as it always did, and he slowed his car to peer inside the windows of the other vehicle and check whether there had been a breakdown or somebody in need of help.

But all the windows were empty, and there was nobody inside the car.

Thinking of how angry the coastguard would be, when they had to fish the vehicle from the water the next day, Ryan continued across the causeway, where Chatterley awaited him.

Anna thought she heard the rumble of a car's engine somewhere nearby, but it was hard to be sure above the crashing of the waves outside, and the whistle of the wind. She kicked out at the wall of the boot, in case anybody could hear her, and screamed Ryan's name over and over again.

When the car continued on, and a few minutes later she felt the first ice-cold trickle of water seep through the sides of the boot, Anna knew real fear. The kind that stops your heart, and loosens your bowels; the kind that came from knowing this was the end of the line.

She fought wildly to be free of the ties at her wrists and ankles, but they were too tight.

Water began to pour in, no longer a trickle but a continuous flow, and she was paralysed for a moment, unable to think, unable to move in the terrifying blackness.

Until the back of her fingers brushed against something rubbery.

Spare tyre.

Anna tried to feel for the air cap, but her fingers were numb with cold, making her movements slow and clumsy.

As the water reached her waist, Anna tipped her head high to gasp at the remaining water, whilst working her fingers against the air cap on the spare tyre, twisting and twisting for what seemed an eternity, until it came loose in her hands and she felt a stream of bubbles against her palm.

She took one last gulp of air and dived beneath the freezing water, feeling her way to the air cap so she could clasp her mouth around it and release small sucks of air. She tried to hold her breath for thirty seconds at a time, using the side of her face as a plug until she needed to take another breath.

She knew, eventually, that the air in the tyre would run out.

Ryan, she silently screamed. *I'm here. Please find me.*

Chatterley was indeed a man of his word, and Ryan found him waiting at the designated rendezvous point, on the beach at the head of the causeway on the island side.

He looked almost exactly as Ryan might have pictured him; a man in his late forties, of medium height and build, with a balding head and clean-shaven face. He could blend into a crowd, and had 'one of those faces', so it was easy to see how Chatterley could have impersonated the late Father Jacob with a few well-chosen accessories, such as the beard and habit, because they were of a type.

It was difficult for Ryan to keep the disgust from showing clearly on his face, when he thought of all this man had done.

"Where are the remains?" Chatterley demanded. "Where are they?"

Ryan indicated a large, brown leather holdall sitting at his feet. "Where's Anna?"

He couldn't see the man's vehicle, nor any sign of his wife, and Ryan felt panic begin to rise.

Chatterley held up a set of car keys, and jiggled them.

"In the boot of the car," he said, with a flash of his teeth.

"Which car?" Ryan asked, and then a dreadful, dawning realisation hit him like a sucker punch to the gut.

He spun around, eyes searching for the shadow of the car he thought had been abandoned, but it was too dark to see it from where they stood.

"Give me the keys!"

"Ah-ah! The bones, first," Chatterley said, curling his fists around the keys he still held in his hand.

Something in Ryan's face must have frightened him, because he took an involuntary step backwards.

Ryan lifted the bag and flung it forward, where it landed with a heavy clatter at the other man's feet.

"Here," he said. "Now the keys. Give them to me!"

"These?" Chatterley said, jingling them again, giggling like a schoolboy now he had what he wanted. "Go and get 'em."

To Ryan's horror, he flung the keys high in the air, in a wide arc over the sand dunes on either side of the road where they stood. The keys seemed to remain suspended for a fraction of a second before falling again, towards the water and oblivion.

Ryan shouted something—he didn't know what—and made a dive for the keys. The tide was still rising—up to his knees already—and he scrambled about for precious moments trying to feel where they had landed.

Dimly, he heard the man's maniacal laughter, before he scuttled off in the direction of the village and the harbour on the other side, where he had a boat ready to go.

Ryan swept his hands along the sand under the water, trying desperately to judge where the keys had landed. Finally, his fingertips brushed against something metallic and he pulled them out of the water. Keys clasped in his hand, Ryan made a dash for his car, but the water was already too deep to drive back across to where Anna was trapped inside a metal box. There was half a mile between where he stood and where the car was half-submerged— and the current too strong to swim the distance and have enough energy to get her out.

Thinking fast, Ryan jumped back inside his car and a minute later was roaring through the quiet streets, with its pretty lights and squat stone cottages, towards the harbour. He passed Chatterley on the way, but didn't care; he had one goal in mind.

Ryan came to an emergency stop outside the Coastguard's Station, and was relieved to see the light burning inside.

Throwing open the door, he was met with a pair of lively green eyes and a broad smile.

"Well, look what the tide dragged in." Alex Walker, the Chief Coastguard in those parts, was an old friend of Anna and Ryan's, but this was no time to catch up.

"Anna's trapped, over on the causeway. I need a boat—now!"

Walker took one look at his friend's face and grabbed the keys to his rib.

"Let's go."

A few minutes later, they rounded the harbour and headed out onto the open water, racing towards the channel to where Anna remained trapped inside the boot of Chatterley's car. Alex knew those waters like the back of his hand, and handled his boat with the ease of long experience. Ryan was look-out, blinking the cold spray of water from his eyes as he searched the water for any sign of the car.

As they neared the causeway, they found it fully covered by the tide, and Alex cut the engine.

"*It was here!*" Ryan cried, wild with anguish. "*Anna!*"

Just then, the waves buffeted the car so it rolled upward, revealing itself to them in the powerful beam of the boat's search lights.

"There! Over there!" Ryan cried.

"I see it!" Alex shouted, and moved them a bit closer.

Before he could object, Ryan had removed his life jacket to enable him to swim more freely, and dived headfirst into the icy depths of the sea.

Anna knew the air was running out.

The tiny sips of air she rationed herself from the air cap were becoming thinner and thinner, and wouldn't last much longer. Her body felt numb and lifeless, and a terrible fatalism threatened to take over, as a prelude to the end.

The last thoughts she called to mind were of Ryan's face, laughing as they walked along the beach, and of her daughter, the first time she'd opened her eyes to look up at her mother.

Exhausted, hypothermic, she let go for the final time.

The first shock of water hit Ryan like a brick wall, but he powered through the waves, thrusting his legs hard until his hands reached the car boot. He rose to the surface to take in a huge gulp of salty air, then dived beneath the surface again, clutching the key in his hand.

The waters were too dark to see, despite Alex's efforts to shine the search light in the right area, and Ryan felt his way along the back of the car until he found the keyhole.

His lungs were starting to scream, but he persevered until the key turned and the boot opened. He had to force it higher, battling the downward pressure of so much seawater, but in a final, monumental effort, reached down to grasp his wife's limp body and pull her free.

Alex dived in after him, armed with a life ring, and took the weight of Anna's inert body as Ryan broke the surface.

No words were spoken, but the two men dragged her back to the rib and through strength of will alone heaved her up onto the boat in record time.

Once there, Ryan went to work on her immediately.

One...two...three...

Breathe, Anna, breathe!

One...two...three...

Ryan performed CPR while Alex rushed to start the engine, radioing his colleagues a couple of miles further down the coast in Seahouses to expect their arrival and order an ambulance.

One...two...three...

Stay with me, Anna.

One...two...three...

Ryan continued to pump his wife's chest, breathing air back into her exhausted lungs, while their friend waged his own battle with the sea, hands gripping the wheel tightly as they negotiated some of the worst waters of the British Isles, passing over the skeleton graveyards of sunken ships as they went.

When the lights of Seahouses Harbour came into view, Ryan didn't so much as look up.

He didn't stop CPR until a paramedic was ready and waiting to take over, this time with a defibrillator device.

CLEAR!

He watched his wife's body jerk once, then twice.

Again!

CLEAR!

Ryan saw his past, present and future pass before his eyes in that one dreadful moment. He heard her laughter, her tears, her singing in the shower. He saw her face as they made love, as he kissed her goodnight, and as he kissed her good morning. He saw all the mornings that might never be, stretching out before him.

Then, she reared up, and took another breath—before twisting onto her side as her body convulsed, expelling what seemed like gallons of seawater.

Only then did he break down, pouring his heart out to the wind as he wept for all that could have been lost, and for all that had been saved.

CHAPTER 43

Christmas Day

It had often been said that the sea was a cruel mistress, who did not like to be scorned.

Though Mother Nature had been unable to claim Anna that night on the causeway, she had claimed another soul, instead.

William Chatterley's joy at having been united with Cuthbert's bones was short-lived, and dissipated as soon as he opened Ryan's leather holdall. For, rather than containing the precious relics that he believed would cure the cancer in his brain, the bag contained nothing more than a collection of trainers and gym gear, which Ryan had thrown in the boot of his car the previous day, in anticipation of some lunchtime running sessions with Phillips.

There had been nothing to live for, then; no hope of a miracle, and William had experienced another epiphany.

It was all meant to be—and in accordance with Cuthbert's plan.

Why else bring him to Lindisfarne, where he had been bishop, and why else steer the boat out towards Inner Farne, where Cuthbert himself had died? It would be a fitting end to a distinguished life and perhaps, one day, others would look upon him as they looked upon Cuthbert.

Yes, he could see it now.

So engrossed was he, in the fantasy of his own veneration, that William Chatterley was too late to avoid the jagged rocks which lurked beneath the shallows, ready to claim their next sailor.

There had been an almighty crunch of metal, then the boat tipped up at the bow, once, before capsizing into the water to join its fellows on the sea bed.

Shipwreck divers were deployed in the aftermath of the accident, and their discovery of Cuthbert's original pectoral cross made worldwide news, before it was restored to its rightful place in the Open Treasures Gallery of Durham Cathedral. Upon his return from a week's holiday in the Canary Islands, Mike Nevis, the Head of Security, was tasked with designing an even more elaborate system, to deter any would-be thieves who'd been inspired by one man's obsession.

"It's been a right ol' year, hasn't it?" Phillips declared, as he whipped up his special Yorkshire pudding mix, ahead of a Christmas feast, fit to end all feasts.

"You can say that again," MacKenzie said, as she added the finishing touches to an enormous Black Forest gateau. "I think we're all ready for the Christmas break."

"And to spend it with good friends, and family," Anna said, coming to slide an arm around them both. "I'm so glad you could join us."

MacKenzie laid her head briefly on Anna's shoulder.

"We wouldn't miss it for the world," she said, then glanced over her shoulder to where Samantha was presently fleecing Charles for all he was worth on the Monopoly board.

"Another hotel?" he said, weakly. "What if I only want to stay in a hostel?"

"Bad luck, grandpa," Sam giggled. "Let's see the colour of your money."

Charles tried to hide a smile, but failed, since he was enjoying every moment.

"You just wait until I get the Cluedo board out," he warned her. "Then we'll see."

Samantha smiled indulgently, and wondered when the grown-ups would ever learn.

Later, when Charles and Phillips both snored in tuneful abandon from the comfort of their armchairs, and the baby slept upstairs, the others settled down to enjoy the last few hours of what had been a wonderful day.

"I was wondering about something," Ryan said. "It's to do with the gravesite I found, supposedly belonging to Edward De Villiers. You know the story about how the switch of the bodies could have been made, which means, in theory, that's Cuthbert lying in St. Mary's churchyard.

I was wondering whether that's something people would want to know. Is it a secret that should be kept?"

Anna frowned, thinking through all that Ryan had told her before, and the timing of Edward De Villiers' death.

"There is another theory," she said, slowly.

All heads turned in her direction.

"I was thinking over this idea of the monks having switched Edward and Cuthbert's bodies, so that Edward's body is the one lying inside Cuthbert's Shrine at the Cathedral, and vice versa—Cuthbert's remains occupying Edward's gravesite in Wooler," she said. "The thing is, it would have been much more fitting for the monks to have tried to keep Cuthbert's remains on-site at Durham, which is where, legend has it, he always wanted to rest. It would have seemed sacrilegious, I think, to have buried him in another monk's grave."

"What are you saying?" Ryan asked. "That he never left Durham? There's always a possibility the Code is a load of nonsense."

"Perhaps," she said. "Perhaps, not. You see, back in the sixteenth century, there were certain formal rites that were followed after a monk died, including time spent in the 'Dead Man's Chamber' and then in the chapel, where the other monks would pray over his body. At the end of it all, the monk was buried in an unmarked graveyard along with all his brothers before him, there at the cathedral."

Ryan began to see her line of thought, and was intrigued.

"So, let's say Edward died around the same time Henry's commissioners turned up—the monks might have taken the opportunity to protect Cuthbert's remains by transplanting him into a grave intended for a monk who'd recently died. Is that what you mean?"

Anna nodded. "Think about it—all they'd need to do is slip Cuthbert's body into the graveyard beside all his fellow monks, and he'd be surrounded by his community for all eternity, thus respecting his wishes. Far from it being Cuthbert's body the monks stole away with, in the dead of night, it could have been Edward's body, which needed to be removed elsewhere so the other monks wouldn't grow suspicious."

"Which would mean that Edward's body is lying in the correct place, after all?" Ryan said. "Beside where he was born?"

"Yes, it means they took Edward home, since he couldn't be buried among his spiritual brothers."

There was a long pause, and then Ryan made a raspberry sound. "I like my version better."

Anna laughed. "I guess we'll never know the answer."

"Some things are best left to the imagination," he agreed, and leaned over to bestow a tender kiss. "How are you feeling?"

Anna looked around the room and felt surrounded by love.

"Better now," she said. "I feel so hopeful about the future."

"So long as I have you, I could withstand whatever life throws at us. Merry Christmas, darling."

"Merry Christmas, love. Here's to many more."

AUTHOR'S NOTE

I love the characters in these books, and it's always a joy to sit down and write about their lives in the context of a fresh setting or adventure. With so large a cast of characters, it's inevitable that some books will focus on certain characters more than others, and such was the case in Cuthbert's Way. For me, this book was about reconciliation and forgiveness, friendship, kindness and living one's life in a way that helps to build up other people, rather than knocking them down. I am, therefore, more interested in thinking about the metaphorical message behind Cuthbert's way of life than I am with the walking tour—though, it is an excellent trail, and I would certainly recommend it!

I began to think of a story involving Cuthbert after stumbling across an article to do with Cuthbert's Code, a couple of years ago—naturally, the thought of sixteenth century monks swapping the body of Cuthbert with another monk, then keeping the secret closely guarded for centuries, was instantly compelling. For my part, I conceived a story not about Cuthbert, but about Edward De Villiers (who is, to my knowledge, completely fictitious). I've drawn upon various real-life facts, places and historic events which, I hope, adds life and texture to the fictional plotline. I've researched thoroughly— however, please do remember this is a work of fiction. Whilst I always try to be accurate, there are times when I choose to deviate from the reality in order to make for a better, pacier story. After all, the idea is to be entertained, not put to sleep!

As Cuthbert's Way is my twentieth novel, I need not tell you how grateful I am for all the kind messages of support I've received over the past six years, nor how shocked I was to see Cuthbert's Way make it to the #1 spot on Amazon, to become my sixteenth UK #1 bestseller (I can hardly believe it). However, at this juncture, I want to say that I approach each new book I write with completely fresh eyes, and never make assumptions based on past successes. I hope that each new story will make for a happy reading experience, and I look forward to bringing you many more adventures to come.

LJ ROSS
November 2020

ACKNOWLEDGEMENTS

Given that this book was written during a lockdown period, in the midst of a global pandemic, I'd like to thank everyone for remaining so sane and normal throughout the process. Chiefly amongst them is my wonderful husband, James—I don't mind telling you, there just aren't enough kind words in the dictionary to describe his generosity of spirit and loving support, throughout all twenty of the books I've written, and it's for those reasons that I proudly include the "J" in "LJ" to acknowledge the important and irreplaceable part he plays in creating the conditions in which I'm able to tell my stories.

To my family, I love you all, thank you so much for cheering me on.

To my friends, I love you all, thank you for keeping my feet on the ground.

To all my readers, you're the reason I write these stories, thank you for all your kind support over the years.

Until the next time…

LJ ROSS
November 2020

ABOUT THE AUTHOR

LJ Ross is an international bestselling author, best known for creating atmospheric mystery and thriller novels, including the DCI Ryan series of Northumbrian murder mysteries which have sold over five million copies worldwide.

Her debut, *Holy Island*, was released in January 2015 and reached number one in the UK and Australian charts. Since then, she has released a further nineteen novels, all of which have been top three global bestsellers and sixteen of which have been UK #1 bestsellers. Louise has garnered an army of loyal readers through her storytelling and, thanks to them, several of her books reached the coveted #1 spot whilst only available to pre-order ahead of release.

Louise was born in Northumberland, England. She studied undergraduate and postgraduate Law at King's College, University of London and then abroad in Paris and Florence. She spent much of her working life in London, where she was a lawyer for a number of years until taking the decision to change career and pursue her dream to write. Now, she writes full time and lives with her husband and son in Northumberland. She enjoys reading all manner of books, travelling and spending time with family and friends.

If you enjoyed reading *Cuthbert's Way*, please consider leaving a review online.

If you like DCI Ryan, why not try the bestselling
Alexander Gregory Thrillers by LJ Ross?

IMPOSTOR

AN ALEXANDER GREGORY THRILLER (Book #1)

There's a killer inside all of us…

After an elite criminal profiling unit is shut down amidst a storm of scandal and mismanagement, only one person emerges unscathed. Forensic psychologist Doctor Alexander Gregory has a reputation for being able to step inside the darkest minds to uncover whatever secrets lie hidden there and, soon enough, he finds himself drawn into the murky world of murder investigation.

In the beautiful hills of County Mayo, Ireland, a killer is on the loose. Panic has a stranglehold on its rural community and the Garda are running out of time. Gregory has sworn to follow a quiet life but, when the call comes, can he refuse to help their desperate search for justice?

Murder and mystery are peppered with dark humour in this fast-paced thriller set amidst the spectacular Irish landscape.

IMPOSTOR is available now in all good bookshops!

LOVE READING?

JOIN THE CLUB...

Join the LJ Ross Book Club to connect with a thriving community of fellow book lovers! To receive a free monthly newsletter with exclusive author interviews and giveaways, sign up at www.ljrossauthor.com or follow the LJ Ross Book Club on social media:

 #LJBookClubTweet

@LJRossAuthor

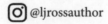 @ljrossauthor